Murder at an Irish Chipper

Carlene O'Connor

Kensington Publishing Corp.
kensingtonbooks.com

KENSINGTON BOOKS are published by

Kensington Publishing Corp.
900 Third Avenue
New York, NY 10022

Copyright © 2025 by Mary Carter

All rights reserved. No part of this book may be reproduced in any form or by any means without the prior written consent of the Publisher, excepting brief quotes used in reviews.

To the extent that the image or images on the cover of this book depict a person or persons, such person or persons are merely models, and are not intended to portray any character or characters featured in the book.

This book is a work of fiction. Names, characters, businesses, organizations, places, events, and incidents either are the product of the author's imagination or are used fictitiously. Any resemblance to actual persons, living or dead, events, or locales is entirely coincidental.

If you purchased this book without a cover you should be aware that this book is stolen property. It was reported as "unsold and destroyed" to the Publisher and neither the Author nor the Publisher has received any payment for this "stripped book."

All Kensington titles, imprints, and distributed lines are available at special quantity discounts for bulk purchases for sales promotion, premiums, fund-raising, educational, or institutional use.

Special book excerpts or customized printings can also be created to fit specific needs. For details, write or phone the office of the Kensington Sales Manager: Attn.: Sales Department. Kensington Publishing Corp., 900 Third Avenue, New York, NY 10022. Phone: 1-800-221-2647.

KENSINGTON and the KENSINGTON COZIES teapot logo Reg US Pat. & TM Off.

First Hardcover Edition: March 2024

First Paperback Edition: February 2025
ISBN: 978-1-4967-4447-0

ISBN: 978-1-4967-4450-0 (ebook)

10 9 8 7 6 5 4 3 2 1

Printed in the United States of America

WHO KILLED MRS. CHIPS?

"We're looking at a very angry killer," Jeanie said.

"Resentment, a grudge, some kind of personal history," Siobhán agreed. *Like an ex-husband after a bitter divorce.*

"I wonder what line of work our killer is in."

"We have a banker, a fisherwoman, a flour supplier, a vegetable supplier, a restaurant equipment supplier, another chip shop owner, a best friend and an out-of-town food critic," Siobhán spouted.

Jeanie shook her head. "Is that all?" she asked sarcastically. "I was told the mural on Mr. Chips across the way was vandalized by our victim."

"There was a can of black spray paint in the shop," Siobhán pointed out. "She seems the likely culprit. Not that I could blame her."

"Indeed."

"I think there's one definite thread we—*you*—*Sargeant Healy*—can pull on." Siobhán waited for Jeanie to stop chuckling. "The hood vent repairman. Tom Cahill."

"Go on, so."

"He claims someone called that morning *canceling* the repair. If he's telling the truth, it has to be the killer . . ."

Books by Carlene O'Connor

Irish Village Mysteries
MURDER IN AN IRISH VILLAGE
MURDER AT AN IRISH WEDDING
MURDER IN AN IRISH CHURCHYARD
MURDER IN AN IRISH PUB
MURDER IN AN IRISH COTTAGE
MURDER AT AN IRISH CHRISTMAS
MURDER IN AN IRISH BOOKSHOP
MURDER ON AN IRISH FARM
MURDER AT AN IRISH BAKERY
MURDER AT AN IRISH CHIPPER
MURDER IN AN IRISH GARDEN
CHRISTMAS COCOA MURDER
(with Maddie Day and Alex Erickson)
CHRISTMAS SCARF MURDER
(with Maddie Day and Peggy Ehrhart)

A Home to Ireland Mystery
MURDER IN GALWAY
MURDER IN CONNEMARA
HALLOWEEN CUPCAKE MURDER
(with Liz Ireland and Carol J. Perry)
IRISH MILKSHAKE MURDER
(with Peggy Ehrhart and Liz Ireland)
IRISH SODA BREAD MURDER
(with Peggy Ehrhart and Liz Ireland)

A County Kerry Mystery
NO STRANGERS HERE
SOME OF US ARE LOOKING
YOU HAVE GONE TOO FAR

Published by Kensington Publishing Corp.

To my sister, Melissa Carter Newman. We may be a much smaller sibling unit than the O'Sullivans, but I couldn't have asked for a more talented or kind sister. Thank you for all that you do.

Acknowledgments

Thank you to my editor John Scognamiglio, my agent Evan Marshall, publicist Larissa Winterbottom, production editor Robin Cook, cover designers, and so many more professionals at Kensington Publishing who work so hard behind the scenes to bring a book to the shelves. I'm grateful to have such a wonderful team. And to my Irish friends and their holiday tales.

Author's note

Although Lahinch is a real place where many go to holiday, I have taken liberties by adding establishments to the town that do not exist. The chippers, the inn, the oil and vinegar shop, the bakery—they are all fictional. Dodi Café, however, does exist and so does the menu quoted in the book.

Chapter 1

It was done. Vera Cowley—or Mrs. Chips, as everyone in town called her—stepped back and admired the handiwork. Her custom-made bookcase for *her* chipper. Hers and hers alone. The bookcase that Corman, aka Mr. Chips, had ridiculed.

"A bookshelf in a chipper?" he'd said in that tone she'd grown to hate.

"No. A *bookcase* in a chipper. A special bookcase. Custom-made." For this exact spot in the corner where it would be a perfect fit. (And it was.)

He'd scrunched up his bushy white eyebrows. "No bookshelves in chippers!"

"*Bookcase*." That was one of his many problems. The man never listened. Now she'd lost a husband but gained a bookcase, and it was perfection. She stepped to the side to view it from yet another angle, trying to ignore everything *else* in the small chipper in need of repair. The old red leather peeling off the booths. The chipped beige-tiled floors. The kitchen equipment that was nearly as old as she was. At least it all worked. All but the hood vent. And that was why she was here early waiting on the repairman. Tom Dowd. He was late. You absolutely could not count on anyone these days, especially husbands and repairmen. Forty years of marriage and Corman leaves her with the same dingy chipper, only to open a brand-new one across the street. Brand-new! The nerve.

For about the hundredth time that morning, she crossed back to the window and peered out. The new Mr. Chips was painted blue, just like she'd always wanted. Corman Cowley had done it to upset her. What a small man. Back then she'd wanted it blue like the sea, and he'd *insisted* they paint it red. An angry color from an angry man. Everything about his new place was designed to rattle her. The pretty blue paint, Mr. Chips on a sign so large one could probably see it from outer space, and that mean-spirited banner announcing his grand opening: *All that and no old bag!*

But the most shocking bit was the mural. She would recognize Tara Flaherty's (her ex–best friend) work anywhere. And what a ridiculous mural it was. A fish—a cod, she presumed—grinning while eating a basket of chips. Now. That was just absurd. A fish eating the chips? Why would a fish eat the chips? And why, when the customers were also going to be eating the fish, would they want to *see* the thing all alive and smiling? And how could Tara do that to her? She was obviously right to accuse her ex–best friend and her ex-husband of knocking boots. The writing was on the shop wall; the proof was in the painting.

A divorce. A divorce all because Vera had asked for two things. One: their sign to read MR. AND MRS. CHIPS. Two: a switch to vegetable oil, which was much healthier than frying the cod in beef fat drippings. Stubborn old goat that he is, he had refused. That is the only reason she delivered jars of beef fat to the doorsteps of their customers. She felt obligated to show them what was going into their bodies. Mr. Chips lost the plot altogether. He threatened to have her committed to a mental health institution. He was the one who needed to be committed. To their marriage. This was when she did something that she hadn't done in forty years. She stood her ground. Using the ladder from their garden shed and old paint they had stored, she'd added a bespoke S to the sign. MRS. CHIPS. That's when he filed for divorce.

They were married in a Catholic church by a priest. That was forever. That only ended in death.

Now there were two chippers across from each other. Unsustainable. But she would never leave Lahinch, a town she fiercely loved. She loved the small beaches, the ocean, the promenade, the shops, the galleries, the restaurants. She even loved the tourists. It was summer, the best time of all. Loaded up with surfers, golfers, and those who just wanted to float in the sea. She crossed to the wall near her new bookcase where she had printed and framed a newspaper article: "Save the Chipper!"

It was a feature on her, and it wasn't just a plea for

charity. They were sending a food critic/restaurant reviewer from a popular website to do a write-up on her new top-secret curry sauce. (She had admittedly raved about it to the reporter, and it had piqued the woman's interest.) Ms. Madeline Plunkett. She was due to arrive today. *Take that, Mr. Chips. You and your smiling cod.*

Madeline Plunkett looked posh. Vera had stalked her Instagram account. Her outfits—they probably cost more than the chipper. A gorgeous young Black woman who had just moved to Ireland from London. She had more than one hundred thousand followers. One hundred thousand! Maybe Madeline would write up something brilliant and entice a few of those followers to her chipper. Which was why Tom Dowd had better get his lazy arse down here and fix her hood vent pronto!

She couldn't serve Madeline Plunkett fish and chips if her deep fryer wasn't working. She needed Madeline to love her—especially her curry sauce. She needed Madeline to be so impressed that she wouldn't notice her chipper was a bit dingy. Vera hoped that Madeline hadn't minded all the messages she had left on her voice mail. The town was going to have to be loyal to her once that article was out. She would see to it that Mr. Chips went out of business. She would bury him for good.

She snatched a pile of bills from a nearby booth and imagined putting a match to them and hurtling the fireball into the front window of Mr. Chips. She threw them back onto the booth, wishing it were a rubbish bin instead. Ruminating on her debt made her furious. And not just at her ex but also at that weasel of a loan officer, Mike McGee. His bank was directly across the street, and she knew plenty about how that man operated. *Shady.* She'd seen his handshake deals with gamblers stumbling out of the empty shop front between the bank and Mr. Chips. She had seen it all. And she was taking names.

At least Detective Sargeant Healy had believed her when she said something funny was going on across the street late at night. He'd approached Mike McGee straight away. She watched the entire thing through her binoculars from her upstairs flat, but sadly she could not read lips. But from the serious expression on Detective Sargeant Liam's face and the shame on McGee's, he was giving it to him good. She had no idea what would become of it, but she hoped it would be something. And to think she always remembered that Mike McGee liked his chips with extra vinegar. She'd give him extra vinegar!

Traitor. This town was full of them, and every single one was going on her list. Still no sign of Tom Dowd, and she could not stop looking at that mural. She poked her head out the front door and scoured the street. Deadly silent, not a soul to be seen. Vera wondered where the tall lady in the yellow hat had gone. She'd seen her early this morning, head down, stride quick. She seemed to be *pacing.* Nothing was open this early, and who took a morning stroll in a fancy hat? *Keep your nose on your own face, Vera.*

She grabbed the can of black spray paint someone had recently left on her doorstep, shook it like she hated it, threw the door to her chipper open, and marched across the street. Halfway there, she stopped. When she'd first discovered the black spray paint on her doorstep, she thought it was in reaction to leaving jars of beef fat drippings on doorsteps. Was this person encouraging her to vandalize Mr. Chips? Or was it Tara or Corman *daring* her to do something about it. Either way, she was doing it. She continued across and shook the can of paint again. Joy spread through her. This was going to be fun.

Mrs. Chips was all smiles when she returned to the footpath in front of her shop and surveyed her work. The nasty message on the banner—*All that and no old bag*—was now obliterated. Blacked out. The mural looked brilliant if she did say so herself. She had sprayed horns and fangs on the grinning cod, then added vomit pouring out of its mouth onto the basket of chips. *Take that, Mr. Chips.* Still smiling, Vera headed back inside. A ladder was leaning up against the wall near the hood vent. *Finally.* The repairman was here at last.

"Tom?" she called. "It's about time you showed up. You'd better give me a discount. Time is money, you know." There was no answer, or any movement anywhere. She turned back to the front door, poked her head out again, and scoured the street for his lorry. No sign of it. She hadn't heard the rumble of his engine, but she'd been hyperfocused on her spur-of-the-moment paint job. Where was he? To be safe, she shut and locked the door. She shouldn't have left it wide open, but she'd been gone only a few minutes. She approached the ladder cautiously. Was it the one from her garden shed? The one that had been missing? It certainly looked like it. Maybe that's where Tom was, rummaging through her things, too lazy to bring his own gear.

The ladder rested just below a shelf near the ceiling, where she had stored a heavy bag of flour. Underneath the bag dangled a piece of twine. Where had that come from? Vera Cowley could not stand when things were out of place. Loathed it. Everyone knew that. Did Tom leave that string?

"Hello?" she yelled. No answer. She was going to give him a piece of her mind, but first she had to deal with that string. She headed for the ladder and put her hands on either side, jostling it to make sure it was steady. Right as rain. She ascended the ladder, and it wasn't until she was on the third step that her feet began to slide. There was something slick on the treads. She should descend and let Tom deal with that piece of twine. But only a few more steps and she could grab it. She'd be careful. She took another step, and her foot nearly slid into the empty space between the steps. She cried out as she scrambled to keep her balance. The ladder rattled and swayed. Someone had coated the treads with grease! She could smell it now, and she'd know that smell anywhere. Beef fat drippings. Was this revenge for leaving jars of the stuff on doorsteps? Maybe someone had slipped on it and this was payback. She'd meant no harm, but now she was climbing a ladder with treads as slick as black ice.

Had Corman done this? What was he playing at? Her heart thudded against her rib cage as she slowly, slowly tried to keep her balance and think. *Tread carefully. Is that where the saying came from? Stop talking nonsense. Hang on until Tom arrives. I never should have locked the door. What if he can't get in? Careful, old girl. Careful.* This wasn't safe. She knew in her gut she was not safe. She was halfway up the ladder. What a sick, sick man.

She was here, so might as well tidy up, get rid of that piece of twine. She reached her hand up and could almost touch it. A baby's breath away. *Let it go, Vera, let it go.* But she could not. She just could not. It wasn't in her nature. She stretched just a little bit farther. *Got it.* She tugged on the string, expecting it to come away easily. What she didn't expect was for the four-stone bag of flour to come with it. She stared in horror as it came straight for her, and that's when she panicked. As she tried to scramble down, her feet flew out from underneath her, and soon the world was tilting backward as the heavy bag continued its trajectory. Her last thought before the bag struck her head and her head struck the floor was that she was going to haunt Mr. Chips until the day he died.

Chapter 2

It wasn't easy for Siobhán O'Sullivan to ignore the whinging of her siblings, even with her head shoved as far into the freezer as it could go. Kilbane had hit 32 degrees Celsius, close to breaking the all-time record—33.3 degrees Celsius logged at Kilkenny Castle in 1887. She wondered if the folks back then had had anything cool to stick their heads in, perhaps an ice bucket, but had a feeling she should count herself lucky. Eoin was pacing and yammering on about the permit delays that were preventing The O'Sullivan Six, his new farm-to-table restaurant, from opening; Gráinne was fanning herself with a fashion magazine and moaning about the styling appointment she had to cancel because mascara kept running down her face; Ann's camogie game through the University of Limerick GAA had been canceled because of the excessive heat; and Ciarán couldn't play his new video game because the internet was out. Instead, he had plopped himself close to their one fan and was talking into it, making his voice wobble. He was in real danger of a blade cutting off his tongue.

Siobhán pulled her head out of the freezer just in time to see Macdara come through the front door. Her handsome husband took a few steps in, then made eye contact with Siobhán as he eyed the freezer.

He grinned and his dimple appeared. "Is it hot in here?"

"It is now," Siobhán said with a grin of her own.

"Ew," Gráinne said without looking up from her magazine.

Ciarán said something indecipherable given he was still speaking into the fan.

"It's going to cut your tongue right out of your mouth," Siobhán said for the hundredth time. She shut the freezer and sunk into a kitchen chair.

Macdara held up his newspaper. "I've got an answer to our woes," he said.

"Which ones?" Ann asked. Eoin laughed, Gráinne snorted, Ciarán cooed into the fan, and Siobhán waited.

"Save the chipper," Macdara said. "There's an article about a chipper in Lahinch in danger of closing."

"Lahinch?" Gráinne said, sitting up and letting her magazine slip to the floor. "I want to go to Lahinch." Situated on the northwest coast of County Clare on the Liscannor Bay, the town was a delightful seaside resort.

"Save the chipper?" Siobhán said, gravitating toward the newspaper.

"Touted to be one of the best in Ireland, Mrs. Chips

is going through a nasty divorce and could use some support."

"Mrs. Chips?" He had everyone's attention.

"That's the name of her chipper, and I suppose it's what everyone in town calls her," Macdara said. He set the newspaper down, grabbed a kitchen towel, and wiped the sweat from his brow.

"I want to save the chipper," Siobhán said. Fish and chips—especially heavenly curried chips—were one of Siobhán's top reasons for living.

"We can have that honeymoon after all," Macdara said.

"The wedding was well over a year ago," Siobhán pointed out. She didn't know how that was possible, but there it was: time was winning the race.

Macdara shrugged, once again flashing that dimple. "Better late than never?"

"That's the last thing I want to do," Ciarán said, finally turning away from the fan. "Go on your honeymoon." His voice was deep now, and although technically he was nearly a grown man, he was a bit immature for his age. That didn't bother Siobhán one bit. If she could bottle him up and keep him young forever, she would do it in a heartbeat. It was nearly impossible to imagine him out of the house fending for himself, although lately she had been dropping hints (and catalogues) about going to University. Despite getting his Leaving Certificate, he was taking a year off before applying to University, a decision everyone supported. He wanted to work at Eoin's restaurant, and he'd agreed to continue with his fiddle lessons. He was quite good at it but had a lazy streak that required a bit of finagling.

He'd be the last of them to fly the coop, although Ann was still living at home while commuting to U of L, the University of Limerick. She hadn't declared a major yet, but she was playing on their camogie team, which had brought everyone a bit of excitement this first year; it had been a thrill to attend her games, even if they were all a bit hoarse for days after from the cheering and screaming.

"Don't worry, pet, it won't be romantic at all," Siobhán said to the youngest O'Sullivan.

Macdara laughed. "Be still my heart."

"I'll stay here," Ciarán said.

"Of course you'll come with us," Siobhán said. "All of you."

Ann cocked her head. "You really want us to go on your honeymoon?" She was probably the most thoughtful one of the brood.

"Why not?" Siobhán said. "We won't honey, we'll just moon."

"No," Ciarán said. "Hard no."

"There's surfing in Lahinch," Ann said. "I want to go surfing."

"And girls in bikinis," Eoin said, clapping Ciarán on the back. The last time Siobhán had been in Lahinch, there were pale middle-aged women in cover-ups, but she kept her gob shut.

"And loads of ice cream," Gráinne said. "For those of you who don't care about your figures."

"I'll go if I don't have to hang around with you lot," Ciarán said.

"That's the spirit," Siobhán said.

Eager faces stared at Macdara, waiting for his reaction. Macdara laughed and threw open his arms. "I guess we're all going on a honeymoon."

"But only if James agrees to come," Siobhán said. "I haven't seen him in ages." Her older brother was always renovating a house somewhere in Ireland. But right now, he was in County Clare so he had no excuse not to join them. They could even take a trip to the nearby Cliffs of Moher. Lahinch was a popular destination for surfers, golfers, and weary folks looking to be healed by a good soak in the bay. It had been ages since she'd been, and she couldn't believe she hadn't thought of it herself.

"Wasn't James just here last week for a visit?" Macdara asked.

"Exactly," Siobhán said. "It's been ages. I'll give him a bell." She lunged for her mobile phone.

"This is shaping up to be the honeymoon of my dreams," Macdara said.

"I think you mean your worst nightmares," Ciarán said. "And I second that."

Just being near the ocean brought an instant relief to the overheated O'Sullivan-Flannerys. They stood on the street where two chippers faced off—one to Siobhán's left, and the other to her right. They were on the side of Mrs. Chips, which indeed had seen better days. But given there was a long line in front of her shop, and no line in front of Mr. Chips, the "Save the Chipper" article must have done the trick. Siobhán's siblings had all dumped their luggage on the footpath, nearly obscuring Macdara, who stood behind the giant pile. Gráinne was the last to add to it, and she let her bag down with a thunk.

"What's in there?" Ciarán asked. "A pile of bricks?"

"Yes," Gráinne said. "In case we end up staying in an inn made of sticks and you huff and you puff and you blow it all down." Gráinne grinned and Ciarán frowned. "We can't check in to the inn until three, and I know this one is going to stand here and drool over the thought of curried chips." Gráinne jerked her thumb in Siobhán's direction before turning to Macdara. "Do you mind if I leave my bag here while I have a wander?"

"Not a bother," Macdara said. "I'll watch all the bags, so if anyone wants to have a wander, go to it, lads."

"Thanks, mate," Eoin said, clapping him on the back.

"Deadly," Ciarán said. "Can I go surfing?"

"Two problems with that," Siobhán said. "One, you don't have a surfboard. Two—and I would consider this the most important bit—you don't know how to surf."

"There's a surfing school," Ciarán said. "I saw it on our way in."

"I want to surf," Ann said. Of all of them, she was the most athletic. "That would be class."

"Why don't you just have a walkabout and we'll figure out all the activities later," Siobhán said.

"We're totally surfing!" Ciarán pumped his fist, and Ann shifted her backpack as she eyed the pile of luggage and then Macdara. Ciarán scooped up Trigger, their Jack Russell Terrier, kissed him on the head, and tucked him under his arm. He was a good little traveler, content as long as he was with one of them.

"Go on, so," Macdara said with a nod to her backpack. "I'll mind it." Ann grinned, slipped if off her shoulders, and placed it gently on the pile.

She whirled around and faced Gráinne. "Race ya." Gráinne didn't hesitate. She began running down the street toward the sea, her flip-flops slapping on the footpath and her silk cover-up billowing behind her as she held on to her floppy hat with one hand. Ann took off and within seconds had passed Gráinne, whipping off her hat in the process. Gráinne's shriek made heads turn. Or maybe it was her nice figure and black hair blowing in the wind. Sometimes Siobhán was jealous of her sister's take-no-prisoners approach to life. She wished she could be more carefree, but then what would she do about all the burdens permanently resting on her shoulders?

"Are you coming?" Ciarán said to Eoin. Eoin looped an arm around Ciarán and nodded.

"Should we race?"

"Nah," Ciarán said. "Racing's for girls." Eoin and Ciarán ambled away, and Ciarán could be heard yammering on about surfing. Eoin had been so focused on his soon-to-open restaurant that, out of all of them, he needed this break the most. Then again, Siobhán and Macdara had been working nonstop since their wedding. Marriage always took a back seat to crime. They all needed this getaway.

"It doesn't look like either of them are open," Siobhán said, looking between the chippers.

"It's not yet noon," Macdara pointed out.

"But their signs say eleven." The chipper across the street was obviously new, the blue paint so fresh, Siobhán could still smell it. Then again, maybe she was smelling spray paint. Someone had vandalized the banner across the top of the chipper and messed with the mural on the side of the shop. The cod had horns and fangs and was vomiting onto a basket of chips. "Yeesh," she said.

"Young lads, no doubt," Macdara said with a shake of his head. "Although it is kind of funny."

"Don't say that to Mr. Chips," a tall man standing at the back of the line piped up. He was dressed in a tan suit, which seemed an odd choice for the weather.

Siobhán had an urge to rip his blazer off and fan it in his direction. Siobhán's mobile phone rang. *James.* She answered it and chatted away and then hung up. "He'll be here by tomorrow afternoon," she said to Macdara. "Hopefully I'll know which chipper is best by then."

"Did you ask if he wanted to send his luggage ahead of him?" Macdara quipped.

A taxi interrupted the moment. It screeched up in front of Mr. Chips and a man jumped out before it had even come to a complete stop. He placed his hands on top of his head and grabbed clumps of his white hair as he vocalized his displeasure at the vandalized mural. Then he dropped his hands and whirled around, fury in his eyes. He was a short older man and had a fire in his belly. "Vera Cowley! I'm going to kill you!" he screamed at the red chipper. He then barreled across the street, cut the line, and began pounding on the door as the crowd looked on. Church bells rang out in the distance, striking twelve noon.

Siobhán and Macdara instinctually moved toward the distraught man.

"Calm down, will ya?" said a man at the front of the line. He wore a gray uniform with his given name: Tom. "She's obviously not in, which is odd. She called me effing and blinding about an appointment that *she* canceled."

"What time did she call you?" Siobhán couldn't help but ask. She was starting to realize that the man throwing a fit was Mr. Chips. Nasty divorce was right. *The War of the Chippers.* It took some nerve, or rage, to open a chipper across from your ex-wife's. And given his temper, Siobhán was already starting to side with Mrs. Chips. And she'd been here less than thirty minutes. No doubt people in this town had been forced to take sides as well. "How did she sound when you spoke with her?" Siobhán added.

Tom looked her up and down. "And who might you be?"

"I might be the Queen of the Nile," Siobhán said.

Tom frowned. "What on earth are you on about?"

"Anything's possible," Macdara said with a shrug.

Siobhán edged closer to the chipper, noting that all the blinds were shut and the sign was firmly turned to CLOSED. "Does she always keep her blinds closed?"

"No," Mr. Chips answered, eyeing Siobhán. "She'd rather spy on everyone. Lately with a giant pair of binoculars. Spying on me, at least." His eyes narrowed at Siobhán. "Blow-ins should mind their own business, like."

Siobhán's hands went to her hips. "I'm Garda Siobhán O'Sullivan, and this is my husband Detective Sargeant Flannery."

Behind her, Macdara groaned. "I thought we were on holiday. I wanted to be someone different."

Siobhán considered this. "Who do you want to be, like?"

Macdara tilted his head to the blue skies. "A man of leisure."

Siobhán turned back to a flustered Mr. Chips. "This is me husband, Mr. Man of Leisure."

"Thank you," Macdara said. "Spot-on."

"The guards?" Tom said. "Is something wrong?" He pointed to the closed chipper. "Did she call you as well?"

"Whatever she said, she's a liar," Mr. Chips said. He pointed to his own shop. "Look what the banshee did to me chipper."

"I take it you're Mr. Chips," Siobhán said.

"I am, so." He straightened up, obviously proud of his moniker. "Me real name is Corman Cowley, but everyone calls me Mr. Chips."

"Is someone going to suss out why she isn't open?" This came from a beautiful young Black woman at the end of the line. She had an English accent. "I'm here to review her new secret curry sauce, but I don't have all day."

"You're a restaurant critic?" Mr. Chips did not sound happy about it.

"I review for the website *Take Aways from Take Aways*. My blog post ended up in a local Irish paper, and now here I am. I'm Madeline Plunkett." She waved as if she were greeting fans from a float in a parade.

"*Take Aways from Take Aways?* Never heard of it," Mr. Chips said. Judging from the look on his face, he wasn't impressed.

"Then you live under a rock," Madeline replied.

"A rock by the sea," Mr. Chips bragged.

"I hear Mrs. Chips's new curry sauce is divine," a woman in line said, tugging on a strand of long blond hair. She was wearing overalls and holding the handle of a large cooler.

"Divine," Siobhán repeated with a sigh.

"I'll believe it when I taste it," Madeline said, her eyes flicking over the woman's overalls with a look of outright fascination. "If she ever opens."

"If she has a new curry sauce, I'm the Pope!" Mr. Chips said. "Or she stole it from someone."

Madeline Plunkett whipped out a notebook and began scribbling furiously. A man at the front of the line handed Mr. Chips a newspaper article. "You can read all about it," he said.

Mr. Chips skimmed the article, let out a groan, then balled it up and threw it at her front door. It bounced off it and landed on the footpath. He pointed at Madeline Plunkett. "Why can't you leave well enough alone? You're going to give her a big head, which let me tell you is already too big for her body."

"Careful now," Tom said, pointing to the discarded newspaper. "The guards here will give you a ticket for littering." He looked at Siobhán as if he expected her to do something.

"We're not local," Siobhán said. She picked up the newspaper. "But I don't like litter."

"I don't have all day either," Tom said. "And I hauled a new hood vent all the way here." He gestured to a lorry parked at the curb. DOWD RESTAURANT EQUIPMENT SUPPLY AND REPAIR.

"Equipment failure," Mr. Chips said loudly. "No wonder she's not open."

"When are *you* going to open?" Madeline inquired, her gaze flicking across the street to his chipper.

Mr. Chips looked as if he wanted to jump to his own defense, but then he took a moment. After all, she was writing for an influential website. "I'll have the doors open in a jiffy," he said. "Been working so hard I overslept." He dug in his pocket and handed her a flier. "Buy two lunch specials, get an extra basket of chips for free."

Madeline stared at it as if it could bite, then handed it back to him. "I always eat for free if I'm there to write a review."

Macdara sidled in and took the flier.

"Did you say you overslept?" The question, directed at Mr. Chips, came from the blond woman in overalls. She was in her twenties and quite pretty. She appeared to be in some kind of work clothes, and Siobhán found herself wondering what this woman did for a living.

"Yes," Mr. Chips said. "I've been burning the midnight oil and didn't hear me alarm this morning."

The blond woman put her hands on her hips. "I saw you racewalking by the water this morning. When I was bringing me boat in."

Boat? Interesting.

Mr. Chips shook his head. "Must have been someone else."

"If I say red tracksuit, does that mean anything to you?" she asked pointedly.

Mr. Chips turned red and looked at his feet. "Nope."

"Liar. It was you."

"If this yoke was racewalking, he must have been going too fast for you to recognize him. A case of mistaken identity." He scanned the crowd as if waiting for the others to jump in and side with him.

"I assure you, I know it was you," the woman said. "And you weren't alone." She gave him a pointed look.

Mr. Chips reddened, mumbled something, and turned away. The crowd was growing antsy.

"Are you sure she heard the knock on the door?" Macdara asked.

"I pounded on it," Tom said. "But feel free to give it a go."

Macdara banged on the door. "Mrs. Chips? I'm Detective Sargeant Flannery. Checking to see if everything is alright." Everyone strained to listen for any sign that she was in there. They were greeted by silence.

"Has anyone tried ringing her?" Siobhán asked.

"Nonstop," Tom said, holding up his mobile phone.

"I have keys," Mr. Chips said. "But I wouldn't want her to accuse me of breaking in."

Macdara stepped up. "Tell ya what. We'll deal with the fallout. This is a welfare check. May I have those keys?"

Mr. Chips held up a finger, then scurried back to his

shop. He returned minutes later with a set of keys. Everyone watched as Macdara attempted to unlock the front door. He turned back. "The key doesn't fit."

"She changed the locks?" Mr. Chips said. "Typical." He turned to Macdara. "Now do you see what I've been dealing with?"

"Why wouldn't she change the locks?" Siobhán said.

Mr. Chips whirled around and glared at Siobhán. "I don't know what it's like where you come from, but folks around here trust each other."

Siobhán did not let him rattle her. "Does she have keys to your chipper, then?"

Mr. Chips's face turned bright red. "That's beside the point."

"Is there a town locksmith?" Macdara asked.

"John Healy," several folks said at once.

"He's a local handyman. Everyone calls him whenever they need anything," Tom added.

"John Healy?" Macdara asked. "We're staying at Healy's Seaside Inn."

"That's him," Tom said. "Good man. Jack of all trades."

"In that case, I have his number," Macdara said. "Will someone else ring 999 and tell them we need guards out here for a welfare check and that we're trying to contact a locksmith. Otherwise they'll have to break down her door."

"There would be war," Mr. Chips said. "She probably had to pop out for an errand."

"Better safe than sorry," Macdara said as he took

out his mobile phone. "And maybe when Mr. Healy is done I can get a ride back to the inn."

"Sure lookit," Tom said. "He'll do anything for a pence."

Ten minutes later, a garish yellow lorry that belched smoke pulled up to the curb. Across it, painted in blue, were the words HEALY'S SEASIDE INN. Below it, painted in green, were the words JOHN HEALY—HANDYMAN. As if that wasn't enough, a third line in back read HEALY'S TAXI CAB. "That would be John Healy now," Tom said.

"Really?" Macdara deadpanned. "I wouldn't have guessed."

A man they assumed to be John Healy hopped out of the lorry carrying a chainsaw and whistling a jaunty tune. He was a spritely man, close to eighty.

"Me grandson Liam is on the way, but he heard you were a fellow sergeant and he's given the okay for me to open the door." John held up the chainsaw and grinned, flashing a set of teeth so perfect they had to be dentures. "Battery-powered."

"A chainsaw?" Macdara asked.

"I'll cut the doorknob off, reach in, and unlock it. Believe me, it's the quickest method."

"Your grandson is a guard?" Siobhán asked.

"Detective Sargeant Healy," John said with a grin. Siobhán was relieved to hear he was on his way. Macdara gestured for everyone to step back as John approached the door with his chainsaw. He made the hole big enough for his hand to fit through, and soon the door was open. John revved the chainsaw and grinned. Siobhán was almost sorry Ciarán wasn't there to see it. They certainly did things their own way in this town.

"Let us take it from here," Macdara said. John shut off his chainsaw and stepped back. Macdara and Siobhán quickly stepped inside. They saw her right away, and it was a right shock. Lying in the middle of the floor, faceup, was a woman. She was covered in white dust. *Flour.* A large burlap bag of it was sitting on her chest, and on top of that was a ladder. Even her face was covered in flour. Siobhán couldn't help thinking she looked like a piece of cod about to be fried. And strangely, next to her head sat a single bottle of vinegar.

"Oh no," Siobhán said. "Poor luv." She stepped closer. Something was written on Mrs. Chips's broad forehead. Siobhán edged in until she could read it. When the word was finally legible, Siobhán gasped. There was little chance that this woman had written on her own forehead. Someone else had been here. Someone who had meant her harm.

Chapter 3

The minute Siobhán and Macdara stepped back outside, the folks who had once been standing in an orderly queue converged at the door in a panicked clump. Everyone began shouting at once.

"Is she there?"

"Is everything alright?"

"You were in there a bit long, like . . ."

Macdara had called 999 from inside the chipper but was now forced to stand guard at the door. "We need everyone to back up, and please stay where you are. If you have to leave, I'm going to need to get your name and digits."

"I knew it," the woman in overalls said. "Something is wrong."

"Is she alright?" Mr. Chips said, his face breaking into a sweat. "You can't leave us hanging."

Siobhán knew the word was going to get out one way or another, and if they wanted these folks to cooperate when the guards arrived—the ones who actually had jurisdiction to investigate this case, it was best to be honest with them.

"I'm afraid Mrs. Chips has passed away," Siobhán said. "The guards are on their way and they will need the space to do their job."

"Passed away?" Mr. Chips said. "You're joking me."

"We would never joke about someone's passing," Siobhán said.

"Are you sure?" he asked. "Not about the not joking part, but is it possible she's pulling the wool over your eyes?"

Macdara frowned. "Are you suggesting that your ex-wife is playing dead?"

"She likes to mess around," he said. "Especially when it involves me."

"Are you saying you're involved in her death?" Siobhán asked. She caught movement out of the corner of her eye and turned to see Madeline Plunkett writing furiously in her notebook.

Tom, the repairman, turned to Mr. Chips. "I've hauled a new hood vent all the way out here. Any chance you need a backup?"

"I'm sorted, thanks," Mr. Chips said, holding his hand up and shaking his head.

"What about a supply of flour?" a woman with red hair in braids at the end of the line said.

The blond woman in overalls chimed in. "Me first. I have a fresh cooler of cod, and the ice is melting." She kicked the cooler at her feet, and it made a sloshing sound. "Mr. Chips, I'll sell it to you for half price."

The man dressed in the tan suit stepped out of line. In his late thirties or early forties, he was fit with a head full of wavy brown hair, so striking that Siobhán suspected he'd had a little help from a hairstylist. Gráinne would be impressed. "Would you consider switching to vegetable oil like Mrs. Chips did?" he called to Mr. Chips.

"Not on your life," Mr. Chips said, shaking his fist. "My fish will be battered in beef fat drippings until the day I die."

"Of clogged arteries," the well-dressed man said under his breath, shaking a flop of brown hair out of his eyes.

"Mrs. Chips—I know it was her—left a jar of beef fat on me doorstep," the redhead said. "Disgusting."

Murmurs of "Me too" rippled through the crowd.

"You've been eating it that way your entire lives," Mr. Chips said. "You've survived, haven't ye? It seems switching to vegetable oil didn't work out so well for Mrs. Chips." A shocked gasp rang through the crowd. Mr. Chips flinched. "I meant no disrespect to the dead," he said. "I'm in shock, that's all it is. May she rest in peace." He crossed himself.

Siobhán was gobsmacked. A woman had just died and they were all being so cavalier and selfish. "What is the matter with ye," she said. "A woman has been murdered and all you can do is try to cut deals?"

She didn't realize what she'd done until Macdara groaned beside her.

"Murdered?" a chorus rang out. *"Murdered?"*

Mr. Chips appeared to vibrate in front of her. "What are ye on about, murdered?"

Siobhán shook her head. "I'm getting ahead of meself. I only meant there's a possibility she was murdered. We'll know more after the state pathologist arrives."

"But why did you say murdered?" Mr. Chips said. "It wasn't a heart attack?"

"No," Siobhán said. "It was not a heart attack." The crowd edged in.

"Was she stabbed?" the redhead said.

"Shot?" someone else in the crowd called out.

"Did she drown?" the man in the suit asked.

Everyone turned to stare at him. The blond woman gestured to the chipper. "How would she drown inside a chipper, like?"

"Maybe she fell in the deep fryer," he said, crossing his arms and glaring at the woman.

Macdara held up his hands. "Settle, everyone, settle. Although there are indications that foul play may be involved, we cannot say anything for sure. The coroner and state pathologist will sort it out."

Mr. Chips wiped his brow. His gaze slid to the crowd of people. "I hope you won't think me demented for conducting a little business, but if Mrs. Chips is truly gone, she won't be needing the cod, and flour, like, and I still have a chipper to run."

"You must be the guards from out of town," a deep voice called out. Siobhán and Macdara whirled around to see a tall man standing in front of the chipper as if he'd materialized out of thin air. He was a ginger, and Siobhán found herself wondering if he had applied sunscreen this morning, as no doubt he burned easily. She soon had her answer, for when he removed his sunglasses the patches around his hazel eyes were pale white while the rest of his face was slightly red. An otherwise good-looking man, the sunburn made him look like an Irish raccoon. Macdara and Siobhán stepped forward and introduced themselves. The man stuck out his hand. "I'm Detective Sargeant Liam Healy. But most folks call me Liam. Are you my grandfather's guests?" His eyes slid to the lorry and his grandfather, who was back in the driver's seat bobbing his head to music none of them could hear.

"We are," Siobhán said. "We will be."

"Welcome, welcome," he said. "I'm sorry we're meeting under such sad circumstances."

"It's a bit more than sad," Siobhán said "It's bizarre at the least, sinister at the most."

"Sinister?" Liam held out two pairs of gloves and booties. "Would you like to put these on and accompany me inside?"

Macdara glanced at the luggage, then at John Healy, who was still perched in the driver's seat of his lorry.

"You go on, so," Siobhán said to Macdara. "I'll catch the sargeant up on the scene and then get myself to the inn."

"Are you sure?" Macdara asked.

Siobhán nodded. "I won't be long."

Macdara leaned in and lowered his voice. "It's not our case."

"We're on holiday," Siobhán agreed, hoping Macdara wouldn't see right through her. She couldn't help thinking of the poor woman's forehead and wondering who would write such a thing. Not to mention the bottle of vinegar placed at her head. It showed rage. Was it the ex-husband? He certainly fit the bill. Wait until she showed the detective sargeant what someone had done. And here Siobhán thought the sea was good for the soul. Was the perpetrator standing in front of them now?

"Mr. Healy, are you sure you don't mind giving me and the luggage a lift to the inn?"

John Healy leaned out of his lorry and tapped the portion that read HEALY'S TAXI CAB. "I dabble in a bit of everything," he said. "I don't mind, but of course there will be a small charge."

"Grandfather," Liam said with a laugh. "They're fellow keepers of the peace. If you must get paid, I'll pay ya."

"Are you sure you didn't gamble your earnings away in that poker game?" the grandfather teased.

"I have enough to pay your taxi fare," Sargeant Healy replied.

"That'll do," John said, giving the side of his lorry a good smack. "I would help you load the bags but me back isn't what it used to be."

"Not a bother," Macdara said, picking up as many bags as he could and waddling to the lorry.

"I'm afraid me passenger seat is a bit full. Someone threw out a perfectly good ladder that I had to fetch." Sure enough there was a ladder jammed in the front seat, the upper portion hanging out the open window. "You'll have to sit in the back with Clancy."

"Clancy?" Macdara asked.

"Don't worry. He's like a dog."

"He's like a dog?" Just then they heard a bleat from the back of the lorry, and a goat stuck his head out and bleated as if he knew the old man was talking about him. "Aye. There's Clancy now. Someone forgot to tell him he's a goat. Except when it comes to eating. You might want to remove those sunglasses, as Clancy will no doubt find them appealing."

"Where did you find the ladder?" Siobhán asked. It could be a coincidence, but she had a dead woman with a ladder on top of her so she had to ask.

"I'm afraid I got to her first, lassie," Mr. Healy said. "If you need a ladder I can direct you to the hardware shop."

Siobhán leaned over to Sargeant Healy. "It might be evidence, Sargeant Healy," she said. "You'll see in a minute."

"Please," he said. "Call me Liam." He looked at his grandfather and donned his gloves and booties. "Pappy. Where did you find the ladder?"

"Out in front of Bisby Fishery." He glanced at the beautiful blond woman in overalls.

She shrugged. "It's not mine. Maybe one of my crew. You can have it."

"How far is the fishery?" Siobhán asked Liam.

He pointed toward water. "About eight kilometers west," he said.

"When did you find it, Mr. Healy?" Siobhán asked.

"I found it early this morning." His gaze slid to the blond woman.

"Why were you at my fishery early this morning?" she asked.

"I was looking for Liam." John's face turned red as he looked at his grandson.

Liam sighed and shook his head. "I wasn't there, Pappy, and I don't need you driving all over Lahinch bothering folks if I don't return your calls straight away."

John sniffed, then shrugged. "Just making sure you were alright."

Liam glanced at Siobhán. "He doesn't like it when I stay out all night playing poker."

"Idle hands!" John shouted. "That's no way to pass the time."

"Relax," Liam said. "I wasn't out playing poker." Liam looked at Siobhán. "Should I take the ladder?"

Siobhán nodded. "It might be best."

"I'm going to take the ladder, Pappy. You can have it back when I'm finished."

John made a face, then shrugged. As Liam removed the ladder, John looked at Macdara. "Are you going to sit up front now, or would ya like to keep Clancy company?"

"I'll sit in the front," Macdara said.

John nodded. "Just watch the back of your head," he

said. "For some reason Clancy fancies curly-haired fellas. He might give you a nibble or three." He laughed. "Clancy fancies," he said. "That's gas."

The lorry took three tries to start, and when it did black smoke belched out of the exhaust. John peeled away from the curb. As promised, Clancy nuzzled up to the back of Macdara's neck. Macdara stuck his head out the window, pointed at Siobhán, and yelled, "Don't forget. We're on holiday!"

Chapter 4

Liam had reached through the hole where the doorknob used to be and was about to stick his hand through it when a petite woman in her sixties came barreling across the street, her chopped silver hair sticking straight up like her finger had just finished a date with a light socket.

"Detective Liam," she shouted. "Me mural has been vandalized by that mad cow. I want to press charges." When she reached them, she had to stop and catch her breath. She placed her hands on the knees of her red tracksuit as she took in gulps of air. Was this the woman that the fisherwoman had eluded to? The one who'd been spotted racewalking with Mr. Chips this morning?

"Tara," Liam said with a sigh. He turned to Siobhán. "This is Tara Flaherty. She was Vera's best friend."

"The key word being *was*," Tara Flaherty said, crossing her arms and lifting her chin.

"Before you say anything else about the woman who *was* your best friend—"

"I was justified in cutting off our friendship. Did you see what she did?" Tara pointed at Mr. Chips, who was still lurking on the footpath, then at the mural across the street. "She spray-painted a pair of horns on me fish. He's getting sick on the basket of chips." She clenched her fist. "I could kill her." Liam's face must have said it all. She stopped raging and dropped her hands. She stared at the hole in the door, then glanced at the crowd.

"What's the story?" Her tone instantly changed to one of concern. Siobhán couldn't help but feel she was witnessing a performance.

"She was your best friend but you painted a mural for her ex-husband's new chipper?" Siobhán said before she could stop herself. *That he opened directly across the street* . . . Siobhán probably should have stayed out of it, but she couldn't help herself. *Outrageous.* Siobhán couldn't imagine her best friends, Maria and Aisling, ever betraying her like that. Not that Macdara would ever divorce her. But if he did, her best friends would side with her hands down. Wouldn't they?

Tara planted her hands on her hips and squinted at Siobhán. "Who are you?" Mr. Chips sidled up and placed his hand on Tara's lower back. She shook it off.

"I'm a woman of leisure," Siobhán said.

Liam let out a surprised laugh that he cut off when the women looked at him. "Tara, this is Garda Siobhán

O'Sullivan, and Siobhán, this is Tara Flaherty. As she mentioned, she and Mrs. Chips were lifelong friends. Tara is our local artist and she owns a gift shop in town."

Tara chewed on her lip. "What's the story?" she asked again.

Liam nodded to Mr. Chips. "Why don't you two go back across the street. Mr. Chips will fill you in. Right now I need to concentrate."

Mr. Chips pulled a reluctant Tara across the street. Liam looked to Siobhán. "Ready?" Liam asked.

Siobhán nodded. "Brace yourself," she warned.

Liam stood just inside the doorway staring at the deceased Mrs. Chips. He shook his head. "Looks like she took a tumble off the ladder."

Just then the door behind them opened and Mr. Chips barged in.

"Vera!" he shouted. "Vera!"

"Stay back, Corman," Liam said, his voice deepening as he physically barricaded Corman from entering. "You cannot trample on a death scene, even if it was a terrible accident."

"She fell off the ladder?" Corman said, getting enough of a glimpse. "I warned her never to get on the ladder by herself. She was too impulsive." His voice sounded anguished, but Siobhán had learned through the years that murderers were often excellent actors. Liam wrestled Corman outside, then returned. He turned to Siobhán.

"I need to call Fergus."

"Fergus?"

"Apologies. Our coroner." He sighed as he took his mobile phone out of his pocket. "He may be on the golf course." He glanced at Mrs. Chips again and shook his head. "If only she'd waited for someone to steady the ladder."

"It wouldn't have made a difference," Siobhán said. "Unless the person had spotted the trap."

Liam tilted his head. "Trap?"

"I'll explain after you call in the brigade." The brigade consisted of the coroner, the Technical Bureau, the crime scene photographer, and eventually the state pathologist. It took a village to solve a murder.

Liam nodded, then stepped outside to make the calls. While she waited, Siobhán spotted a pile of bills on the booth. It was situated opposite where Vera's body lay. Given she had gloves on, Siobhán quickly thumbed through the pile. A note on a napkin slipped out. The napkin featured a blue fish eating chips from a basket and read MR. CHIPS across the top. *All that and no old bag!*

Written on the napkin was a note.

Binoculars are for the birds. Stop spying on us!
You've been warned.

"They're on their way," Liam said a few moments later when he returned.

"I noticed a pile of mail on the booth, and this fell out." Siobhán handed him the napkin.

Liam read it and sighed. "It's been a really nasty divorce," he said. "We've all had to suffer through it."

"What if it's more than that?" Siobhán asked.

Liam raised an eyebrow. "Such as?"

"What if this was no accident?" She gestured to poor Mrs. Chips. Liam had not yet clocked the two key pieces of evidence that convinced Siobhán this was anything but an accident. This was murder.

"I take it you have a theory you'd like to share?" He set the napkin back on the booth. "I'll get it in an evidence bag if I deem it necessary."

Siobhán nodded. She hoped he would see the two clues unprompted. Together they told a diabolical tale. "I believe this was murder."

"Murder?" He frowned as he looked around. "There's no sign of a break-in."

"I believe she left the door open when she picked up that"—Siobhán gestured to the can of black spray paint that sat on a nearby booth—"and marched across the street to vandalize the mural on Mr. Chips's new shop."

Liam mulled it over. "Go on, so."

"She returned to find a piece of twine, rope, whatever it turns out to be, dangling out, most likely tucked just underneath the enormous bag of flour that's lying on top of her." Siobhán pointed out the piece of twine that was just visible underneath the large bag. She then gestured to the high storage shelf where she believed the bag of flour had been resting. "I believe the ladder was propped just there."

"Ladder," Liam said. "That's why you wanted my grandfather to leave the one he picked up."

Siobhán nodded. "I don't know for sure, but either

someone switched the ladders or your grandfather picking one up is a coincidence." Siobhán O'Sullivan did not like coincidences, but she left that bit out. "Either way, she was expecting the hood vent repairman. And given the ladder was propped next to the hood vent, and the repairman was waiting in line when we arrived, then it wasn't his ladder. Either Mrs. Chips placed the ladder herself or someone else did." Siobhán pointed, although Liam was already looking at the hood vent.

"I don't think I'm catching what you're throwing."

"If I was waiting on a repairman I wouldn't supply my own ladder. I would assume he'd bring his own."

"Maybe she grew tired of waiting and climbed up to see if she could fix it herself."

"Perhaps. But there's more to it."

"Such as?" Siobhán could tell from his tone that he was growing impatient with her.

"Because the treads of this ladder are greased." Siobhán knelt next to the ladder and pointed it out.

"Greased?" Liam reluctantly knelt down and peered closer. "What's that smell?" He jerked back.

"Grease. Fat. Look at the rest of the treads. They're all shiny. Every single one of them is greased with something."

"Greased with what?" Liam didn't sound as if he believed her.

"I don't know for sure. Beef fat drippings?" It certainly smelled like it.

"Beef fat drippings?" Liam said. "But Mrs. Chips switched to vegetable oil recently."

Interesting. Was this some kind of message? Siobhán recalled someone in the queue from earlier saying something about Mrs. Chips leaving jars of beef fat dripping at people's doorsteps. Did one of those people do this? Siobhán asked Liam about it.

"I did receive several calls about that," he said. "I intended on having a word with Mrs. Chips today." They stood. Liam scratched his head. "But why would she climb a greased ladder?"

"I'm only guessing here, but given she worked around that smell for forty years, she probably didn't pick up on it, or didn't think it was unusual."

"That doesn't explain why she climbed the ladder."

"My guess is someone expected her to climb the ladder to figure out what that piece of twine was doing dangling from underneath her flour bag." Siobhán pointed out the twine. "And I believe it was someone who knew her well enough to predict her behavior, because that's exactly what she did."

"She climbed the ladder and pulled on the string," Liam said, slowly piecing it together. "Bringing the bag of flour down on top of her."

Siobhán nodded. "And as she scrambled to get away, she slipped on the grease treads and sadly fell to her death."

They stood in silence for a moment, thinking it through.

"That is an interesting theory, Garda. But it seems a bit far-fetched. I don't know how we would prove it."

"You can check CCTV cameras. One of the nearby

shops or restaurants is bound to have them. Especially the bank across the street."

Liam glanced out the front window. "That would prove whether or not someone snuck into the chipper while she was across the street."

"It would be a good start."

"That still doesn't prove it was murder. Someone could have seen the door open, thought the chipper was open and stepped in." He held his arms out palms up. "That doesn't mean they greased her ladder."

"True. But if someone innocently stepped inside and they discovered her lying on the floor like this, wouldn't they call 999?"

"Most likely a person would. But people get funny around dead bodies. I'm sure you're aware."

"The chipper wasn't open yesterday, was it?" Siobhán asked.

"She's closed Mondays and Tuesdays." He frowned. "How did you know that?"

"I don't smell fish and chips. Just the sour smell of old grease from the ladder."

"Observant," he said.

Siobhán smiled. "Comes with the job." Today was Wednesday. Siobhán looked up at the ceiling. "Does she live in the flat upstairs?" Many businesses in Ireland had flats above, often where the owner of the shop lived. Out back there would be a small garden. It was the exact setup of her old shop, Naomi's Bistro back in Kilbane. They had been in their new farmhouse only a year. She loved it and was super excited about Eoin's new restaurant opening, but sometimes she missed the old bistro right on Sarsfield Street.

Liam looked at the ceiling. "She used to live up there. She hasn't been staying here since the divorce. But you still haven't told me what's convinced you it was murder."

Siobhán edged closer to the body and pointed. "Do you see that beside her head?"

Chapter 5

Detective Sargeant Healy paraphrased Siobhán's words as if she was working his last nerve. "Do I see *what* beside her head?" He frowned, looked, looked, looked, then finally spotted it. "A bottle of vinegar?"

Siobhán resisted the urge to clap. "Why would a bottle of vinegar be on the floor?"

"It's a chipper," Liam said. "Maybe it fell on the floor." He sounded aggrieved that she had put him through all this about a bottle of vinegar.

"It's standing upright," Siobhán said. "Right next to her head." Liam chewed on his bottom lip. "And look at the booths. They all have a bottle of vinegar but they're not the same style of bottle." The bottles on the tables were new, the typical vinegar bottles you see in chip shops everywhere. The bottle by her head looked antique. It was tall with ornate glass. It didn't fit in with the rest.

Liam looked. He crossed his arms. "They don't match, I'll give you that." He continued to stare. "Maybe it was her personal bottle. A wedding present, a family heirloom, some such."

"Quite possible. But I don't see why she would set it on the floor and then happen to fall right next to it, do you?"

"It's a bit odd, I'll give you that. But it doesn't exactly scream 'murder.'" He still hadn't clocked the most important piece of evidence. "If the ladder was coated in grease, why didn't she see it?" He sniffed. "Or *smell* it?"

"I had to be right up next to it to see it. As far as the smell, my guess is that she's so used to it that she didn't think twice." It was also possible that as an older woman her sense of smell wasn't as sharp as it used to be.

"The Technical Bureau will send samples out for testing," he said. He glanced at the deep fryer. "Do you think it came from there?"

Siobhán shook her head. "It hasn't been used in two days and is not giving off any kind of heat." And if it was vegetable oil, and the rungs were coated with beef fat drippings, that wouldn't match either. It was Mr. Chips who still used beef fat drippings. Siobhán began to pace. "Vera came in this morning to open the shop. According to the hood vent repairman—"

"Tom Dowd."

Siobhán nodded. "Tom Dowd said that Mrs. Chips called him several times this morning to give out to him for being late. But Tom also insisted that she was the one who called and canceled the appointment."

"Maybe she was experiencing stress-induced memory loss."

"Stress-induced memory loss?"

Liam nodded. "After all the arguing she and Mr. Chips have been engaged in, not to mention falling out with her best friend, it's enough to knock anyone off their game."

"I think someone *else* canceled the appointment. And that someone was waiting to slip inside the chipper after she marched across the street to spray-paint the mural."

"Let's go with this scenario for a moment," Liam said as if he were being generous. "How would someone know she was going to march across the street?"

"We will have to check with her, but I believe Tara Flaherty didn't vandalize the mural until early this morning. The blond fisherwoman—"

"Sheila Bisby—"

"I believe Sheila Bisby saw Tara Flaherty and Mr. Chips racewalking early this morning. She eluded to him being with someone in a red tracksuit. Mr. Chips said she was mistaken. But Tara Flaherty was wearing a red tracksuit."

"That's not exactly a shocker. Everyone knew they were dating."

"Then why did he deny it?"

"Maybe they like all the secrecy. Some people do."

"My point still stands. The killer knew Mrs. Chips well. One might say he or she knew her intimately. The killer knew that the minute Mrs. Chips saw the mural, she would want to do something about it."

Just like the killer knew that the minute she saw a

piece of twine dangling from underneath the flour bag, she would need to pull on it. "I'm even starting to wonder if the killer brought the can of spray paint."

"Why are you wondering that?"

"Because I find it a bit far-fetched that she just happened to have a can of black spray paint the moment she needed it most."

"What does it even matter?"

It mattered a great deal. It was another piece of evidence that could trip up the killer. They could find every establishment nearby that sold spray paint, maybe even catch someone on CCTV camera purchasing it recently. Siobhán explained this to Liam.

"I did mention Tara Flaherty is an artist," Liam said. "Vera could have taken a spray can from her."

"That's a strong possibility," Siobhán said. "And Tara Flaherty did the one thing she could that she *knew* would get Mrs. Chips's attention."

"Are you saying that Tara Flaherty deliberately painted the mural just to lure Mrs. Chips out of her shop?"

"That, or someone hired Tara and instructed her to have this painted by this morning."

"And by someone you mean Mr. Chips?"

Siobhán nodded. "I assume he's the one who would have hired her."

Liam walked to the door. "My grandfather had to cut out the doorknob to get in?"

"Correct."

Liam frowned as he looked around as if imagining it. "Was there a queue in front of the chipper when you arrived?"

"Yes. And I got the feeling that they'd been waiting for a bit."

"How did the killer get out if the door was still locked from the inside?"

Liam wasn't the only one missing clues. Siobhán hadn't thought of that yet. "I don't know." She looked toward the kitchen. "Back door?"

"Let's check it." Liam strode toward the back, and Siobhán followed. Just past the small kitchen they found it. Siobhán assumed it led to a garden, but the door had small curtains and they were pulled shut. Even before Liam tried to open it, Siobhán could see the dead bolt was on.

"They didn't go in and out of this door," Liam said.

"They didn't go *out* that door," Siobhán said. "But isn't it possible they came in that door?"

"I thought you just said the entire point of the mural was to lure her out so that the killer could slip inside?"

"It's an evolving theory," Siobhán said. "But I can't rule out entry through the back door."

"Except for the fact that the dead bolt is still on," Liam said. Still gloved-up, he unlocked the back door and opened it. They stepped into a small but tidy backyard and garden. Flowers had been planted along with tomatoes, and a small shed was situated in the back. The door to the shed was open. They took a few steps toward it and got close enough to see that the shed was also tidy and well organized. "She came out for the ladder," Siobhán said. *Or someone did* . . .

Siobhán turned and studied the back of the house.

She saw no visible cameras. Liam picked up on her thought process.

"She didn't have cameras in the front either. They've been here forty years. She said the day she needed cameras was the day she closed up shop."

"Ironic for someone who liked watching everyone through binoculars," Siobhán said.

Liam nodded. "She was a woman of contradictions."

"Let's hope not everyone on the street felt that way about security cameras," Siobhán said. Security cameras were a garda's best friend.

"I'm sure we can pull plenty of CCTV footage." Liam headed for the side of the building. There wasn't much space between the chipper and the buildings next to it. There was barely enough for a person to squeeze through. But it could be done. However, if someone had entered this way, there was no obvious signs of a disturbance. No footprints, no trails of dirt or debris. Everything was tidy. Mrs. Chips had been an organized woman. The place may have been a bit run-down but it was still well maintained. There was pride here. "Let's check the other side," Liam said.

Unlike the right-hand side, the left was overgrown with weeds and bramble. No one could have walked through it. "I don't know what we're looking at," he said. "The back door was locked *and* dead-bolted. The front door was locked . . ."

A locked-door mystery. Siobhán had to remind herself she was on holiday. She could hear Macdara reminding her of that fact. She was on holiday. No matter how intriguing this case was shaping up to be. *H-O-L-I-D-A-Y.*

"I think we're back to my first theory," Siobhán said. "She left the front door open when she came out to spray-paint, and while she was doing that, the killer slipped inside. The killer would have had enough time to grab the ladder from the shed, grease the treads, and set it up."

"And then the killer slipped back outside all while she's still spray-painting?"

"I don't see any other possibility," Siobhán said. "There's not many places in here to hide—although possibly the killer hid by the back door—but even once Mrs. Chips is dead, I believe the queue had already formed outside."

"It really leaves us with only one possibility," Liam said. "The killer snuck in and out while Mrs. Chips painted the mural."

"Given the details she put into the fish getting sick all over his chips, I'd say the killer had enough time."

Liam gave it a beat. "But I still don't see a strong case for murder. Do you think it's possible this was an accident after all?" His voice was kind but firm.

Siobhán shook her head. "I do not." He raised his eyebrows but didn't say another word. "Maybe I'm wrong about the killer slipping in while she was spray-painting. But someone could have still greased the ladder in the shed, thus causing her 'accident.'"

"And the string hanging down that you believe was under the bag of flour?"

"Twine," Siobhán said reflexively.

"*Twine*," Liam repeated. "If no one was lying in wait, how did the twine get under the bag?"

"Maybe someone had enough time to come in and

place it"—Siobhán hesitated—"or maybe they came in on Monday or Tuesday when she was closed." They would have to track her whereabouts on her days off.

"In this scenario, a person would also need the ladder. So are you saying the killer simply left the ladder here? Wouldn't Mrs. Chips have walked in this morning and wondered who did that?"

"She was expecting a repairman. Tom Dowd."

"But she wasn't expecting Tom to somehow gain access to her shop and set up the ladder without her present. Believe me, she would have been quite alarmed in that scenario."

"I don't think so. She probably realized she left the door open while she was across the street, and when she returned she saw the ladder and assumed it was Tom's. Then she stepped out to grab more tools."

"And if it turns out to be her ladder?" He shrugged. "Not that I know how to even figure that out." True, it was a standard old ladder most likely found in a dozen different sheds.

"There's a lot to be discovered," Siobhán said.

Liam shook his head. "No disrespect and I appreciate your input, but as your husband pointed out, you're on holiday."

"A woman of leisure," she said. He was right. It wasn't her case. Even if it was utterly fascinating. It wouldn't be long before he asked her to leave his crime scene. She couldn't blame him; she would do the same thing. But given he hadn't done that yet, she wanted to see everything she could in the meantime. "Can you show me how you get to the upstairs flat?" *Maybe someone had been waiting up there?* Was there was a way to climb up to the roof, a second-floor window that could be accessed and slid open?

"I can show you where the stairs are to the upstairs flat, but until the Technical Bureau processes the scene, we can't go up there." Liam led her once again through the back door. To the left was a set of stairs going up. A door was closed at the top.

"What if—" She hesitated. He was already slightly annoyed with her, even though he was doing his best not to show it.

"Yes?"

"What if someone is *still* hiding up there?"

Liam stared at the door and thought through that possibility. When he spoke next, his voice was a whisper. "Someone snuck in while she's doing her thing. Brought in the ladder, slid the deadbolt closed. Propped the ladder near the hood vent. Climbed it. Placed a piece of string—"

"Twine."

He sighed. "What's the difference?"

"Twine is stronger."

He nodded. "Placed the twine under the bag of flour. Climbed back down. Greased the ladder with . . . ?"

"Beef fat drippings that she literally left on the killer's doorstep in a jar."

Liam took this in. At the thought that someone might be hiding in the flat listening to them, Siobhán's heartbeat ticked up. "And then what?" Liam whispered. "The upstairs door just happened to be unlocked and that's where one or more killers are still hiding?" He continued to stare at the door.

"Or the killer had a key," Siobhán said, also lowering her voice.

"And you think someone is *still* hiding up there?" Liam took a slight step back and placed his hand on his gun.

"I think we . . . *you* . . . should check it out. Otherwise a killer could slip away."

Liam nodded. "I need you to stay down here."

"Of course."

"I'm reaching for my firearm," he told her. Siobhán nodded and stepped farther back. Technically she could act as backup, but was it not smarter to wait for the team? But Liam was already in motion, his gun aimed at the door as he inched up the old wooden stairs. They were sure to creak at any moment. Siobhán hoped she hadn't given bad advice. She was already getting too involved.

At the top he rapped on the door. "It's the guards," he yelled. "Detective Sargeant Healy here and I'm armed. If anyone is in there, you need to make yourself known before I break down the door." He was greeted with silence that stretched on for minutes. He tried to open the door. "Locked," he said down to Siobhán. They stared at each other, breathing hard and waiting for their adrenaline to ease up.

"I can stay here and watch the door," Siobhán said. "I think you should have backup." Noises from the front of the shop rang out.

"Speak of the devils," Liam said, coming back down the stairs. "Backup has arrived."

* * *

When additional guards arrived, Liam and his team entered the upstairs unit by force. It did not take long to search the entire flat and find it empty.

"Neat as a pin," Liam said when he came back down. Siobhán was dying to have a peek, but this was it. She was not going to insert herself in the case any further. Liam was on it, and given this was his hometown, she could tell he was motivated to solve the case. Siobhán had a feeling this was not going to be easy. A right puzzler this one. The shed door had been left open, and possibly the front door, but now all the interior doors were locked. *From the inside.* Maddening. Siobhán felt a sudden lightheadedness. And it wasn't the kind you felt while on holiday. It was an anxious feeling. She couldn't help but hope that Liam would keep her up on any developments. Liam stood near the front door as the Technical Bureau began moving into the space.

Siobhán quietly approached. "I'm about to head off but before I do, do you mind if we go over one more thing?"

He held up his hand. "Listen. I've been thinking. I know you assumed this was murder, but what if she did this to herself because she wanted to frame Mr. Chips?"

"Frame him? For her murder?"

He gulped and nodded. "It was such a nasty divorce."

"Do you know if Mrs. Chips was right-handed or left-handed?"

He frowned. "No clue. Why?"

"Make sure the technical team and coroner get a

look at her fingertips, see if there is flour on her dominant hand's fingertips—at least on one of her fingers."

"Her fingers?" From his expression she could tell he thought she'd gone off the edge.

"Do I have time to show you that something?"

"You have me curious," he said. "I insist." Siobhán headed toward Vera's body, and Liam followed. The Technical Bureau held back a moment.

Siobhán knelt and so did Liam. "Not only is there a bottle of vinegar near her head, there's literally writing on her forehead." She pointed to the word someone had written in flour on poor Vera Cowley.

Liam's mouth dropped open as he followed Siobhán's finger to Vera's forehead. There, in all caps, was a single word: FRIED.

Chapter 6

Despite thinking that she was going to be in Liam's way, he said that if she could stay on until he was finished he'd give her a ride to the inn. She called Macdara and gave him the scoop. He said that he and her siblings were headed off to Lahinch Beach. She felt a twinge of regret that she wasn't with them and assured him that once she was finished here she would officially be on holiday. Macdara was his usual jovial self about it with a touch of sarcasm. But he said the inn was delightful and John Healy, jack-of-all-trades, was a gracious host. Apparently, apart from being an inn owner, a taxi cab driver, and the town's handyman, he also loved to garden and cook. He was busy showing her brood his new plants and discussing his mam's recipes with Eoin. They were all in a buoyant mood, which warmed her heart. She couldn't wait for James to arrive, and then they'd be all together.

As soon as she hung up, she saw a man carrying a golf bag on one shoulder and a black satchel on the other while wearing a protective suit, gloves, and booties striding toward her.

"Fergus," Liam said, intercepting him. "The town coroner," he said to Siobhán. "Good man."

"Morning, Liam," Fergus said with a booming voice. "You yanked me off the golf course, had to leave old McGee without a partner."

"Couldn't be helped," Liam said. "We've got a fishy one here, I tell ya."

Fergus raised an eyebrow. "Accident?"

Liam glanced at Siobhán, then gave a slight shake of his head. "Doubtful."

Fergus seemed to enjoy the answer. "Intriguing. Perhaps you made ruining me golf day worth it." Folks were still gathered outside the chipper, but they were getting restless: voices raised in concern, pacing, and the same story being told whenever someone new joined the clump. *It's Mrs. Chips—she's dead—this garda here on her holiday thinks it's murder* . . .

Great. They were talking about her. All small towns were alike. Chin-waggers, curtain-twitchers. Gossip, gossip, gossip.

"This is Garda Siobhán O'Sullivan," Liam said, interrupting her thoughts.

Fergus grinned as he dropped his golf bags on the bench of a nearby booth, on the opposite side of where the body lay. She found herself staring at his bushy mustache. "New in town?" he asked.

"On holiday," Siobhán answered.

"Siobhán," Liam said. "I hate to ask, but do you mind getting the names and digits of our witnesses here?" He gestured to the crowd outside. "They're getting ready to bolt I'm guessing."

"I don't mind at all," Siobhán said. "Happy to help."

Liam held up a finger as he patted himself down. "I have a notebook and biro in me car," he said. He was parked across the street and returned a moment later with them.

"Should I ask a few questions too?" Siobhán asked. "Might be good to get statements before—"

"They have a chance to make up a story," Liam finished.

"Sadly, yes."

"I'd really appreciate it, Garda."

"No worries." Liam and Fergus headed back inside the chipper. She wanted to start with Tom Dowd, the hood vent repairman. He was standing by his vehicle smoking a cigarette.

"I'm Garda O'Sullivan," Siobhán said as she approached.

"You're not in uniform," he observed casually.

"Right place, right time," she said with a smile. "If you're willing to answer a few questions, I can make sure you get back to work." She wondered if he'd sold the hood vent to Mr. Chips, but given he was driving a van it was impossible to tell if he'd put it in the back or sold it. "Did you make a deal with Mr. Chips?" she asked.

Tom shook his head. "Do you think her estate will pay for it?" he asked.

"I doubt it."

He stubbed out his cigarette on the side of the van. "Wasted morning."

"It was a bad morning for Mrs. Chips too."

His face reddened. "You're right, you're right, you're right." He crossed his arms. "Ask away."

"You mentioned that Vera called you to order the hood vent but then she canceled, but then she called again and gave out to you about missing the appointment?"

Tom arched an eyebrow. "You remembered all that?"

"I did, so."

He nodded. "I was due to repair it yesterday. But then she called and canceled."

"Did you actually speak with her?"

He shook his head. "My secretary, Caitlin, spoke with her, I believe. Or she left a message, I'm not sure which."

"I need you to write down her name and number." She handed him the notebook and biro. "Please add your name and digits as well."

"Not a bother." He jotted them down and handed back her things.

"If Mrs. Chips left a voice mail, do not erase it. The guards will want to listen to it."

"Understood." He tossed his cigarette at his feet and crushed it with his giant boot. "I did speak with Mrs. Chips this morning, if that's important."

"I would think it's very important. What time was this?"

"By the time I answered, it was half eight."

"By the time you answered?"

He nodded. "I missed her earlier calls. So by the time I answered she was screaming at me and I couldn't even think. I tried to tell her she'd canceled it the day before. She went mental. I wish I did have a recording of it. She was out of her mind with rage." He took out his mobile phone. "I finally agreed I would try to be there before eleven." He shook his head. "She did not like that answer. I finally agreed to do me best to be there by half nine."

"And were you?" Siobhán asked. "Here at half nine?"

"I was here by half ten. Ten forty-five at the latest." He shrugged. "I had a bit of a drive to pick up a hood vent."

"And where did you pick up this hood vent?"

"I have a warehouse outside of town."

"Was anyone at this warehouse?"

He laughed. "Are you looking for me alibi?"

"Yes," Siobhán said without a trace of a smile.

Tom frowned. "No," he said. "It's my warehouse and it's simply for storage."

Siobhán skimmed her notes. "Let's go back to this call where she supposedly canceled her appointment."

"Alright."

"When you spoke with her later, she denied that she ever called to cancel?" Tom swallowed hard and nodded. "Did you discuss it with your secretary?"

"I haven't spoken to her today. Caitlin is salt of the earth. If she says Vera Cowley canceled, then Vera Cowley canceled. I'm thinking the poor woman was losing it." He mimed someone tipping a bottle to suggest that she'd been drinking. "You never know." He began shifting his weight, looking at his lorry. He was anxious to go. "What exactly happened to her?"

"I'm afraid I can't answer that at this moment."

Tom removed a set of keys from his pocket and began to jiggle them. "I need to get out of here. I've already wasted half the day already."

"I'm sure Detective Sargeant Healy appreciates your patience," Siobhán said. "Murder has a way of interrupting the day."

"Murder?" he said, sounding eager for the gory details. "It's definite then, is it?"

Siobhán felt a hot flash of dread. She should have kept her piehole shut. "Death," she said. "I should have said death."

Tom leaned in, his breath stinking of cigarette smoke. "But you didn't," he said. "You said murder."

Several other witnesses heard his comments and edged in. Given Siobhán had already heard *them* bat the word *murder* around as if it were a beach ball, she felt she didn't deserve the heat. Then again, she was a guard and she should have known better.

"I misspoke," Siobhán said. "The cause of death will not be determined until the state pathologist makes an official determination."

"I think she doth protest too much," Tom said. "Am I free to go? Time is money."

He was way too callous about poor Vera's death. "You're free to go. But expect an official interview with Sargeant Healy."

Tom gave a nod as his van door squeaked open. "I'd be happy to chat with Liam anytime. He knows that." He climbed in, slammed the door shut, and peeled out.

"Can we go too?" Siobhán turned to find Sheila Bisby, the blond fisherwoman, staring at her.

"As soon as I get a name and contact information and you answer a few brief questions, each one of you is free to go."

"I'm next," Sheila said. "I have fish to clean."

"You're next then," Siobhán said.

Madeline Plunkett strode over and handed Siobhán a calling card. "This is where I can be reached. I'm afraid I must get to work or I'm going to miss a deadline." With that she strode away. Siobhán copied her name and number into the notebook and then tucked her calling card inside. She wasn't responsible for physically keeping the witnesses at the scene. Next to Madeline's name she wrote, *Refused to stay and be questioned, claimed she had a deadline.*

Siobhán then scanned the crowd and noticed that Mr. Chips and the ex–best friend Tara Flaherty were no longer in the crowd. She marked them down as absent. Typical. They were the pair Siobhán wanted to question the most. She glanced at the chipper across the street; the sign was still turned to CLOSED. Not that she could blame him. It would be downright callous to open after his ex-wife was found dead. Sheila Bisby gave an exasperated sigh as she flipped a strand of her long blond hair over her shoulder. "Your turn," Siobhán said.

Sheila continued to play with her hair. She probably wore a cap while fishing, but it seemed she was one of those women who could take off a cap, shake her head, and have her shiny tresses cascade back to perfection. Whenever Siobhán took off her garda cap, her auburn hair stuck up like a science experiment. She was envious, but that was petty given the circumstances.

"What would you like to know?" Sheila asked in an impatient manner.

Siobhán handed her the notepad and biro, asking her to write down her contact info. Sheila laughed, and it was a pretty sound. Siobhán raised an eyebrow. "Liam has my digits. He and I have known each other our entire lives," she said. She leaned in. "He has a little crush on me." Siobhán wasn't surprised; she was a very beautiful woman.

"I've no doubt that's true," she said. "But it's pro forma." Sheila shrugged and scribbled down her information. "Take me through your morning," Siobhán continued.

Sheila didn't hesitate. "I was out at sea—"

"What time did you set off?"

Sheila laughed. "Three days ago."

Siobhán felt foolish. She knew nothing about fishing. "Wow."

Sheila beamed. "That's actually nothing. Many commercial fishermen spend six months or more at sea. I fish only for the local chipper—or now chippers—and if the tides are in my favor I can get her done in a few days."

"Right, right. Catch anything?"

A look of pride came over her face. "I should hope so. Been doing it since I was a colleen. My family owns a fishery in town."

"I inherited a family business too," Siobhán said. "A bistro. My brother mostly ran it, but recently we moved to a new farmhouse, and soon he'll be opening a farm-to-table restaurant." Siobhán wasn't usually so chatty with witnesses unless she was trying to soften them up. But she was on holiday and she liked Sheila. "Do you like being a fisherwoman?" Siobhán had never met one and she was fascinated.

"I love it. Although it is getting challenging. These waters are overfished. And we have to cross our fingers that the kelp beds will stay plentiful. But I don't suppose you're here for a lesson on sea angling and fisheries, are ya?"

"Just curious. What time did you come back to shore?"

"This morning at half four."

If she truly spent three days fishing, it was hard to imagine she had time to pull off a complex murder. But people lied all the time. Or, in this case, told a fish story. "Take me through the rest of your morning, so."

"I was knackered, and my brothers and father came out to unload me haul. I took a shower, made a cup of tea, and decided to walk the promenade."

"Even though you were just back from being out to sea and you were knackered?"

"I can never go to sleep after days at sea. A walk always helps me transition. Shake off me sea legs."

"Right, right. Go on, so."

"When I was on my walkabout, I saw Corman and Tara racewalking. I said hello, but they seemed to be in an intense conversation and they didn't even notice me."

"What time was this?"

"I'd say it was half five, close enough anyway."

Did everyone in this seaside town wake up early? "Did you happen to go by this street?"

"No. I only walked the promenade." Sheila glanced at the vandalized shop front. "You're wondering when Vera did that, are ya?"

"How do you know Vera did that?" Siobhán knew it was the most likely scenario, but you never knew how someone would answer even the simplest questions. This job never failed to surprise her.

"Are you joking me?" Sheila let out a musical laugh. "Who else would do that?" Siobhán kept a neutral expression. She didn't want to give anything away, especially when Sargeant Liam was counting on her.

"And after your walkabout?" Siobhán said. "What did you do then?"

"I went back home, took a catnap, and then was in line for Mrs. Chips at half ten to deliver fresh cod."

"Was it unusual that her shop was closed?"

"Unusual? It was like Santy not showing up for Christmas." Her eyes took on a glint of mischief. "That is, if you believe."

"Was anyone else here when you arrived?"

Sheila tilted her head and gave it some thought. "There were folks out and about. Lahinch is always busy in the summer. And the weather's been gorgeous, so we're full-up."

"Understood. But was anyone else waiting for Mrs. Chips to open?"

"Tom Dowd's lorry pulled up, but I believe he stayed in it for a spell."

"What time was this?"

Sheila sighed. "I know these questions are important for your investigation and I'm not trying to be obtuse, but I just wasn't paying that close of attention to the time."

"But he arrived after you?"

"Yes. I did let Tom ahead of me in the queue."

"That was kind of you." Sometimes a little flattery went a long way.

Sheila gave a modest shrug. "He said Mrs. Chips needed a new hood vent installed and she was irate about it." She looked around, then leaned in. "To be honest, we were all a bit afraid of her lately."

"Afraid?"

"She was a bit intimidating when she was on a rant. And since the divorce, she'd been on one big rant. Did you know she was putting jars of beef fat drippings at people's doorsteps?"

"I heard. Did she put one at your doorstep?"

Sheila shook her head. "I'm lucky, she probably didn't want to step foot in the fishery."

"Can you think of anyone who meant Mrs. Chips any harm?" Often these types of open-ended questions generated interesting answers, even if you did have to take them with a grain of salt.

"Are you asking me to guess which one of us is a killer?" Sheila raised an eyebrow.

"I'm not asking for guesses," Siobhán said. "I'm just trying to figure out what was going on with Mrs. Chips."

Sheila rubbed her chin. Her fingernails were bitten to the quick. It had to be a lonely job being adrift in the ocean for days at a time, let alone months. It probably made a person go a little bit mental. Sheila presented herself as a calm woman. Her fingernails told a different story. "I thought maybe it had something to do with the mural. I figured she saw it, spray-painted it, and then was on a warpath after Tara and Corman."

"Why do you think Corman denied that he was out racewalking?"

"Because he was with his girlfriend. They've been denying their affair. It's ludicrous, because we all know about the two of them." Once more Sheila looked around, then lowered her voice. "It's been going on for ages."

"Do you mean they were having an affair while he was still married to Mrs. Chips?"

Sheila put her hands up. "You didn't hear it from me, like."

"But now they are officially divorced, are they not?"

"I think you mean *were* divorced," Sheila said. Her forehead scrunched. "Are you still divorced when you're dead?"

"Technically, yes, I suppose so." Siobhán leafed through her notes. "But even though they were officially divorced, it sounds like there was still quite a bit of tension between the two."

"Tension? It was all-out war. In Vera's mind, marriage was forever. She was doing everything she could to prove that the affair between Tara and Mr. Chips began *before* the divorce. I bet it would have made a difference in their settlement." Sheila glanced at the Mrs. Chips shop front. "The chipper could use a bit of a face-lift, and she made no secret of the fact that she needed money to fix it. Then again, Mrs. Chips most likely would have done the same thing regardless. I think she just wanted revenge."

Revenge.

"I'm sure that's very common during a messy divorce." Mrs. Chips had been turning up the heat on Tara Flaherty and Mr. Chips. She'd also been keeping tabs on who frequented the new chipper. Had someone grown tired of her rage? Siobhán was in no way blaming Mrs. Chips—after all, a person could not predict their own reaction if their entire world were turned upside down by the person one loved the most. But learning about the fallout from their divorce and what it prompted Mrs. Chips to do could be the key to unraveling the entire mystery. Part of being a guard was to ask unsavory questions. This was no time to be polite.

Sheila glanced at her mobile phone. "Will that be all?"

"Two more questions. Did Mr. Chips buy your haul of fresh cod?"

Sheila frowned and studied Siobhán. "He did," she said. "But before you read into that—everyone has to earn their living. Even if there's been a tragedy."

Siobhán nodded, although she still thought the timing was in poor taste. "This morning you said you saw Corman and Tara racewalking when you pulled your boat in."

Sheila arched an eyebrow. "We literally just went over that." Sheila's friendly demeanor had vanished.

"The story we went over didn't match your original story." Siobhán tried to keep her tone neutral. *Not accusing here, just clarifying.*

"What are you on about?" Sheila was clearly agitated.

"You either saw Corman and Tara when you were pulling your boat in or saw them much later when you were having a walkabout. I was just wondering... Which is it?"

Chapter 7

Sheila Bisby stared at Siobhán as she pondered the question, making Siobhán wonder if the fisherwoman was trying to buy herself time to concoct an answer. Innocent or guilty, most folks did not like to be called out about their inconsistencies. But Siobhán had no choice. Either Sheila had seen Tara and Mr. Chips either while she was pulling her boat in or while on a walkabout. The answer mattered.

"Wow," Sheila said. "Good memory. I saw them on the promenade. On my walkabout."

"Why did you tell them it was when you were pulling your boat in?" Siobhán was genuinely curious.

Sheila sighed. "I just thought if I told him I saw them when I was pulling me boat in, Mr. Chips might try to correct me and confess that they saw me when we passed on the promenade." Sheila grinned, and a twinkle came into her eye.

Siobhán found her answer a bit puzzling. "Do you fancy yourself an amateur detective?"

Sheila placed a hand on her chest. "Me? Not at all. But Corman's as slippery as a fish, so I thought I'd give it a go. Obviously it didn't work."

He wasn't the only slippery one around here. "But you have no doubt that it was Corman and Tara?"

"Do you think I'm telling a fish story? Hoping you'll buy it hook, line, and sinker?" She appeared thrilled by her own deceipt.

"Are you?"

Sheila shook her head, then chewed on a fingernail. "I don't mean to make light of the situation. I liked Vera. And I thought Corman was horrible for carrying on as he has been. With her best friend! I mean, I know there's only so many old people in the dating pool, but he could have ventured a bit further outside the circle. Opening a chipper across the street, using the paint colors she'd always wanted, and not only dating her best friend but getting that same best friend to paint a mural on his chipper? She had to look at that sign every single day, like." She sighed as she stared at his chipper. "He'd better go to confession, because he's been a very bad man. And Tara has a lot to answer for as well, like. There are just some lines you don't cross. Especially with a supposed best friend."

Siobhán was inclined to agree. And yet Sheila still sold Mr. Chips the cod. Business before ethics, apparently. "That's it for now," Siobhán said. "Liam may be contacting you to set up an official interview."

"Not a bother," Sheila said. "I hope you get to enjoy the rest of your holiday." As Siobhán watched Sheila walk away, a guilty feeling washed over her. There was little doubt—and here is where the guilt came in—that she was *already* enjoying her holiday. She couldn't help it. The murder was intriguing and so were the folks she'd met so far. Sheila was likable, but Siobhán found herself wondering if the woman had been lying. She was quick with an explanation, but *had* it been a fish story? One thing was for sure. In this delightful seaside town, everyone in Vera Cowley's orbit seemed to be keeping their share of secrets. Perhaps an ocean of them.

Healy's Seaside Inn was so close to the bay that Siobhán was afraid Ciarán would sleepwalk, wander out, and tumble into its watery depths. He wasn't a child anymore, but she still didn't trust his young brain. The exterior of the older inn was delightful, painted yellow with turquoise trim. It had aged nicely; it didn't look brand-new by any means, but the outside was tidy and the planter boxes showcased an array of colorful flowers. Seagulls would be their alarm clock. She opened the old wooden door and stepped into a small foyer. In front of her, a set of stairs led up to the second floor; a cozy living room was situated to the left, and just beyond that was the dining room and kitchen. That's where she found Ciarán and Eoin conversing with the handyman himself. John Healy was rummaging around his cupboards as Eoin nattered on about recipes. Ciarán had his face shoved into an old fan on the kitchen counter. As he'd done with the one at home, he was talking into it, enjoying the sound of his own voice as it wobbled. Indeed, the gap year would be a blessing. "You'll cut your tongue off," Siobhán said.

Ciarán turned and stuck it out at her. "Still there," he said.

John turned to greet Siobhán. "How ya," he said. "It's good to see you away from that nasty business at the chipper." He shuddered.

"You have a beautiful inn," she said.

"Thank you. It's been in my family sixty-some years but it's still a work in progress." He grinned and gestured to a dining chair. "Sit, sit, I'll put on the kettle."

"I'm a robot," Ciarán cooed into the fan. "We don't have tongues." He said that, or something like it, it was hard to tell.

Siobhán rolled her eyes as she took a seat. It was his tongue. If he wanted to lose it, so be it. She turned to Eoin. "Talking shop as usual, I see."

"John started it," Eoin said with a grin.

"'Tis true, 'tis true," John said as he ferried a tin of biscuits and a cup of Barry's tea to the table.

"Ah, thank you, brilliant," Siobhán said. She could definitely use a cuppa.

John stood over her. "When you registered as a guest, I had no idea you were a garda and that your husband was a detective sargeant." He placed his hand on his heart. "Given me grandson is a detective sargeant as well, consider me family."

"Aren't you a luv," she said. "But please, treat me husband like a man of leisure or we'll never hear the end of it." She winked as John tilted his head in confusion.

"I might be talking shop, but you're walking shop," Eoin said, wagging his finger at her. "But given you've been at a murder scene, I'd say you're talking *and* walking shop." He crossed his arms and grinned.

"Touché," Siobhán said.

"Are you sure Mrs. Chips was murdered?" John asked. "I mean, I know it was a nasty divorce and all, but I just cannot see anyone in Lahinch doing such a horrific thing."

"I'm sure your grandson will sort it all out," Siobhán said. "But you'd be surprised what even the nicest people are capable of when under a tremendous amount of pressure." *Or hatred. Or rage. Or fear. Or greed. Or revenge. Or heartbreak.* She sighed. There were too many reasons people were driven to murder. Macdara was right. They needed this holiday. She would make every effort to keep her nose out of this case. She should feel relieved that it wasn't her problem. Even if she did want to start canvassing the entire street for CCTV footage.

As she sipped her tea, her eyes landed on a pile of wet towels on the kitchen floor near Ciarán. He was wearing swim shorts and a T-shirt. "Ciarán O'Sullivan!" she said. Startled, Ciarán actually pulled away from the fan. Siobhán pointed at the towels. "You should be ashamed of yourself. It is highly disrespectful to dump your disgusting wet towels on the floor." It was then she noticed the pile was bigger than she first thought. Shame filled her. What must John Healy think of them? "Is that a sheet?" She shook her head and pointed to the pile. Had he already messed up his sheets? "Did ya grow up in a barn?"

"No," he said, frowning and not sounding one bit sorry. "I grew up in a bistro." He flashed a grin.

Siobhán made eye contact with Eoin, who was also grinning.

Eoin shrugged. "He's not wrong."

For some odd reason both Eoin and Ciarán were happy out despite her reprimands. Ciarán was usually very sensitive to scolding. Perhaps it was hard to be scolded by your sister, not your actual mammy, or perhaps when you were as tall as the person scolding you, it was nearly impossible to tolerate. But a grin was different. She knew instantly that whatever this was, it was going to be a story that was told and retold until the day she died. She sprung out of her chair. If they wouldn't pick up their messy towels and sheets—what was he doing with a sheet, anyway?—she was going to have to do it herself. *Typical.* She'd give out to them more when they were alone. Just as she bent to pick up the laundry, John Healy sheepishly raised his hand.

"I'm so sorry," Siobhán said. "His manners are usually much better than this. Is there a hamper or a laundry room?"

John shook his head. "I'm afraid I'm the one who dropped them on the floor."

Ciarán and Eoin roared with laughter. "You should see your face," Ciarán said. "It's about twelve shades of red."

"Sorry to leave them on the floor," John said. "You'd think I was raised in a barn, but that's not the case." He looked truly embarrassed, which made Siobhán want to crawl under the table and hide. "I had to scramble to get a room ready for our additional guest, and then, well, the young one was having so much fun talking into the fan that I was just waiting to use the washer." He pointed to where Ciarán was standing, which was indeed in front of a small built-in washing machine.

"I'm so sorry," Siobhán said. "That's not a bother at all. Ciarán should have moved out of your way." Additional guest? She thought there were only six rooms in the inn, and she was still waiting on James to let her know whether he could make it. Then again, James could always room with Eoin, and she was certainly not going to make a fuss about it. "Ciarán, would you put those clothes in the washer for Mr. Healy?"

"I won't hear of it," John Healy said, as Ciarán moved out of the way and John scooped up the pile of laundry. "You're the guests."

Ciarán had the decency to open the washer and wait while John shoved the clothes inside and set about starting the machine.

"I'm terribly sorry, Mr. Healy," Siobhán said, "and of course I wasn't implying that you . . ." *Were raised in a barn*. Perhaps it was best just to forget that part altogether.

"Are you going to apologize to me?" Ciarán said. "For accusing me of doing something I didn't do? And then apologize to Mr. Healy for saying he was raised in a barn?" The grin didn't fade, and he held up his smartphone as if to record her. *Cheeky*.

"Mr. Healy, I was only giving out to Ciarán, and now that I see you were only being polite so he could play with the fan—"

John Healy held up a hand. "Don't mention it," he

said with a chuckle. "I took no offense." He patted Ciarán on the back. "And this one reminds me of Liam when Liam was his age."

"Aren't you going to ask who the surprise guest is?" she heard a familiar voice say. She whirled around and there he was, James O'Sullivan, the oldest of the clan standing before her.

"James!" She launched herself at him. "*You're* the additional guest!"

"I couldn't let ye have a holiday by the sea without me," James said, tolerating her as she squeezed the life out of him.

She stepped back to have a proper look at him. He was skinnier than she remembered. "Are you eating enough?" Siobhán asked. "Have you lost weight?"

"Ah, stop." He gently shoved her away, then patted his very thin stomach. "I burn a lot of calories working on houses."

He was now in the construction and remodeling game and it suited him. He'd come a long way from the drinking lad of his youth. Sobriety was a gift from heaven, and even though he'd been sober for many years, Siobhán still had a wedge of fear in her that he would relapse. She knew it was part of the program, but secretly she prayed that he would never touch a single drop again.

"How was your trip?" She wanted to hug him again, but he was already moving through the space.

John Healy pulled out another chair at the dining table and gestured to James. "Sit, sit." He scrambled to fix another cup of tea.

Siobhán gladly took her seat again and felt some of the stress of the afternoon melt away. James sat across from her. She loved having all her siblings together again. Well, almost together. "Where's Gráinne, Ann, and Dara?" she asked.

"Exploring the beach," Eoin said, "and Macdara is having a snooze."

"A snooze?" For a moment, she thought about shaking her husband awake. She'd love to bounce some details of the case off him. In the end, she settled back. He had a right to holiday however he wanted. As long as he didn't sleep the day away.

"How is me grandson getting along at the chipper?" John asked as he poured the tea. "Miserable business altogether."

"Sure lookit," Siobhán said. Although she'd be happy to discuss the case with Macdara, she was definitely steering clear of gossiping with the detective sargeant's family. Liam could dish out the news he wished; she'd leave it with him.

"What kind of miserable business at the chipper?" James asked. "Did Siobhán eat them out of curried chips, like?"

"Hilarious," Siobhán said. "But no. The owner of the chipper was found dead in her shop this morning, and we believe there's foul play involved."

"Foul play," John repeated, shaking his head. "Right here in Lahinch."

"Your kind of holiday," James said under his breath to Siobhán. "But jokes aside, that's a shame." Siobhán and James crossed themselves in unison.

"John was telling me all about his mother," Eoin said. "Supposedly she has some deadly recipes he'll let me have if I play me cards right." He winked at John.

"You've already won the hand, lad," John said. "I'll let you have them. They're no good to me now."

"I don't believe that," Eoin said. "You've still got a hearty vegetable garden out back. You're even growing beans."

"I'm hoping for a beanstalk," John said with a grin. "In case I ever need to climb on out of here."

"Speaking of cards," James said. "I could use a game of poker."

Siobhán tried not to react. She always feared that gambling could lead to drinking. All those addictions tended to get tied up in a messy knot. But he was a grown man and she had no control over his actions. That didn't stop her from worrying.

"My grandson attends a game around here now and again," John said. "Next to the bank, across from Mrs. Chips as a matter of fact. But I'd stay clear of it if I were you."

"Why's that?" James asked with a grin. "Are they sharks? Big spenders?"

"They can get a bit vicious, so they can." John's face clearly showed his disapproval.

"Ah, stop. Isn't that always the way," James said. "I'm good at knowing when to fold." He trained his gaze on Siobhán as if challenging her to respond. She mimed locking her lips and throwing away the key.

"Why don't you ever do that when it comes to me?" Ciarán sulked. "I'm a full-grown adult capable of making his own bad decisions." Everyone laughed, and Ciarán frowned in confusion.

"I rest my case," Siobhán said. John brought over James's cup of tea, but John's hands were shaking so badly that the cup rattled on the plate. James jumped up to help him.

"Thank you," John said. "I've been a bit weak lately."

"Is there anything we can do?" Siobhán asked. "Maybe Eoin can fix you something to eat?"

John held up his hand and shook his head. "I'm not able for it," he said.

"Maybe you should have a seat."

"Don't mind if I do." John hobbled over to the table and sat down across from James. Siobhán hoped he could retire soon, if that's what he wanted. She shouldn't assume he couldn't work because of his age, but she had a feeling it wasn't easy to keep up an old inn by the sea. And if the place was empty when they'd arrived, but there was a room he was just now getting around to cleaning, Siobhán had a feeling it was indeed difficult for him. And Liam wouldn't have much time to help; being a detective sargeant was a full-time job, which she well knew. Macdara was gone for long stretches at a time, even longer than the hours she put in as a guard. There were days it was dark when she left the house and dark when she returned. She aspired to be a detective sargeant herself, hopefully in the next few years. She'd already been studying for the exams. "Thanks a million," Siobhán said as John Healy pushed the tin of biscuits closer to her and nodded for her to take one. What she really wanted was a good lunch, but it was so late in the afternoon that it would have to be supper. Given they weren't going out to eat any time soon, she helped herself to a biscuit.

"How does one get in on this evil game of poker?" James asked.

John pursed his lips. "Mike McGee runs the dirty game, but you can ask Liam, me grandson, when you meet him. Watch yourself, or they'll bilk you out of your hard-earned money."

"I might be a chancer," James said, "but I'm no fool."

"Sure, you know yourself," John said.

Siobhán nibbled on her biscuit while she mulled something over. "This Mike McGee—you said his games take place across from the chipper?"

John nodded. "Used to be a touristy shop. Knick-knacks and whatnot. Then bigger ones moved in and it's been vacant for about a year now. McGee runs the bank next door. I suppose he was too lazy to go much further after work for his shady game."

John had made several derogatory comments about this game. There had to be more to the story. She also wondered if maybe an unsavory character had been hanging around after the poker game. Perhaps this person had been watching Mrs. Chips. And although she hadn't been allowed into Mrs. Chips's upstairs flat, she'd noticed that a window faced the bank and of course Mr. Chips. Maybe Siobhán had it backward. Had Vera been spying on a gambler? Someone earlier today had mentioned they'd seen her with binoculars, peering out at Mr. Chips. For most folks, a poker game was probably just a bit of craic, and maybe they'd lose a hundred euro or so. For others, it could become an all-consuming addiction that took them to their knees. If Liam did open up to her about the case, she'd mention this—even if nothing as drastic as her imaginings had taken place. Siobhán couldn't help running through a scenario. Mrs. Chips spies on a gambler—maybe he loses too much, maybe she threatens to tell the man's wife. Then again, how could one see all that even with high-powered binoculars? But maybe *something* had occurred, maybe she had witnessed something someone didn't want her to see. Whoever this killer was, the person had planned it out well in advance. It had been too polished to be an impulsive kill; there were too many moving parts. An old rotary phone on the counter rang, making Siobhán jump. John sprang from his chair and reached it before it could ring again.

"Speak of the devil," John said. "How are you getting on? Right, right, right. She's sitting right here with meself and her brothers. I'm threatening to give one of them some of Mam's recipes. And we've a new arrival here, James O'Sullivan and he'd like to join that nasty poker game. I warned him off it, but you know yourself." At this, John turned to James and winked. "Let me see." He held the receiver to his chest and addressed Siobhán. "Liam would like to know if you and your husband would join him and the woman he's chasing after for dinner tonight." He glanced at Eoin again. "All of you are welcome. He's taking you to a fancy restaurant with a great view of the sea, and if you're lucky you can catch the sun set over the bay."

"Lovely," Siobhán said. "We'd love to."

John repeated that to Liam and hung up. "Dinner's on him. I'll come too. Any time me grandson is offering to pull his wallet out of his trousers, I'm there."

"We'll be looking forward to it," Siobhán said. *Woman he'd been chasing?* That must be Sheila Bisby. Why was she stringing him along if she only thought of him as a friend?

John grabbed a book on his counter and began scribbling in it.

"Are you a writer?" Siobhán asked.

"Me? A writer?" John laughed. "Not at all. I just like to write down me thoughts, feelings, and observations day by day."

"A diary," Siobhán said. "That's wonderful."

"A diary?" John looked horrified. "Not at all, go away with you, it's not a diary at all." He scoffed. "A diary." At that he picked up a tiny key and locked the book before setting the not-a-diary diary back on the counter. "I use this to lock it up just in case someone wants to have a snoop."

"My mistake," Siobhán said. "Not a diary at all."

John nodded seriously. "Don't let it happen again. Maybe you were right in the first place. You could call me a writer and this is my work."

"In that case, I would love to give it a read."

John perked up. "You would?"

"Absolutely."

He looked thoughtful. "Maybe when it's finished."

She nodded. "How long have you been at it?"

John began to count on his fingers, and his lips continued moving when he ran out of them. "About forty years."

Siobhán choked on her tea, then began to cough. "Well," she said. "I won't hold me breath."

"That's for the best," he said. "But you can read it when I'm dead."

Chapter 8

The table Liam reserved at the fancy restaurant by the surf school faced the ocean, and that evening their large group arrived just in time to see the sun set, spreading its glorious colors across the horizon as it appeared to sink into the bay. It had been a while since the O'Sullivan-Flannerys had dressed up to go out, and it was even more festive to be joined by Sargeant Liam and Sheila Bisby. Unfortunately, John Healy said his old bones weren't up to an outing this evening, so he stayed back at the inn. Sheila sported a little black dress, so dolled up Siobhán found herself questioning her assertion that she had no romantic interest in Liam. That is until she started flirting with James, and James beamed like a lighthouse. *Fantastic*. He was going to become infatuated with a suspect.

And that was before Gráinne, who had been sitting next to James at the end of the table, switched seats with Sheila and was suddenly laughing at everything Liam said, playing with her hair, and touching the detective sargeant's arm every chance she got.

Liam didn't seem outwardly bothered by it, but he did look as if he was out of his depths, and unfortunately he was right. Gráinne was intense even when she was flirting. Liam needed to be able to focus on this case, but if Siobhán tried to stop Gráinne from chasing after love, there would be war. Eoin was studying the menu as if he were about to write a thesis on it and peppering their server with questions about the chef. Siobhán could feel his excitement; opening his own restaurant was a major life event, which came with a mix of extreme stress and extreme joy. Right now, he was in the extreme joy phase, and she wanted it to last as long as possible. Ciarán and Ann were excitedly going over their day combing the beach. They'd found shells and rocks, and the pair of them were still mad to take surfing lessons. The very thought of it made Siobhán nervous, but Macdara thought it was a grand idea. Youth was for taking risks. It seemed everyone was in holiday mode but her. She was dying to talk to Liam about the case. Macdara, most likely sensing this, ordered drinks for the table. Nonalcoholic for James, and for Liam, who said he wouldn't be drinking given he had a very early start in the morning.

"See?" Macdara said, leaning in and whispering in her ear. "He's got this. You can let go."

"I agree. He's competent," Siobhán said. "I am officially letting go." Macdara continued to stare at her, and she forced herself to relax her shoulders. "Bring on the cocktails," she said uncharacteristically loud.

"I'm on holiday." Macdara laughed, then reached for her hand under the table and gave it a squeeze.

"I've always been fascinated with fishing," James said, his eyes sparkling as he stared at Sheila.

"You have?" the rest of the O'Sullivan Six said in unison.

James didn't miss a beat. "It's been a dream of mine to go out in a fishing boat."

"You're welcome to come out on me trawler with me tomorrow morning," Sheila said.

"Really?" James said. "I would love to."

"Me too?" Ciarán piped up.

"And me?" Ann said.

"Of course," Sheila said as James's face fell. Sheila looked to Gráinne and Eoin. "My trawler is big enough for all of you."

"What do you say, boss?" Macdara leaned in. "Might be a fun thing to do."

"Fun," Siobhán said, forcing a smile. It was the last thing she wanted to do, but if everyone else wanted to go, she needed to be a good sport. She was also a firm believer that holidays were about having new experiences, and going out on the ocean on a fishing trawler would certainly be a new experience.

Gráinne glanced at Liam. "Are you joining the expedition?"

He shook his head. "I have a lot on me plate right now, and I'm not just talking about me lobster."

Gráinne threw her head back and roared with laughter. She then turned to Sheila. "I'm afraid I have some important clients I need to visit tomorrow." She snuck a look at Liam. "I'm a personal stylist."

He gave her the once-over. Whereas Siobhán was wearing a lovely but simple sundress, Gráinne was decked out in a silk dress as bright as the sun. "Personal stylist," Liam said. "I can picture that now, I can," he said. Gráinne beamed. Siobhán stifled a groan. Their food and drinks arrived on heaping plates that looked to-die-for.

Once they were all served, Eoin jumped back into the conversation. "I'm actually going over some recipes with Mr. Healy tomorrow," he said. "I'm afraid I won't be able to join either."

"Nan was an excellent cook," Liam said. "And no doubt me grandfather will appreciate the company."

"What time do you set off?" Macdara asked Sheila.

"Half four," she said with a wicked grin.

Macdara nearly choked. "In the morning?"

"Perfect time," James said. "But are you sure you all want to go? Four in the morning. That is awful early." He turned to Sheila. "For *them*. I'm in the remodeling business, so I'm always up before the sun." James turned his attention to Macdara, hoping for an ally. "Don't you all want to have a lie-in?"

Macdara shook his head. "I've done plenty of that."

James tried another tack with the young ones. "Ciarán and Ann, didn't you say you wanted to take surfing lessons?"

Ciarán narrowed his eyes. "Can't we go on the boat and then take surfing lessons?"

"You can, so," Siobhán said. "We're here for ten whole days."

James gave her a look. Siobhán gave it right back. He fell in love too fast. It would be wise to have Ciarán and Ann along. And if Sheila were a murderer, at least they would all be there to protect each other.

"You might even see a dolphin," Sheila said. "Or a whale."

"A whale!" Ciarán enthusiastically stabbed at his chicken breast. "Deadly."

Sheila took a deep breath as she stared at her seafood pasta, which she'd barely touched. "It feels wrong to be out having such a good time when there's been a murder in town."

"It is a shock," Liam said. He looked at Siobhán and Macdara. "And here you lot are on holiday when something like this happens. I swear to ye, this is a once-in-a-million occurrence."

"Everyone in town is going to be afraid to go out," Sheila continued. "'Tis horrible for business."

"At least the fish will still bite," James said with a grin.

Sheila smiled and gave a little shrug. "I suppose they will, so." She shivered. "I'm just worried the killer will come after one of us next."

"Unlikely," Siobhán said. "This was personal."

All heads snapped to Siobhán. Liam wore an expression that was hard to decipher other than: *Not happy.*

"What?" Sheila's eyes were wide with curiosity, and she was waiting for an answer.

"I just mean—I don't think anyone else is in danger." *At the moment.* Then again, Siobhán didn't know that for sure. All killers were unpredictable. But this one had specifically wanted Vera Cowley dead; there was nothing random about it. "Honestly, I think the travel and the sun has gone to me head. I take it back. You should be worried. Very worried."

Apparently, if the open mouths surrounding her were a clue, that wasn't the right thing to say either.

Liam stood up. "Garda Siobhán, may I speak with you outside for a moment?"

"Of course."

Macdara lowered his head and his voice. "Do you want me to go with you?"

"No," she said. "I got myself into this, and I'll get myself out." She turned to Liam and smiled even though her stomach was doing flip-flops. "Not a bother."

"I apologize," Siobhán said to Liam the minute they were outside. Streetlights shone along the footpath, a nearby boat horn sounded, and the smell of ice cream mingled with the sea wafted through the night air. Plenty of folks were out and about, and the sound of lilting voices and children pleading to stay out just a little longer made Siobhán feel as if she were well and truly on holiday. *No more talk of murder.* "I promise from now on I won't say another word to anyone about the case."

Liam shrugged. "The same talk is going on all over town, and there'll be no stopping it." Siobhán had expected more of a scolding. Apparently that's not why he asked to speak with her. He got right to it. "The state pathologist is arriving tomorrow morning, and I hear you have a good rapport with her."

"Doctor Jeanie Brady?" Siobhán perked up. She had developed a close relationship with Dr. Jeanie

Brady through the years. More than colleagues, they were friends.

"Dr. Brady. That's the one."

"She's the best. Very, very thorough." This meant the town coroner had already realized this would be a tricky case. Staged to look like an accident, yet deliberately placing several clues to indicate it was anything but. Siobhán was fascinated by it, and she knew Jeanie would be too.

"Would you mind meeting us at the chipper tomorrow?" Liam asked. "After you go out to sea with Sheila, that is."

"Do you mean it?" She should say no. She'd promised Macdara a full day of holiday activity. Then again, after being out on the boat, she'd want to shake off her sea legs, wouldn't she? And a woman on holiday might certainly want to have a walkabout. Lahinch was a small town, so it wouldn't be shocking to stroll past the chipper—and of course if she spotted Jeanie Brady through the window or some such, why, she'd have to stop and say hello. It would be rude not to.

"I'd be happy to join ye after we return from our boat ride."

"Sheila won't do her usual haul. She's very good about entertaining out-of-towners on her trawler," Liam said.

"Wonderful." Siobhán worried she sounded way too enthusiastic. *Tone it down.* "Happy to help."

Liam attempted a smile, but he wore an expression of concern. "Your older brother, James," he said. "Is he married?"

Uh-oh. Liam wasn't happy that James had been flirting with Sheila. Siobhán cleared her throat. "No.

He's a bit of a wild one. He flirts with every woman, so I wouldn't worry about that."

"I suppose it's the lady's decision," Liam said.

"It is," Siobhán said. "And I'm sorry if my sister came on a bit strong."

"Don't be," Liam said. "She was the best part of me day." A smile lit up his face.

"Brilliant," Siobhán said, the lie already souring her stomach. Whatever else happened, Siobhán was not going to repeat that to Gráinne. Holiday or not, they all needed their heads firmly attached to their bodies.

Chapter 9

The next morning at the Healy Inn, Eoin rose even earlier than the fishing squad, and by the time everyone was dressed and at the table, there was a full Irish breakfast sitting in front of them. Eggs, rashers, sausage, black pudding, white pudding, potatoes, and toast. Siobhán hesitated by the table with the rest of their brood as John Healy made appreciative noises and scrambled to his seat.

"What's the story?" Eoin said as he copped on that they were standing in an awkward clump.

"We're about to go on a trawler on the choppy ocean, luv," Siobhán said.

Eoin slapped his forehead. "I wasn't thinking. What am I to do with all this food?"

John Healy jumped up from the table. "Don't you worry, lad. All it will take is a few phone calls and we'll have every seat filled up."

Eoin brightened up. "Brilliant."

Siobhán kissed him and said he should tell them all about his restaurant before they headed out the door. Macdara was the last one out. "It wouldn't be the worst thing in the world if you made that brekkie again tomorrow morning," Siobhán heard her husband yell before he shut the door.

The five of them took two taxis to the fishery, and had the sun been up, it would have been a pleasant ride up the coast. Even in the dark Siobhán could feel the energy of the ocean. They were dropped off twenty minutes later, and for a moment they just stood, taking it all in. Exterior lights illuminated the grounds. Bisby Fishery consisted of two large warehouses and an office. A variety of grounded boats were situated near a small hill of large black rocks, and the place hummed with activity. Workers carrying crates wrapped in twine entered the warehouse on the left, while workers in the warehouse on the right were hosing down surfaces. Everyone wore overalls made of some sort of plastic, no doubt so they could easily wash off the fish slime. And although a fishy smell was about the place, the smell of the sea mingled with it enough to make it tolerable.

Sheila greeted them, all suited up in her fishing attire. She pointed to a row of hooks where more "outfits" hung. They were a waterproof material—a jacket and trousers that one could pull on over their regular denims. Siobhán smiled, imagining that if Gráinne had come with them, this would be the point that she would announce a personal emergency and slip out before even seeing the fishing trawler. The vessel was smaller than Siobhán had pictured. It was painted a cheerful red with black trim and was loaded up with fishing rods. The sun was peeking out, thanks be to the heavens, as Siobhán had no interest in being out to sea in the rain. She wasn't even sure she wanted to be out to sea with the sun shining down on them. She found herself wrestling with excuses as to why she suddenly could not join them, but given she hadn't yet sounded convincing enough to herself, she stopped trying.

After they were suited up, Sheila helped them onto the boat. The smell of yesterday's catch was evident, and Siobhán was curious why Sheila would want to do this for a living. Then again, many probably wondered how Siobhán could be a guard, spend her life immersed in crime.

"Had you always wanted to be a fisherwoman?" Siobhán asked as Sheila finally stepped onto the boat, pulled up the anchor, and shoved off with the help of two burly men.

"It's the family business," Sheila said. "It's in me blood."

"Brilliant," James said, grinning ear to ear. The last time her older brother had been up this early he was no doubt just coming home from an all-night poker game. Sheila was just that pretty. But James had not seen the murder scene. The greased ladder, Vera Cowley sprawled faceup covered in flour, the word *FRIED* written on her forehead, and the bottle of vinegar deliberately placed at the side of her poor head. Once again Siobhán couldn't help but wonder if making Mrs. Chips look like a piece of cod about to be fried was the work of this local fisherwoman. Siobhán wanted to warn James to tread carefully before it was too late, but she knew that could blow up in her face.

"I've always wanted to live by the sea," James said. "You might just have a new neighbor."

Indeed, it was probably already too late.

Sheila was at her element as she steered them out to sea, and a spray of water made Ann squeal with delight. "Life jackets are at your feet, lads. You might want to put them on." Everyone did except for James, who no doubt wanted to look cool, and if Sheila wasn't going to wear one, neither was he. Sheila grinned before she gave the trawler a jolt of speed. "Everyone settle in and make sure you've got something to hold on to when it gets choppy."

"Can I just hold on to you?" James said. If Siobhán didn't give him a couple of whacks before this ride was over, someone would have to make her a saint.

"I'll be at the wheel," Sheila said. "I'll come back out when we find a good place to anchor and take up our rods."

"Do I get a rod?" Ciarán pleaded, his eyes glued to them.

"Me too?" Ann asked.

"Absolutely," Sheila said. "I'm thrilled to have the help."

Ann and Ciarán cheered.

The trawler bobbed up and down as they headed out. Siobhán found herself grinning as they undulated with the waves, and she was grateful they hadn't partaken in Eoin's Irish breakfast. If he didn't repeat it for them tomorrow, maybe she'd go to the shops herself later and be the one to surprise the lot with an Irish breakfast. Vera Cowley would never get to indulge in the pleasures of life again. There was never any true justice when a life was taken too soon, but Siobhán would settle for whatever kind of justice they could get. And getting a killer off the streets no doubt saved lives—ones the killer might have taken had that person not been caught. This was the mantra that made Siobhán addicted to her job. Her thoughts returned to the ex-husband and the supposed best friend. But if the divorce was done and dusted, what was the motive to kill Mrs. Chips? More business for Mr. Chips? Revenge?

The word *fried* implied revenge. Anger. Without that single word and the bottle of vinegar, one might assume it was an accident. Then again, the slippery treads also told of the evil deed. Why hadn't the killer brought a towel to wipe them off after she took a fall? Was it possible he or she didn't have time? Was it because a crowd started to gather outside the shop? Or was this killer just that brazen?

It was puzzling. Why not make it look more like an accident by wiping down the treads? Or, better yet, replace the ladder? Perhaps the killer intended to do so but was interrupted. Or forgot to bring the extra ladder to the scene. Siobhán couldn't help but think of the ladder in the back of John Healy's lorry. What if that was the killer's ladder? It wasn't out of the realm of possibility that it fell out of the back of the killer's lorry. And given that ladder was found at the entrance to the Bisby fishery, wasn't it her due diligence to question Sheila about it?

No. Liam was the detective sargeant, and this was his case. There may not have even been a second ladder. Was the killer confident that the guards wouldn't even cop to the slippery treads? No. Not a chance. True, Vera hadn't noticed they were slick until she climbed the ladder, but any guard worth their salt—let alone a coroner, member of the Technical Bureau, or state pathologist—would have eventually noticed it. But even clever killers didn't always think everything through. This brought Siobhán back to the first two possibilities: either the killer forgot or lost the replacement ladder or the killer had been interrupted. If so, by whom? And how on earth did the killer slip in and out leaving all the doors locked from the inside?

"Earth to Siobhán," she heard Macdara say. "I hope you're having holiday thoughts only."

"Absolutely," Siobhán said. "Nothing but seashells and the sun."

"Uh-huh," Macdara said.

They were far out now. Siobhán could barely see the shore. The trawler slowed, and soon the engine cut off.

"Honestly, pet, I'm just meditating," Siobhán said.

Macdara gave her a look. "Uh-huh," he said again.

"Isn't that what holiday is for?" Siobhán said. "Staring out at the ocean and reflecting?"

"Not if you're reflecting on murder," he said as he raised an eyebrow and waited for her answer.

"I told ya. I'm focused on nothing but sunshine and wet, slimy fish," Siobhán said.

Macdara laughed. "Talk that love talk," he said as he leaned back and watched James, Ann, and Ciarán get schooled on how to set the bait and hold the rods.

"How much cod do you think you'll catch?" Macdara asked.

"October to February is the best time to catch cod," Sheila said. "But Mrs. Chips always prefers me to catch a few live before accepting the frozen," she said.

Everyone fell silent, reflecting on the fact that Mrs. Chips no longer had any preferences.

"What about Mr. Chips?" Siobhán asked.

"He usually goes with frozen cod. He'll take anything as long as there's a discount," Sheila said. "And since he fries his cod in beef fat drippings, it's impossible to tell that the cod was frozen. To be honest, it's impossible to tell either way, but I never minded fishing, especially for Mrs. Chips. I grew up going to that chipper, and she always treated me right." Sheila crossed herself, then bowed her head.

"Did you hear that the morning Mrs. Chips died, John Healy found a ladder discarded near your fishery?" The words were out of Siobhán's gob before she could stop them.

"I did hear that," Sheila said.

"Did you see a ladder discarded near your fishery?" James gave her a look but she ignored it. Sheila was chatty and not at all defensive.

"Where exactly did he find it?" Sheila asked.

"He was driving by, so I assume it was somewhere near the road."

"We do use a lot of ladders in the warehouses," Sheila said. "If you have it, I can have a look and let you know if it's one of ours."

"Brilliant," Siobhán said. "I'll mention it to Liam."

"He is the one in charge," James said, treating her to another unmistakable look: *Back off*.

Siobhán sighed, leaned back, and took Macdara's hand. She forced herself to relax and think holiday thoughts. Perhaps she'd do a little shopping, find a good beach read, and spend the rest of the day relaxing. That is, after she "accidentally" ran into Jeanie Brady.

They spent the next half hour in relative silence as they waited for fish to bite. When he couldn't take it anymore, James started on his flirtation campaign again and Siobhán overheard him asking Sheila about the local poker game. James was thrilled to discover that she played too. Maybe they were a match made in heaven after all. She wondered if he would eat fish for the rest of his life.

"Isn't the poker game run by a man named Mike McGee?" Siobhán asked, trying to sound casual and hoping James wouldn't be too browned off that she was nosing in on his conversation yet again.

"Is it ever," Sheila said. "That man only goes three places. The bank, the golf course, and his all-night poker game."

Before Siobhán could ask any follow-up questions,

a neon green speedboat cut across the water, sending a generous spray over their heads and jostling the boat.

"Hey!" Sheila stood and began shaking her fist at them.

"Who was that?" James asked, staring after the boat now disappearing into the distance.

"Natalie O'Brien and Daniel O'Grady," Sheila said through clenched fists. "O'Grady loves his toys. He's a grown-child."

"That's the way I am," Ciarán said.

Sheila laughed and everyone else shook their heads. *Natalie O'Brien* and *Daniel O'Grady*. Those names sounded familiar. Then Siobhán remembered. They had both been in line the morning of the murder. Natalie was the flour supplier, and Daniel the suited-up vegetable oil supplier.

"Are they a couple?" Siobhán asked. Both fit and good-looking shop owners, they seemed well matched.

Sheila scoffed. "They say they're not dating but then everyone sees them going out on dates. Daniel came into money, it looks like."

Interesting. "Why do you say that?"

"Do you have any idea what that little speedboat costs?"

"Not a clue."

"More than I'll make in me lifetime." Sheila stared after it, her expression dark.

"Perhaps it's Ms. O'Brien who bought the speedboat?"

Sheila shook her head. "It's Daniel's. You cannot be

around the man five minutes before he's giving you all the specs. You'd think it was his newborn baby."

"And before the purchase of the speedboat he wasn't a wealthy man?" Siobhán asked. Macdara slid her a look. She'd better not go too far.

"He owns an oil and vinegar shop," Sheila said. "He does always dress well, but I don't know anything about his finances. He doesn't own a car and he lives in a modest flat near the shop, so I suppose I made an assumption that he's not a wealthy man." Sheila suddenly handed her fishing rod to Macdara. He wasn't expecting it, so he held it awkwardly as he stood. If Siobhán wasn't mistaken, he was looking a little seasick.

"I'll teach you," Ciarán said, picking up on his distress and giving him a hearty slap to the back.

Macdara lunged forward, grimaced, then forced a smile. He knew Ciarán meant well. "Good man," Dara said to Ciarán, who beamed and began giving Macdara "lessons."

Sheila disappeared into the cabin. Siobhán gave it a beat and then followed. Sheila stood near a small sink and counter. She grabbed a large bottle of whiskey, and as Siobhán watched she took a sip straight out of the bottle, slammed it down, then turned and punched a wall behind her with a guttural cry.

Siobhán froze. What in the world? Whatever this was about, one thing was certain. Sheila Bisby had a temper. She felt a presence behind her and whirled around to see James halfway down the steps to the cabin. He was staring adoringly at Sheila. Sheila, who now had her hands on the wall and her forehead plastered to it, still had no idea she wasn't alone.

Siobhán crept up to join James on his step. "Did you just see her drink out of a bottle and punch a wall?" she whispered. Perhaps this was the wake-up call her cow-eyed brother needed.

"I did," James said. "She's a freaking goddess."

Chapter 10

After the morning on Sheila's trawler, they returned to the inn, showered, changed, and were treated to delicious ham and cheese toasties, compliments of Eoin and John Healy. Once all that was sorted, everyone wanted to plant themselves on the beach for the rest of the afternoon. Siobhán and Macdara sat on lounge chairs watching Ciarán and Ann take a surfing lesson. Ciarán kept losing his balance and was exasperated that Ann was making a go of it. She was truly an athlete and took a shine to nearly every physical activity she tried. It only took her four spills before she was standing on the surfboard. Gráinne had joined them, wearing yet another fancy hat and a matching cover-up. She and Siobhán combed the beach for shells while Macdara reclined on a lounge chair reading one of his westerns.

After collecting some pretty seashells, Siobhán returned to the lounge chairs to find Macdara snoring away, his book lying on his chest. She gently shook him awake. He cracked open one eye.

"If you want to go golfing, you should go," Siobhán said.

Macdara squinted. "I didn't bring me clubs."

"I'm sure you can rent some clubs."

"I'm not going to take off golfing on our honeymoon." He gave her hand a squeeze. "That would be rude."

"It would be rude not to," Siobhán said.

Macdara sat up straight, grabbing his book as it slid down his chest, and gave her a quizzical look. "What's the story, boss?"

Siobhán gave an innocent smile. "I just want everyone to get everything they can out of this holiday."

Macdara squinted, and it wasn't because of the bright sun overhead. "Does this have anything to do with this banker? Mike McGee?"

He remembered the name, which meant he was paying close attention to the case despite pretending otherwise. Siobhán perched on her lounger. "I knew you were interested."

Macdara held up a finger. "I was listening. That doesn't mean I'm interested."

"His bank and the abandoned storefront where they play poker are directly across from the chipper. I've heard that Mrs. Chips was often seen peering out her upstairs window through a pair of binoculars. I'm guessing her biggest target was Mr. Chips, but what if she happened upon something else?"

"Something to do with McGee?"

"Something to do with the poker game maybe?"

"And this something is what got her killed?"

"It's possible."

Macdara sighed. "We've both said Detective Sargeant Healy is more than competent."

"He is. He's competent. But . . ."

"Go on, so."

"Don't you think he's a bit too close to the people in this town to investigate properly?"

Macdara shook his head. "People in Kilbane could say the same about us. We're still able to do our job."

"That's true."

"And I'm sure Liam Healy doesn't appreciate us nosing in on his big case."

"He does actually. In fact, he wanted me to meet him and Jeanie Brady at the chipper this afternoon." She had already texted him to inform him that she wasn't going to be able to make it. Besides, he wouldn't need a buffer with Doctor Jeanie Brady. She was the ultimate professional.

"You're joking me."

"I am not."

Macdara studied her. "And you didn't go because?"

"Because we're on holiday." A fat seagull swooped and landed a few feet from them, staring them down.

"Very convincing," Macdara said. "But even the seagull doesn't swallow that story."

"I don't see why we can't holiday and help out where we can."

"Exactly what are you asking me to do?"

"Play a little golf, and if you see Mike McGee, see if you can get on his team—" Siobhán stopped. "Are there teams in golf?" Macdara gave a little nod. "Great. I heard he doesn't like to lose. So, if you're on his team, play great. If you're on an opposing team, make sure you let him beat you."

"You're asking me to cheat at golf?" He sounded outraged.

"I'm asking you to realize this is one of the most fascinating cases I've ever encountered—"

"Not our case."

"Don't you want justice for poor Mrs. Chips?"

Macdara sighed. "Why is it the most fascinating case you've ever encountered?" The bait had worked, the fish was biting. Siobhán weaved the tale from the beginning, details she knew would intrigue him. Man of leisure notwithstanding, he was the best detective sargeant she knew, and at his heart of hearts he, like Siobhán, could not let go of a puzzler.

"Fried?" Macdara set his book down. "Someone actually wrote 'Fried' on her forehead?" She knew he was upset with himself for not noticing it first. She gave him a minute to sulk.

"With a finger, I'm guessing, and then the killer placed a bottle of vinegar next to her. Dressed like a piece of cod ready for the fryer."

"That is intriguing."

She reminded him of the ladder John Healy had found dumped by Sheila Bisby's fishery that morning.

"Are you saying Sheila Bisby had something to do with this?"

Siobhán had already told him about Sheila punching a wall in the cabin of her trawler. What had she been so angry about? Macdara had listened but warned her once again not to get too involved. Was he changing his tune? She hoped so. "It's too early to say if she had anything to do with Vera's death. But something made her punch that wall. Maybe she's being framed, or maybe the killer was driving with the ladder on the roof of the car and it fell, or it fell off the back of a lorry..."

"I'm starting to feel like I fell off the back of a lorry," Macdara said. He stood up and brushed sand off his legs while the seagull watched. "Sheila went down into the cabin right after Daniel O'Grady jostled us in his little speedboat. Could that be why she was angry?"

"Yes," Siobhán said. "But it means she angers easily."

"That doesn't make her a killer."

"She's smart too—and this killer was smart."

"Writing 'Fried' on Vera's forehead and placing a bottle of vinegar next to her was smart?"

"Not that bit, no. I have a feeling that was the killer's ego getting in the way of common sense. A taunt. A killer who couldn't help themselves. The intriguing bit is that all the doors to the chipper were locked from the inside," Siobhán continued. "I can see how the killer might have snuck in, but how did the killer get *out*?"

"You always did like a good locked-door mystery," Macdara said.

"And outside, in Vera Cowley's back garden, the door to the shed was open, but everything else? Tidy. Locked."

"Okay," Macdara said. "I'm playing golf. But listen. You and Jeanie Brady are friends, are you not?"

"We are, so."

"You should definitely stop in and say hello."

It worked. Macdara was hooked and reeled in. "It would be rude not to," she said. Then she threw her arms around him and kissed him. They were, after all, on their honeymoon. "I love you," she said.

Macdara jerked his head toward the seagull, which had moved closer and hadn't taken its eyes off Macdara. "You've got competition," he said.

Siobhán turned to the seagull. She pointed at it. "Don't even think about it, he's mine," she said. "Fly away." Siobhán tried to shoo the bird. It moved a few inches back, then jumped forward with a cry, making Siobhán shriek. It ruffled its feathers and left a gooey black-and-white deposit at Siobhán's feet. "Okay, okay," she said, stepping back. "He's all yours."

"That's all it takes?" Macdara said, outraged. "A little bird poop and you let someone else have a go?"

"You need to get your eyes checked," Siobhán said. "That's more than a little."

Macdara had just got off the phone with Liam. McGee didn't golf for another couple of hours and Jeanie Brady and Liam were on a lunch break, so they settled back into their beach chairs. That was when a woman with a floppy yellow hat and matching bikini was passing by just as the wind kicked up. Mother Nature whipped the hat off her head and delivered it into Gráinne's lap. Siobhán looked up to find Natalie O'Brien standing in front of them, patting her head as if to make sure the hat was truly no longer atop it.

"Here it is," Gráinne said, waving the hat. "What a lovely shade of yellow." She held it out.

"Thanks a million," Natalie said, taking the hat. "That's exactly how I lost my first one, only Tara Flaherty refused to give me a discount on the first."

"Never mind that," Gráinne said. "Yellow suits you."

Natalie glowed under the compliment, then held her hand out. "I'm Natalie O'Brien, a local. Where you from yourself?"

"Kilbane," Gráinne said. "We're on my sister's honeymoon." They shook hands.

"I own a flour mill and a bakery in town. Stop by and I'll give you a discount."

"We'll do that," Siobhán said.

Startled, Natalie looked over. "You're the visiting garda," she said. "You were at Mrs. Chips that awful morning."

"I was."

Natalie shook her head. "I'm afraid you've been given a very bad impression of Lahinch. I'm glad you decided to stay and give us a chance."

"Ah, stop," Gráinne said. "We love it here."

"Were you friends with Mrs. Chips?" Siobhán asked.

Natalie fussed with her hat. "I wouldn't say we were friends, no. She was a client. She paid on time. When she was with Mr. Chips and he ran the show, they were often a bit late with payment. That's why I won't sell to him anymore. He still hasn't settled the full bill."

Interesting. "He's certainly spent money on his new chipper," Siobhán said.

"Right?" Natalie put her hands on her hips. "That's what I told him. But the bill is from when he ran the *other* Mr. Chips, which became Mrs. Chips and each of them refused to pay that bill."

"But you forgave Mrs. Chips the debt and decided Mr. Chips was responsible?" Siobhán hoped this didn't sound like an accusation, she just wanted to keep Natalie talking.

"I did. What he did to her was just plain wrong. And he refuses to switch over to vegetable oil. He's going to give everyone heart attacks!"

Gráinne sighed. "You did the right thing. That's why I ask my clients to pay up-front."

Siobhán gritted her teeth. She was trying to gather vital information and Gráinne was just shooting the breeze.

"Oh?" Natalie beamed at Gráinne. "What business are you in?"

"I'm a personal stylist."

Natalie clapped her hands in delight. "Of course you are!" She placed her hand near her heart. "I was complimented by a personal stylist. You made my day."

"Do you want to chat some more?" Gráinne asked.

"If you'd like to join me for a walk on the beach."

"Love to," Gráinne said. She hopped up, and the two of them walked away before Siobhán could even open her gob again.

"Did you have anything to do with that?" Macdara asked.

Siobhán tilted her head. "With what?"

"Is Gráinne on a secret mission to suss out intel on Natalie O'Brien?"

"I wish." Siobhán sighed. "It seems they actually like each other."

"My word," Macdara said. "She's acting as if she's on holiday!"

Siobhán picked up Gráinne's magazine and swatted Dara. Out of the corner of her eye she saw Eoin approaching, but he wasn't alone. Walking by his side was Madeline Plunkett. The food critic. Siobhán had nearly forgotten about her. They passed by and, in lieu of stopping to talk, Eoin simply raised his hand in a wave and then they kept going.

"Smart," Macdara said. "He's buttering up a food critic."

And yet another person of interest. Then again, why would a food critic want to kill the subject of her article before she'd even tried the fish and chips? Attention? It didn't seem strong enough of a motive. So, unless Madeline was hiding some other secret, Siobhán just couldn't see her for it.

Thirty minutes later, the aspiring surfers were knackered, Siobhán and Macdara were starting to get a bit red, and Gráinne returned alone from her walkabout.

"Did you have a good time?" Siobhán said. "She seems nice."

Gráinne nodded. "She is certainly put together. Her jewelry alone must have cost her a fortune. I asked, 'Did ya win the lotto?'"

"What did she say?"

"She said she sells flour. So she makes a lot of dough." Gráinne threw her head back and laughed. "I think she got a loan." Gráinne held out her hand, and tucked inside it was a calling card:

MIKE MCGEE
LOAN OFFICER
BANK OF IRELAND

Gráinne began gathering her things from the lounge chair. "Don't say I never helped you with a case," she said.

Macdara grinned and gave Siobhán an I-told-you-so look.

Siobhán studied the card. All roads led to Mike McGee. Macdara was definitely going golfing.

Chapter 11

Siobhán was on her way back to the inn to get changed when her mobile rang and Jeanie Brady's name came up on her screen.

"I was about to pay you a visit," Siobhán said. "Are you still at the chipper?"

"Just left," Jeanie said. "And before you say anything more, why don't we hold off until tomorrow morning. Say, half five."

"Tomorrow morning? Half five?"

"I'm calling to see if you'd like to go racewalking bright and early."

Siobhán stopped herself from audibly groaning. Another bright and early start to a day. "Racewalking?"

"I hear it's a thing here, and given I'm hanging around for a few days and it's summer by the sea, I'm going to pretend I'm on holiday and eat a lot of carbs.

Therefore, I need to walk it off. Meet you in the morning at the promenade."

Jeanie clicked off without waiting for a good-bye. That wasn't like her. Siobhán had the feeling that someone else was around and Jeanie didn't want them to hear anything she had to say. Smart. In a town like this, no doubt everyone knew everyone else's secrets. At least tomorrow she'd get a chance to discuss the case without worrying she was getting too involved. She couldn't wait for the morning, even if it did involve racewalking.

Doctor Jeanie Brady was sporting a fitted tracksuit, and her curly brown hair was tucked into a ponytail. She wasn't as thin as when Siobhán had seen her last, but she looked her perfect weight, and given they were about to exercise at half five in the morning, Siobhán didn't have to ask whether her recent health kick had stuck. It had been a while since Siobhán had gone for a jog—their new farmhouse had so much land that Siobhán felt she was walking more than ever—but as she and Jeanie started off, legs moving, arms pumping, her lungs reminded her that she needed to get back to her morning jogs around the abbey. It meant she'd have to drive in town and park, but her health was worth it.

"Detective Sargeant Healy said you were one of the first people on the scene," Jeanie said. She kept her head straight and her pace quick, but her gaze slid to Siobhán.

"Right place at the right time, or wrong place at the right time, or right place at the wrong time, depending on how you look at it," Siobhán said.

"All your thoughts on the case. Go," Jeanie said.

Siobhán, knowing Jeanie Brady would ask, was ready. She went from the top and didn't stop until the sun was up and the streets of Lahinch had filled once more with folks enjoying their holiday. Siobhán even told Jeanie about James's crush on Sheila, Natalie and Daniel nearly knocking into them on their speedboat, Mike McGee and his gambling den right across from Mrs. Chips, and the calling card for Mike McGee that Natalie had dropped in the sand in front of Gráinne.

"The word *fried* on her forehead," Jeanie said. "We're looking at a very angry killer."

"Resentment, a grudge, some kind of personal history," Siobhán agreed. *Like an ex-husband after a bitter divorce.*

"Gallows humor to the extreme," Jeanie said. "I wonder what line of work our killer is in."

"We have a banker, a fisherwoman, a flour supplier, a vegetable supplier, a restaurant equipment supplier, another chip shop owner, a best friend, and an out-of-town food critic," Siobhán spouted.

Jeanie shook her head. "Is that all?" she asked sarcastically. "I was told the mural on Mr. Chips across the way was vandalized by our victim."

"There was a can of black spray paint in the shop," Siobhán pointed out. "She seems the likely culprit. Not that I could blame her."

"Indeed."

"I think there's one definite thread we—*you, Sargeant Healy*—can pull on." Siobhán waited for Jeanie to stop chuckling. "The hood vent repairman. Tom Dowd."

"Go on, so."

"He claims someone called that morning *canceling* the repair. If he's telling the truth, it has to be the killer."

Jeanie whistled. "I do hope that the detective sargeant is all over that one."

"He's competent," Siobhán said.

"And handsome," Jeanie added.

Siobhán groaned. "Don't let Gráinne hear you say that. She's already over the moon about him."

"I can see the two of them together," Jeanie said. "You don't approve?"

"It's not that at all," Siobhán said. "I think he's a good detective, but according to another local, he's in love with her. So I'm not sure whether he's a player or just looking for love. And either way, he doesn't need to be distracted right now."

Jeanie nodded. "I'm excited for Eoin," she said.

For a minute Siobhán was thrown by the non sequitur. "He's another one who's over the moon. Just waiting for a permit to come through. I was hoping this holiday would get his mind off it, but he's still been in restaurant mode."

"I figured as much. I don't blame him. If I were him, I'd be checking all sorts of suppliers. Vendors.

Restaurant supply companies. The lot." Jeanie slid Siobhán a pointed look.

Mystery of Jeanie's abrupt change of subject solved. Jeanie wanted Siobhán on this case. She was hinting that Siobhán could use Eoin as an excuse to talk to Tom Dowd again. Once again Siobhán was caught off guard. Jeanie knew this wasn't her case, and Siobhán was supposed to stay out of it. "Do you not like Sargeant Healy?"

Jeanie stopped abruptly, and Siobhán had to go wide to the right not to crash into her. "I need to catch me breath." Jeanie placed her hands on her knees and kept her head down.

"It's actually better if you stand up straight and raise your hands above your heart to catch your breath," Siobhán couldn't help but say. It took a moment, but Jeanie finally straightened up and raised her hands.

"Much better," she said after a few moments. She reached into her pocket for a handkerchief and dabbed her face. "I think he's competent, alright," she said. "But he knows the people in this town too well. He probably has connections, friendship, biases. You don't have to do a thing, it's your holiday, but unless headquarters brings in another detective sargeant, I'm worried this case isn't going to get solved."

"I've only recently been able to convince Dara to nose around a bit—he's joining a golf team comprising at least one person of interest." Siobhán had already filled Jeanie in on Mike McGee, the location across the street, the all-night poker games. "I wonder if Mrs. Chips saw something. No disrespect but I do believe she kept a very close eye on the goings-on about town."

"It is ironic that you finally take a holiday and murder follows you," Jeanie mused. They gravitated toward a hand rail and began a stretch routine.

"Speaking of our holiday," Siobhán said, finishing her stretches, "I'd better get back to the inn. I'm spending some time with Ciarán and Ann while Macdara goes golfing."

"Not a bother," Jeanie said. "I'll be headed back to the chipper. I want to get a look at the shed out back and her upstairs flat."

"Brilliant," Siobhán said. "I so wanted to have a nose around up there meself."

"Funny you mention that," Jeanie said, watching a seagull circle above. "I've had a funny habit of dialing people lately when I don't mean to. Don't be surprised if you get a video call from me while I'm having a gawk at the upstairs flat. Me arse accidentally dials people all the time! Purely accidental, of course."

"Of course."

"So, you should accidentally have your mobile phone with you around half eleven today, and when I accidentally ring ya, you should accidentally answer."

The ice cream was sublime. Creamy, melt-in-your-mouth heaven. Siobhán, Ciarán, and Ann walked about town holding up their two scoops in a cone as if they were wielding fire-lit torches. Siobhán went with strawberry and chocolate, Ciarán cookie dough and chocolate, and Ann chose mint and chocolate. Apparently, their love for chocolate was genetic. It was 11:15 and Siobhán wanted to finish hers before Jeanie's "accidental call."

By the time they'd window-shopped, and Siobhán made a mental note of the location of Tara Flaherty's gift shop, their ice-cream cones were finished and Ciarán and Ann were mad to go into the town's arcade. Luckily, there was a nearby bench. "One hour," Siobhán said. "If you aren't finished then, give me a text." Soon they disappeared into the land of fun. A video call came in just as she sat down.

She accepted the call, and at first all she could see was Doctor Jeanie Brady's chin from underneath. Then a bit of wrestling and mumbling as the room turned upside down as Jeanie tried to set it right. Finally, Siobhán could clearly see the upstairs flat, and much like the downstairs the upstairs flat was neat as a pin.

"Doctor Jeanie Brady here recording me notes. The room is orderly, not a thing out of place, except near the window." She panned the room and landed on the window. "Here we have another pair of binoculars, a teacup, and a notebook."

"A notebook," Siobhán said. "I would definitely want to have a look at that."

Jeanie headed to the notebook and with gloved hands began to leaf through it. "It looks as if she was keeping a list of names." She quickly showed the list before taking it away. "It seems she was writing down the name of anyone who entered Mr. Chips." Siobhán heard the rustling of pages. "Here's another list. It looks like a Vendetta List."

"I wonder how a person would know a list is a vendetta," Siobhán said. "That's pretty specific."

Jeanie Brady zoomed in on a notebook page. Written in capital letters above the list of names, it read VENDETTA LIST!!!

Jeanie turned the page. "Someone appears to have been collecting money from various folks in town." She briefly showed a ledger in which Vera had been writing down amounts from fifty to one thousand euro. Siobhán wished Jeanie could snap a photo of the list but making an "accidental video call" was one thing and sending evidence that could be tracked was another. Siobhán wasn't even sure why they were being so clandestine when Sargeant Healy had basically come out and said he welcomed the help. But they were in it now, and she'd have to make sure she didn't mention any of this to him. If he wanted to discuss any of these topics, she'd let him bring it up.

Jeanie hovered the camera over the Vendetta List. Mike McGee's name was circled in red.

"Did you ask Sargeant Healy about this?" Siobhán said.

"Note to self," Jeanie Brady said. "I asked Detective Sargeant Healy if he had any theory as to why a Mr. Mike McGee was circled in red. He surmised that Vera may have been trying to get a loan, as it took his father ages to get one to fix up the inn. Perhaps someone should speak with this innkeeper about McGee and loans. If only I were staying there."

"On it," Siobhán said. Jeanie swung the camera around the room once again. The bed was made up. "Wait," Siobhán said. "Are there any signs that she was actually living up there?"

"Bed is made, the small bathroom is neat. No wet towels, no toiletries. The closet doesn't look as if anyone has rifled through it recently, and several pieces of luggage are missing from a set." *She wasn't living there. So where was she living?* "Additional notes to self," Jeanie continued. "It's been confirmed that the ladder was coated with beef fat drippings, and underneath the bag of flour we found a long piece of twine. It had a fishy smell. Best guess from a fishery. Working theory—the twine was situated beneath the giant bag of flour and dangling down. Vera Cowley noticed this and climbed the ladder to pull on it. Unfortunately, that was exactly what our killer wanted her to do."

Siobhán had already surmised this, but she shivered as she imagined the bag of flour coming at poor Mrs. Chips, then her slipping on the greased treads as she panicked. This killer knew her, and knew her well enough to predict what she would do once she saw the twine hanging down. Jeanie's words came back to her. The twine smelled "fishy." *The fishery*. Siobhán recalled seeing crates wrapped in twine at Bisby Fishery.

"Note to self," Siobhán said out loud. "I know a fishery nearby owned by local fisherwoman Sheila Bisby and her family. When she took us out on her fishing boat I noticed crates wrapped in twine. I bet they smell fishy."

"Racewalking tomorrow at five," Jeanie said. "This is progress."

That snapped Siobhán out of her thoughts. "Five? What happened to half five? Or six. Half six?"

"Half four for racewalking it is." Doctor Jeanie Brady hung up.

Four. Half four in the morning. Maybe a Vendetta List wasn't such a strange idea after all.

Chapter 12

The O'Sullivan-Flannerys finally gathered together to watch the sunset on the beach. Macdara hadn't had a chance to fill Siobhán in on his golf game, but just as she was about to press him, Mike McGee showed up, still holding a golf club. Siobhán waited for Macdara and McGee to exchange words, chat about the game, but instead Mike glared at Macdara and then headed straight for the beach, where he began swinging the club, perhaps hitting seashells or stones into the bay.

Siobhán's gaze slid to Macdara. "Did anything happen at the golf game?"

"Yep," Macdara said with a sigh. "I won."

"Dara!"

"I know, I know, I was supposed to lose. But he was so annoying! He's a strange, bitter man—he was going on and on about his golf game, calling me a beginner! A beginner. I couldn't take it."

Siobhán sighed. "We'll have to find another way to suss him out."

"I already did. Poker game is tonight. James, Gráinne, and Eoin are coming with me. You're welcome too if you feel comfortable leaving Ann and Ciarán alone."

"They're not children anymore. I'd have no problem leaving them alone." She hesitated. "But one of us needs to have a clean slate with Mr. McGee just in case tonight goes sideways."

"Smart."

"And I agreed to meet Jeanie Brady for racewalking at half four in the morning."

"Half four?" Macdara shuddered. "What's with everyone getting up so early? We're on holiday, we should sleep until noon!"

"I know. It was supposed to be a five-thirty start, but when I opened me gob to push it off until later, she decided even earlier was better."

Macdara laughed. "Well-played herself."

Eoin was getting restless and began to say his goodbyes. "Not so fast," Siobhán said. "How did you and Madeline Plunkett end up hanging out?"

Eoin grinned. "Never hurts to befriend a critic—although in this case I definitely do not want her reviewing my restaurant."

That wasn't the answer Siobhán expected. "Don't think like that. You're a fabulous chef."

"It's not that." He leaned in with the look of someone with a juicy secret. "Madeline Plunkett writes hit pieces."

"Hit pieces?"

Eoin nodded. "She writes for a sleazy online website, which is not the impression she gives everyone. I don't think she had planned on doing Mrs. Chips any favors."

Did Vera find out? What if she confronted Madeline? Was there some kind of altercation?

As the lads headed off, Mike McGee left the beach and was walking back to the promenade. Siobhán cut him off at the pass. "How ya?"

He nearly jumped out of his skin. "What is wrong with you?" he said. "You put the heart in me sideways."

"Sorry, sorry, I just wanted to introduce myself." Mike stood and waited. "I'm Siobhán O'Sullivan. Well, technically Siobhán O'Sullivan-Flannery."

"Flannery," he said. The darkness had ascended quickly and his face was lit by distant street lamps, which made him look slightly green and menacing. "Detective Sargeant Flannery? Is that the one you're on about?"

"'Tis." Maybe this had been a mistake. "He said you're an excellent golfer. He had to practically cheat to win!" Macdara would kill her. But it was too late to take it back now. McGee tilted his head and his face softened.

"Did he now?"

"He said he'd take you as golf partner any day."

McGee nodded. "Nice to meet you, Mrs. Flannery."

"Please, call me Siobhán."

"I'd rather not."

Everyone was right. He *was* a strange man. "I was

wondering if Mrs. Chips had applied for a loan through your bank before she passed away?" No use throwing the word *murder* around him. He was already on edge.

McGee frowned as he twirled his golf club. "Is your husband investigating this case?"

"No."

He stilled the golf club and made eye contact. "Then why are you asking me personal questions about another member of this town when you're nothing but a blow-in?"

Nothing but a blow-in. She clenched her fist and imagined snatching the golf club and beating him over the head. "Sargeant Healy has requested a bit of help with the case," she said instead.

"And the wife of a detective sargeant is qualified?"

"I am a garda, sir."

His eyes narrowed. "Why didn't you say so when you introduced yourself?"

"Because this isn't a police inquiry, it was a personal hello."

"If it's not a police inquiry, then why are you inquiring?"

This had been a huge mistake. "I just thought you might want to help figure out who killed her."

"Killed her? I thought she fell off a ladder." He held steady eye contact and waited for her to respond.

She knew darn well he'd heard she was murdered. His innocent act wasn't fooling her "The state pathologist has arrived and has concluded foul play was involved."

"You mean someone *pushed* her off the ladder?"

"I don't have all the details."

"Something tells me you do."

"Did you or did you not approve of a loan for Mrs. Chips?"

He started to walk away. "I did not."

"Did she apply for a loan?"

"If you don't mind, I'd rather talk to a well-regarded garda over you." With that, he walked away, leaving her to wonder what garda he held in such high regards. She had a feeling the answer was: *none*.

By the time Siobhán, Ann, and Ciarán returned to the inn, the two of them, knackered and happy out, pounded up the stairs to their bedrooms while Siobhán headed to the kitchen for a glass of water. A dim lamp was on, enough for her to see inside the cupboards. She pulled out a glass and was just about to fill it when a male voice interrupted her.

"It's Liam," the voice said. Siobhán yelped and nearly dropped the glass. Liam was indeed seated at the dining room table, a beer in front of him. "Sorry," he said. "That's exactly the reaction I was trying to avoid."

Siobhán's heart thudded as she tried to control her breathing. "Why are you sitting here in the dark?"

"It calms me," he said. "Helps me think."

She understood. She often went for walks when thinking through a case. Everyone had their ways of coping. "Do you mind if I join you?"

"Only if you help yourself to a beer," he said. "There's a Bulmers in the fridge."

Why not? She was on holiday. Getting up early was going to be torture anyway. One beer wouldn't hurt.

"Don't mind if I do," Siobhán said. She poured the water into the sink and retrieved the bottle of Bulmers.

"Here," Liam said, taking out his keys and holding his hand out for the bottle.

There was a little opener dangling from the set. She popped the cap, handed it back to him, and sank into a chair.

"Go on, so," he said with a grin.

"What?"

"I have a feeling you've been chatting to folks. What have you discovered?"

She gave it a beat. "Mike McGee is high on my radar and not just because he's a bad sport at golf."

Liam laughed. "He is that."

"I learned that Madeline Plunkett writes hit pieces."

"Hit pieces?"

Siobhán nodded. "Bad reviews. She lied straight to my face, said she worked for a well-reputed blog. She was right that it has quite a bit of eyes on it. But it's meant to drive people away from restaurants. A bad review there could even put a dent in tourist business."

"And you think she was hired to write a hit piece on Mrs. Chips?"

"I think it's a good thread to follow."

Liam nodded. "Talk me through that possible scenario. Did Vera find out? Threaten her?"

"That's the only thing I can come up with—if she threatened to out Madeline as a liar—but even so, it just doesn't seem like a strong enough motive."

"The strongest motive lies with Mr. Chips and his mistress."

"What if he is the one who hired Madeline Plunkett to write a hit piece?"

"It wouldn't surprise me at all. We'll be bringing him in for an official interview soon. I'll make sure to ask him about it."

Siobhán sipped her beer and they sat in silence for a moment. "I've been meaning to pop into Tara Flaherty's shop."

"Listen." Liam set his beer down and leaned across the table. "I feel I owe you an apology."

"An apology? What for?"

"You're on holiday. Not an official part of this case." He let the rest hang in the air.

Was he saying he didn't want her help after all? Did he know about her video call with Jeanie Brady? "I don't mind helping you out." She hoped she sounded casual.

"I appreciate that. But headquarters called and there are going to be a lot of eyes on this case. It's probably best if they don't think outside hands have been all over it."

"Ah, right, that makes sense," Siobhán said. She had been debating whether to bring up Vera's Vendetta List, but now she was definitely keeping her piehole shut.

"I'm sorry. You're a brilliant garda, and I would have loved the help."

"I completely understand. I will go back to being on holiday, not a bother."

"But if you do happen to hear anything . . ." He left it hanging.

"You'll be the first to know." *Or the second after Macdara. Or the third after Jeanie Brady. Best let him think he'll be the first.*

He held up his beer, and they clinked. "Slainté," they said.

He was going to need all the cheers he could get with his case. Perhaps it was best she was stepping back. As the thought of no longer keeping abreast of this case swirled through her mind, she couldn't help but think of a quote from Oscar Wilde that her da used to recite: "Man can believe the impossible, but man can never believe the improbable."

Chapter 13

Siobhán O'Sullivan was taking a liking to racewalking. She and Jeanie Brady set off from Mrs. Chips; passed McGee's bank, which had a single light on (What was someone doing there so early? Was it McGee himself?); passed Daniel O'Grady's oil and vinegar shop, which looked darling so she was going to pop in there later; and then, as they progressed a ways, Siobhán could see the sign for Natalie's bakery. By the time Siobhán and Jeanie reached the promenade, Tara Flaherty was headed in their direction, racewalking twice as fast as they were. Apparently, from the perspiration coating Tara, she'd been at it awhile. Tara wasn't alone. Behind her, at a slightly slower pace, was Mr. Chips.

Siobhán heard their voices raised in anger. She grabbed Jeanie's arm and dragged her to a nearby bench. "Shhh," she said the minute Jeanie opened her mouth to protest. "It's Mr. Chips and his mistress," she said in a whisper, jerking her head back. Tara stopped, and everyone's heavy breathing filled the void until Mr. Chips caught up.

"I'm not fit for this today," Mr. Chips said. "Not after that visit from Liam." They began stretching.

"Call him Detective Sargeant," Tara said. "Or he'll think you don't respect him. That's the last thing we need right now."

"I've known him since he was in short trousers! He'll always be Liam to me."

Tara shook her head. "You are so stubborn. Why won't you ever listen to reason?"

Because you're a woman, that's why he won't listen to you, Siobhán couldn't help but think. *That's what you get for hooking up with your best friend's husband.* I mean, really. Vera had to have complained about her husband to Tara all these years. And Tara wanted him anyway. They were both fools. But she was still going to eavesdrop in case they said anything incriminating.

"Do you think he believed me about Natalie and Daniel?" Mr. Chips asked in a hushed panic. *Natalie and Daniel?* They must be referring to Natalie O'Brien and Daniel O'Grady. The image of Natalie's floppy yellow hat floated in front of Siobhán. "They're in it together," Mr. Chips continued.

In what together?

"We'll make sure Liam knows all about it," Tara said. "But he can't know it came from us."

"I thought you said we shouldn't call him Liam!"

"I did. But you said he'll always be Liam to you," Tara reminded him.

"*You* shouldn't call him Liam. But he doesn't mind it from me."

"Where is all this moodiness coming from? Are you having second thoughts about holding the wake at your chipper?"

Jeanie and Siobhán exchanged eye contact.

"It's not technically a wake. There's no body and it's not a pub. It's a fundraiser. For her family and whatnot," Mr. Chips said.

"I like her family," Tara sulked. "But it wouldn't look right if I took the money."

"Are ya out of your mind? Why would you take the money? The money isn't for you."

"I just said that," Tara said. "But humor me. Who is the money for exactly?"

"We'll raise money for a memorial bench or some such," Mr. Chips said. "Like that one." Siobhán tensed, as she had no doubt that Mr. Chips was gesturing to the very bench where they sat.

"We were both at war with Vera," Tara said. "Or in my case, Vera was at war with me. Everyone in town knows that. If we host a memorial they'll find it suspicious."

"That's not fair," Mr. Chips said. "I'm only trying to be nice. And if we don't do something nice, everyone will talk about that, now won't they?"

"I don't think Vera would want this," Tara said softly.

"What's done is done." He scoffed. "Besides if I was the one found dead, she'd throw a party."

"For heaven's sake. Think of this as a party then, just don't *act* like it's one." She took off, pumping her arms, leaving Mr. Chips scrambling after her.

"I thought we were finished," he yelled. "We stretched!"

"I still have energy to burn," Tara called back. He grumbled and caught up to her, and soon they were out of sight.

"Interesting," Jeanie Brady said after a beat.

"A memorial," Siobhán said. "That is interesting."

"Let's mull it over during round two." Jeanie popped up and took off.

"Round two?" Siobhán said as she scrambled after her. "You never said there was going to be a round two."

After they finished an excruciating round two, Jeanie went back to her hotel and Siobhán returned to the inn for a shower. Soon Jeanie Brady would be headed to the hospital to carry out the postmortem. Afterward she would be going back home, but she told Siobhán she would give her a bell to say good-bye.

When Siobhán was finished showering and dressing, Ann and Ciarán wanted to practice surfing, so Siobhán went with them clutching a large mug of coffee. Gráinne, Eoin, James, and Macdara must have had a late night at the poker game, for they were all having a lie-in. Siobhán had been fast asleep and had no idea what time they came in. Maybe that's why there had been a light on in the bank—because it had been an all-nighter. Maybe Mike McGee was afraid to go home lest he fall dead asleep and miss a day's work. Siobhán was dying to see if they'd learned anything, or won anything, or at least didn't lose anything other than hours of sleep. But for now, she had to wait. And waiting wasn't her strong suit.

She just needed to drink her coffee, watch the waves roll in, and truly be on holiday. She waded into the water cheering on Ann and Ciarán (mostly Ciarán) as he practiced standing upright on his surfboard and Ann focused on catching a wave. After a valiant hour, they resorted to lying down on their boards and letting the waves take them up and down. Even that brought Siobhán's heart into her throat. They weren't experienced, and the ocean, gorgeous as it was, could be unforgiving. Luckily, they'd soon had enough and everyone was on board with going back to the inn, changing clothes, and figuring out breakfast. Siobhán was also hoping the mad poker players were awake and she could get the scoop on the evening.

The gang was up, but given the dark circles under their eyes and all the groaning and shuffling they were doing, it was obvious the lot was in need of resuscitation. Siobhán knew if they stayed in for breakfast they'd likely fall back asleep. John Healy had given them a list of local eateries, and Dodi Café, the number one choice for breakfast according to the locals, was only a short stroll away. It took a bit of effort, but she finally convinced everyone to go. She'd have to pump them full of sugar and caffeine before she quizzed them about the poker game.

Soon they were pushing tables together in the cafe and drooling at the menu. Siobhán, Gráinne, and Ann ordered the breakfast bap, described in the menu as

"Smashed sea salt avocado, crispy streaky bacon, sunny fried egg, herb pesto." Ciarán went for the buttermilk pancakes with blueberry compote, maple syrup, and mascarpone creme. Macdara quizzed everyone on their choices, peppering the young woman behind the counter with questions before also choosing the pancakes; James went back and forth before he too ordered the bap; and Eoin was the most adventurous, choosing the grilled Halloumi salad bowl: "Toonsbridge Halloumi on a zesty pearl couscous and red cabbage salad, pickled chili, topped with chopped pistachios and served with sourdough toast." This place had been absolutely the right choice for brekkie. *Brilliant.*

Pistachios made Siobhán think of Jeanie Brady, who had a mad addiction to them, although she'd recently curbed it a bit. Given she was leaving soon, Siobhán took a photo of the menu and texted it to her.

"What's Halloumi?" Ciarán asked.

Eoin grinned. "The cheese of Cyprus," he said. "You melt it. It has a high melting point but also holds its form."

Ciarán frowned. "Are you going to make normal food at your restaurant?"

Eoin laughed. "You might surprise yourself and like it. I'll let you have a bite. It's traditionally made from ewe's or goat's milk, but Toonsbridge makes it with cow's milk. The edges are caramelized. Thick and delicious."

Ciarán wielded his fork like a pointer. "Pancakes are thick and delicious."

Eoin grinned and winked at him, and Ciarán shook his head. Ciarán's voice was so deep now. And Ann, while still athletic and outdoorsy, had poise. She didn't slouch when sitting, unlike Gráinne, who was so low in her seat that Siobhán was afraid she was going to slide to the floor. She was wearing sunglasses, which meant she had way too many jars last night. Given the poker game wasn't in a bar, people must have brought in their own spirits.

When their food arrived, they fell into an unusual silence as everyone lost themselves in their food. The bap was delicious and filling. Siobhán hadn't even stayed up all night and she was already knackered. More coffee should do the trick.

"Well?" Siobhán asked, turning to Macdara as they waited to settle the bill.

"It was strange," he said. Eoin and James nodded in agreement, and Gráinne gave a sly smile. There was nothing more she loved than keeping a secret from Siobhán.

"Strange how?" Siobhán had waited long enough and had even let them enjoy their breakfast, and she was going to blow like a kettle if they strung her any further along.

"It was more like a swap than a betting game," Macdara said.

He might as well have been speaking a foreign language. "Pardon?"

The waitress returned with their change. "I'm going to tell you everything, but can we have a walkabout?" Macdara said. "If I sit here any longer I may never get up."

"Let's get our legs under us then," Siobhán said, popping up from the table. Soon they were all outside, where the skies had turned gray for the first time since they'd arrived. Siobhán couldn't help but worry it was a bad omen. The wind had kicked up, and a paper cup and a torn kite rattled past.

Macdara knew Siobhán had little patience left, so he began filling her in as they walked. "This poker group recently changed their rules. They can't bet money. Instead they swap."

He was repeating what he'd already said in the cafe, but Siobhán figured the way to a happy marriage was to give it a beat before biting the husband's head off. He had one more chance. "Swap what?"

"Products," James said.

Macdara, probably sensing that her patience was dangling off a cliff, chimed back in. "Daniel O'Grady puts in a case worth of olive oil. Tom Dowd a gift certificate for restaurant equipment, Natalie flour, Tara a gift certificate to her gift shop, Corman Cowley a gift certificate to his chipper, Sheila Bisby fresh-caught fish, and so on."

"Don't tell me Liam gives get-out-of-jail-free cards," Siobhán quipped.

"He gives away a night at the inn," Gráinne said. Her eyes took on a dreamy look.

"You should know," Eoin said. "You spent all night glommed onto him."

"Like you with Garda Dabiri," Gráinne shot back. Eoin reddened. He did have a crush on Garda Aretta Dabiri.

Siobhán wished she were here with them. Aretta was becoming a great investigator, and she had a calm demeanor that balanced Siobhán's feisty side. But right now, Siobhán's mind was on Liam. He had a serious case to investigate and he was out all night? Then again, a number of their suspects were in attendance, so maybe it was work after all. "How did Liam seem?" Siobhán asked.

"Liam, is it?" Macdara said. "What happened to calling him Detective Sargeant Healy?"

"He asked me to call him Liam," Siobhán said.

"Did he now?" Macdara said. "He didn't ask me to call him Liam."

"No need to be jealous," Gráinne said. "He fancies *me*."

Siobhán kept her gob shut.

Eoin was next to comment. "Madeline Plunkett came and was flustered because she didn't have anything to swap. No one wanted a subscription to her reviews."

"Except," Gráinne said, thrusting a finger in the air, "I overheard Mr. Chips offering to let her use his gift certificates if she gave him a good review."

"You're joking me," Eoin said. "What did she do?"

"She stormed out," Gráinne said.

"I found it interesting," Eoin said. "I suppose despite writing hit pieces she has an honor code."

Perhaps she did have an honor code, but that didn't mean she wasn't a killer. Anyone could be driven to kill. It was a terrifying thought but one Siobhán believed. A person had to recognize their dark side or it would take over. Secrets thrived in the dark. Raw truths rotted in the dark. Humans needed to understand that it wasn't the *thought* of doing something evil that they had to shun. It was the act. And if a person confronted their demons, admitted that the demons lived inside them, then perhaps they could find healthy outlets for dealing with these dark feelings. Siobhán's healthy outlet used to be whittling. The past several years it was throwing herself into work, and now her farmhouse, siblings, and relatively new marriage.

"What did any of you lot throw in the pot?" Siobhán asked.

"We didn't get to play," Gráinne said, sticking out her lower lip. "We watched for a while, then hit the pubs."

That explained the state of them. "Nothing more on Mike McGee?" Siobhán asked.

"Only that he didn't play either. He watched everyone from the corner of the room," Macdara said.

"It was creepy," Gráinne added.

"Was there any talk of murder?" Siobhán asked.

"Not while we were there," Macdara said.

"Murder?" James said, shaking his head at Siobhán. "There's no murder in poker. Unless someone calls your bluff."

Chapter 14

The next evening Siobhán, Macdara, and the rest of the O'Sullivan Six stood in front of Mr. Chips. People were flowing in with flowers, and in the case of Natalie O'Brien a bag of flour wrapped in a bow. Given how Mrs. Chips was found, it made Siobhán shudder, but either Natalie O'Brien was a sadistic killer or Sargeant Liam had done a good job of keeping the details of how Mrs. Chips was found from slipping out. Most likely the latter. *Good man*.

The mural had been entirely painted over in white paint, and a message read, *RIP Vera Cowley aka Mrs. Chips*. Bracketing the message were a pair of angel wings. As Siobhán took it in, she wondered if Vera would be touched by the message or outraged. Human emotions were so fragile, especially when one was hurt. No matter what, Siobhán couldn't imagine how it felt to be betrayed by one's ex-husband and best friend.

And if said ex-husband and best friend were not murderers, most likely they were hurting now too. It always pained Siobhán when people who loved each other had a falling out. Her family had their issues, and squabbles, and faults, and warts, like all families, but they would never let any of those things tear them apart. *Ever*. Flesh and blood was forever. And as her siblings stood with her, heads bowed in respect at the wall, she was flooded with pride. What a beautiful family she had. Overcome with emotion she began hugging them one by one. Gráinne, who was stiff at first and smelled like vanilla, finally hugged her back; Ann laughed and patted her on the back as she squeezed her; Ciarán struggled like a fish on a hook, then wilted into her; and then Eoin and James, who'd had time to see it coming, held their arms open wide and grinned as the three of them hugged. When she came out of the embrace, Dara took her hand and swung her into him for a hug of his own. Siobhán had to wipe away tears, and Gráinne made a crack about death and hormones, and then they all filtered into the chipper.

Unlike Mrs. Chips, whose shop was old and in need of updating, Mr. Chips's was shiny and new. Blue leather booths and silver tables gleamed, and a new steel counter and decked-out kitchen stood out behind it, including a scrolling electronic menu board. On the back booth sat a blown-up photo of Mrs. Chips, a younger, smiling Mrs. Chips standing in front of their former chipper across the street. John Healy had let it slip that Vera had always wanted the sign to read MR. AND MRS. CHIPS, an argument that played out over forty-odd years. That explained the bespoke S that had been added to the sign. Did Mr. Chips regret his stubbornness now? And how had he been able to afford new, new, new in his chipper when he hadn't updated a single thing in the one across the street? Had Mr. Chips ended up murdered, Siobhán would have pegged Mrs. Chips for it and she could have sympathized to an extent.

Surrounding the photo were additional flower arrangements, and mass cards and donation baskets overflowing with cash. Who was going to oversee how the funds were allocated? Siobhán had heard no mention of their having children. Once again, Siobhán couldn't help but feel the late Mrs. Chips would have been enraged over this memorial-slash-charade. She hoped that the money was going to a charity Vera supported. In normal circumstances Siobhán would take the time to suss it out, but this was not her town, and butting into their personal matters was not her place.

The smell of fish and chips and curry sauce filled the air, and Siobhán regretted stuffing herself at brekkie. The lads had no such qualms. They were already standing in line for free fish and chips. This was probably the most generous Mr. Chips had ever been in his whole life. Was it inspired by grief or guilt?

A notice at the "memorial booth" informed folks that an informal wake would be held at a nearby local pub this evening and all were encouraged to attend and share fond memories of Vera Cowley. Siobhán couldn't help but wonder whether the killer would be there. And, as she looked around the crowded, noisy chipper, she wondered which one among them was that killer. A coldblooded one to boot. It took a while before she saw Mr. Chips standing alone by his front windows, and she hurried over to Macdara, took a small bite of his fish and chips (delicious, truly wonderful), then headed over to speak with him.

Mr. Chips looked genuinely sad, but then again it could have been his appearance—sinking jowls, mussed-up white hair, and puffy eyes.

"Hello," Siobhán said. "I just wanted to say what a lovely tribute this is, and the fish and chips are delicious." She felt a strange twinge of guilt; in her heart she was in solidarity with Mrs. Chips.

He gave a small nod. "Beef fat drippings," he said. "I tried to tell Vera not to switch to vegetable oil." He immediately looked away, as if he'd said something he shouldn't, and continued to look away, giving her an obvious sign that he did not want to engage in further conversation. She was dying to know how he had afforded to open the chipper, let alone throw in all the bells and whistles, but she had to approach it carefully. Given he'd already mentioned the vegetable oil, and Daniel O'Grady was the vegetable oil supplier, she decided to follow that track. People were less guarded if they thought it was someone *else* they were focused on. She recalled the conversation she'd overheard the other day between Mr. Chips and Tara on the promenade. Something about Natalie and Daniel and how they were "in on it together." In on what? An image of Natalie and Daniel zipping through the ocean on his speedboat hovered in front of her.

Siobhán looked around until she saw Daniel in the crowd. It didn't take long to spot his mop of blond hair.

He and Natalie were standing together. "They make a nice couple," Siobhán said, pointing them out.

Mr. Chips frowned and looked like he was about to say something when Tara glided over, took him by the arm, and steered him away, as if Siobhán was not visible to the human eye. *Rude.* Was she afraid Mr. Chips was going to say something he shouldn't? Or perhaps she just didn't like outsiders. Siobhán would have to pay a visit to her gift shop and see if she could strike up some sort of conversation. If Vera didn't have any family to speak of, to whom did she leave everything in her will? Did everything belong to the best friend and husband? Had Mr. Chips taken out a loan to build his chipper knowing he would pay it all back after his ex-wife was dead and he had collected the inheritance?

To whom did Mrs. Chips leave everything?

Siobhán did not know Vera Cowley that well, but any woman who took the time to write out a Vendetta List had probably also taken the time to hire a solicitor and change her will. Siobhán wondered how many solicitors were in Lahinch. Then again, even if she did figure out who this solicitor was, that person would hardly give Siobhán anyone's personal financial information. Was Liam also following the money?

A familiar voice filtered through the air. James and Sheila stood in one corner, Gráinne and Liam in the other. *Flirting.* Once again Siobhán had an urge to rip each couple apart, an impulse that probably made her an excellent garda but a terrible sister. Life was full of choices, and those choices were never easy. Then again, she had no power to separate all the lovebirds even if she wanted to. What she really wanted was to ask Sheila Bisby if she happened to bring twine. For all Siobhán knew, the fisherwoman carried it in her pocket. Then again, Siobhán had no doubt that Jeanie would have forwarded the information about the twine to Sargeant Healy. But as she looked at Liam now, relaxed and receptive to Gráinne but still occasionally flicking his gaze to Sheila and James, she couldn't help but worry that Jeanie Brady was right. Liam was way too close to the people of this town. Too close to see any of them as a killer. And just as Siobhán was thinking she'd had enough of this sham of a memorial, the door swung open and in walked Madeline Plunkett.

"You're watching her but you don't want people to think you're watching her, is that it?" Macdara asked. He had sidled up behind her and whispered into her ear before she could even clock he was there. He wasn't wrong—that was exactly what she was doing and hoping.

Siobhán batted her eyelashes. "Whatever do you mean? I'm on holiday."

"Funny. Standing here I have a clear sightline of all our suspects. I suppose that's just a coincidence?"

"No matter where I stand, I can see all our suspects," Siobhán said. "That's just how eyes work."

"I see. Then I don't suppose you're interested in what Madeline Plunkett is doing right now?"

"What's she doing?"

Macdara chuckled. "She's looking at the memorial notice."

"I wonder if she's going to attend."

"Are *we*?"

Siobhán shrugged. "We aren't really a part of this community. They certainly wouldn't expect us to go, I don't think."

"Then again, it's at a pub, which isn't torture, and we wouldn't have to stay long."

Siobhán took his hand and squeezed it. There was nothing better than a husband who anticipated his wife's needs.

"Interesting," Madeline said loudly. She held up a basket of fish and chips. Mr. Chips, who had been shaking hands at the door, whirled around. When he saw who it was, he edged closer and swallowed hard. Madeline made eye contact with him.

"I hope you like it," he said.

"It's not my first time tasting it," Madeline said. "But I am a little confused."

The room, which had been filled with voices, fell silent. "I'd be happy to help you clear up any confusion," Mr. Chips said.

She tilted her head and stared at her basket of curried chips. "Did you change the recipe for your curry sauce?"

"I was saving it for a surprise," Mr. Chips said. "You have highly developed taste buds."

"It's almost as if I'm qualified to do my job," she deadpanned.

Siobhán couldn't keep her gob shut. She stepped forward. "I thought it was Mrs. Chips who had a new curry sauce in the works."

Madeline turned to Siobhán and nodded. She lifted

her plastic fork and jabbed toward Siobhán with it. "Exactly," she said. "Mrs. Chips did have a new curry sauce she'd intended to unveil."

Once again, all heads turned to Mr. Chips. Tara floated up to him. "We thought it was in poor taste to mention it, but it's true. When Vera announced that she had a new curry sauce, I suggested Mr. Chips should expcriment with his as well, like. They were competitors, were they not?"

"Did anyone ever taste Vera's new sauce?" Liam asked. Heads shook all around. "Interesting," Liam said. He took out a notebook and jotted something down.

"What are you trying to say, Detective?" Tara said. She glanced at Siobhán, then Macdara. "It's not always easy to call him that. I remember him when he was a lad in short trousers."

"He liked to chase the seagulls," Mr. Chips said.

"He did more than that," Tara said. "He was a cheeky boy. You threw rocks at them. I saw it myself."

"Are you joking me?" Liam said as the sides of his neck flushed red. "I used to skip stones at the water. I never aimed them at seagulls."

Tara shrugged. "Lads will be lads." She was taking the detective sargeant down a peg in front of everyone. *Interesting.*

"I swear to ye," Liam said, his voice squeaking. "I never aimed them at seagulls."

Tara seemed intent on winding Liam up. There was no doubt she wanted the attention off Mr. Chips and his new curry sauce. Correction, his copy-cat curry sauce.

"There *was* someone who tasted Vera's curry sauce."

This came from Sheila. Once she had everyone's attention, she pointed at Mr. Chips. "You did."

Mr. Chips took a step back, then glanced at all the people staring at him. "Me? Why do you say that?"

"Because the day before her accident I saw her march over with it. I even watched you taste it."

"It was nowhere near as good as she claimed," Mr. Chips said.

Liam stepped toward Mr. Chips, and from the expression on his face he wasn't a happy man. "Why did you lie?"

Mr. Chips waved his hands as if trying to erase everything that had just happened. "I didn't lie, I just didn't come forth with the information."

"When Sheila asked if anyone had tasted the curry sauce, you shook your head no," Liam said. "We all did."

Mr. Chips shrugged. "What does it matter anyway?"

"How do we know you didn't steal her recipe?" Madeline asked. "Did you have anything to do with her 'accident'?" She used air quotes with her forkless hand.

"That's an outrageous accusation!" Mr. Chips yelled. Sheila Bisby wasn't the only one in this town with a temper. But it reminded Siobhán that she still didn't know why Sheila punched the wall in the cabin of her trawler.

"You two certainly were at each other's throats," Natalie O'Brien chimed in, staring at Mr. Chips.

Daniel O'Grady nodded in agreement. As per usual he was dressed to the nines, this time in a light blue suit with a pressed white shirt and a blue-and-white tie. His blond hair was slicked back. Every time Siobhán laid eyes on him she had a hard time imagining him living in this seaside town. He looked way too buttoned-up. Maybe he thought it helped his sales at his oil and vinegar shop, or maybe he just felt better when he dressed up. "And you were furious when she wanted to switch to vegetable oil when the evidence is clear," Daniel announced. "Vegetable oil is the lighter, healthier option." He raised his voice on this last bit, trying to convince the crowd.

Out of the corner of her eye, Siobhán saw Eoin move toward Madeline's basket with a fork of his own, and he must have asked if he could taste, for a moment later he was doing just that. Siobhán couldn't make out from his expression whether he liked it or not, but he did go in for a second taste.

"I don't think you should be in charge of that donation basket," Tom Dowd said to Mr. Chips. "Just until this dreadful business is all sorted out."

"Until what business is all sorted out?" Tara said. "There's no crime here."

"Even so, I'm sure you don't want the appearance of any impropriety," Liam said. "Maybe it's best if a neutral party handles the donation basket."

"I'd be willing to help," a male voice said. It was Mike McGee. Siobhán hadn't even noticed he was in the room. *Interesting.*

Liam turned to Mr. Chips. "Do you have any problem with our trusty local banker handling the donations?"

Mr. Chips crossed his arms and shook his head. "Be my guest." He might have outwardly agreed, but there was no doubt he was browned off.

Siobhán tensed. She wanted to shout that she for one did *not* trust the trusty local banker. And neither had Mrs. Chips. In fact, Mike McGee had been the very first name on her Vendetta List. But surely Liam had seen that list as well. Either he planned on keeping a watchful eye on what McGee did with the money, or he was making the move so that McGee would feel confident that Liam trusted him, or . . . her worst fears were coming true and Liam Healy was too close to the people of this town to see them as killers.

Chapter 15

The argument over the donation basket quickly brought the memorial to a close. Everyone agreed it was best to wait and celebrate the life of Mrs. Chips in the pub this evening instead. Siobhán, Macdara, and the rest of the six stood on the footpath along with Sheila Bisby. The gray skies of the morning had turned blue, the sun was shining down on them, and the wind was now a soft breeze. Liam was still inside the chipper speaking with Mr. Chips, which was no doubt why Gráinne's eyes were glued to the windows.

"What are we going to do now?" Ciarán said. "Ann and I want to go surfing."

"You surfed plenty this morning," Siobhán said. She was too antsy to go back to the beach and watch over them, and it was one activity she wasn't ready to let them do solo.

"The arcade then," Ciarán said. "We're old enough to go where we like, and stay as long as we'd like."

"Yet still cheeky," Siobhán said.

"I'll go back to the arcade," Ann said.

"You don't have to do that." Siobhán sighed. "You're right, Ciarán. You and Ann are old enough to do what you like on holiday."

"Yes!" Ciarán pumped his fist.

"I still want to join ya," Ann said to Ciarán.

Siobhán was suspicious. "You do?"

Ann shrugged. "Why not?"

"Why not, indeed," Siobhán said.

"Don't use your garda voice with me," Ann said. Ann was usually mad to be outdoors doing something sporty. Had she made a friend at the arcade? From the way she was blushing, Siobhán had hit the mark.

"Use common sense and text me in a few hours," Siobhán said.

Ciarán whooped and was gone in a flash. Ann lingered, but before Siobhán could figure out why she was lollygagging, Macdara had pulled out twenty euro and handed it to her. *Good man*. Siobhán should have realized they needed money, but despite her assurances that she was on holiday, she was clearly too involved in this case.

"Thanks a million," Ann said.

"I hope we get to meet your new friend," Siobhán called after her. Was it a girl? Siobhán was pretty sure it was a girl. She'd been wondering about Ann's sexual orientation for quite a while now, waiting for her to initiate the discussion. It wasn't because Ann was athletic, which she was, or because she never seemed interested in fashion, or makeup, or boys (she'd shunned all male attention). The main reason was that when Ann talked about certain girls over the years, she seemed to light up, then clam up if Siobhán asked too many questions. But despite Siobhán's thinking of her as a young one, Ann was a grown woman now, and if she wanted to tell her sister about her preferences it was her place to do so, in her own time. And maybe she hadn't quite figured it out yet, and maybe it would take a lifetime. Siobhán had no doubt that Ann knew she would be respected and supported, so there was nothing to do but wait. Still, a few hints never hurt. "Anyone you want to tell me about?" Siobhán grinned.

"I have no idea what you're on about," Ann called back. "I never do."

"You know," Siobhán added. "Hopefully I will know soon as well, like." This time Ann didn't respond. Siobhán watched her walk away.

"Hope is like a balloon," Sheila Bisby said. "It can't fly to the heavens if you're hanging on to the string."

"Brilliant," James said enthusiastically. "That's class."

Siobhán was starting to regret inviting him on this holiday. "Maybe I don't want it to fly to the heavens," she couldn't help but say. "Maybe I want to carry it around on a string forever."

James shook his head. "That's just sad."

Tara Flaherty came out of the chipper and breezed past them without a word.

"We all know you're going to either look into this case or spontaneously combust," Macdara said.

"Whatever do you mean?" Siobhán said. "I'm just

trying to figure out my next enjoyable holiday activity."

"You've got one ear on every conversation around us," Macdara said.

"My other ear can hear you just fine."

"Well, then. What holiday activity have you decided on?"

"I was thinking of doing a bit of shopping. Shopping is something one does on holiday."

"Indeed." She knew she wasn't fooling Macdara one bit, but he seemed amused rather than annoyed, so there was no harm in it. She turned to Eoin.

"Why did you want to taste the curry sauce?"

"Because I told Eoin I tasted Mrs. Chips's new curry as well," Sheila Bisby said. "And I think they stole it. But don't tell Liam I tasted it, because I shook my head. He'll think I'm a liar."

"Well," Siobhán said, "if you shook your head, then you did lie."

Sheila stared at her and shrugged, but James glared.

"We're going to try to replicate Mrs. Chips's recipe," Eoin said, probably trying to break the tension. "Then see if it matches Mr. Chips's new sauce, or—"

"Or see if Tara and Mr. Chips stole it," James finished.

"Well, well, well," Macdara said. "It appears you're all in the same 'holiday mood' as me wife."

It was true, they were all playing detective. Siobhán turned to Sheila. "When did you taste her curry sauce?"

Sheila glanced around. "I don't want to talk in front of everyone. Shall we get our legs under us?"

"That sounds lovely," Siobhán said. *A walkabout with a liar.*

"Count me out," Gráinne said. "I'm going to enjoy some alone time."

"Is that what you're calling it?" James teased. "Alone time?" He glanced through the shop windows to where Liam was standing. "I smell a fib."

"Smell me later, then, will ye?" Gráinne said, sticking out her tongue and shooing them away with her hands.

They walked through town as the sun shone down on them. Colorful kites dotted the skies, and it was a sight to see. Blue, red, yellow, green—even kites in animal and other fun shapes. So far Siobhán had spotted a dog, a dolphin, and a leprechaun. The latter was no doubt flown by a tourist.

"I forgot about the kite festival," Sheila said. "Shall we go closer to the promenade? It's great craic."

"Brilliant," Siobhán said. Life was too short not to watch colorful things in the sky. Ciarán and Ann must have noticed the kites on the way to the surf shop and arcade, and she hoped they ditched their plans and joined the festival instead.

"To answer your earlier question," Sheila said as they walked, "I tasted Vera's curry sauce the night before her terrible accident."

Accident. Siobhán had noticed that despite knowing foul play could be involved, everyone continued to refer to her fall off the ladder as an accident. It could be wishful thinking, or did this group of people have a difficult time facing the truth?

"How did that come to be?"

"We have a standing order for me to deliver fresh cod on Wednesdays. My last haul was short, so Tuesday evening I had to stop by the chipper and see if she'd agree to take some of her order frozen."

"What time was this?"

"We were supposed to meet at half four, but she didn't show up until five."

"Didn't she live in the flat above the shop?" Siobhán was working with the theory that Vera was living elsewhere, and she wanted to see if Sheila would confirm this.

"All I know is that she wasn't in, so I waited."

"Where did you wait?"

"Does it matter?"

"It's a long time to stand on a footpath, so I was just curious."

"I stood on the footpath for about ten minutes, then went in my lorry and made some calls while I waited."

Siobhán nodded. "Go on."

"She pulled up at five. Didn't really apologize, but she did have a few bags from the market in her hands. I followed her into the chipper, and she told me she had popped out to the shops when she ran out of ingredients for her new curry sauce."

"And then she asked if you would like to taste it," Siobhán said.

Sheila nodded. "And then she asked if I would like to taste it."

"And so, you did?"

"And so, I did." They turned a corner and, as Sheila predicted, stands were set up loaded with kites in every shape and color. Sheila stopped to marvel at one shaped like a dragon.

"What did you think of the curry sauce?" Siobhán asked after a minute.

"Between you and me, I thought it was too spicy."

"Then it wasn't identical to the new curry sauce supposedly created by Mr. Chips?"

"Well . . . I'd say they were identical, but the Mrs. Chips sauce had more of a kick."

Had Mr. Chips stolen the recipe and tweaked it slightly? Surely he hadn't murdered her over a secret curry sauce. Then again, people murdered for all sorts of reasons that didn't make sense. "What kind of mood was Vera in? What did she talk about?"

"She was in a funny mood. If I had to put a word to it, I'd say she was gleeful."

"Gleeful," Siobhán repeated. "Because of Madeline Plunkett's upcoming arrival?"

"I suppose that was it, like. She was very focused on her curry sauce."

"Was there a ladder leaning up against the wall?"

"Definitely not."

"Was the mural painted on Mr. Chips?"

"It may have been," Sheila said. "But it was covered up."

"Covered up?"

She nodded. "Covered in brown paper."

Someone had planned on unveiling it the next morning. This was carefully planned. But unless it was Mr.

Chips and/or Tara, how had this person arranged for the mural to be finished at that precise time? Siobhán was going to have to ask Liam about it and hope it didn't ruffle his feathers. In her mind, this was a key piece of evidence. And yet she wasn't even officially interviewing Sheila. She hoped that Sheila would be willing to repeat everything she had just said in an official interview at the garda station.

"Did Vera—" Before Siobhán could finish the sentence, Sheila flinched. "Are you alright?"

Sheila laughed. "I'm sorry. Every time you call her Vera it takes me a second to realize you're on about Mrs. Chips. Hardly anyone called her Vera. I've been calling her Mrs. Chips me entire life."

"That makes sense. Mrs. Chips it is. Did Mrs. Chips accept that you would be delivering frozen cod the next day?"

"Only a portion of the order was frozen and she would have fresh to fry for the critic, so she didn't make a fuss about it."

"And she didn't cancel or change the appointment?"

Sheila arched an eyebrow. "Why would she?"

Because someone pretending to be her did that with Tom Dowd. Siobhán didn't answer. She was distracted by Sheila touching the string of a nearby kite, running her fingers down it. It reminded her of Jeanie's phone call and the piece of twine the killer situated underneath the flour bag. *The bait.* "Is there any chance that while you were in the shop you had twine on you?" Maybe Sheila had dropped it when she came inside. The killer could have picked it up off the floor and perhaps it was then and there that the diabolical plan was born. If only there had been a security camera inside the chipper. Then again, given the binoculars and her Vendetta List written on paper with a biro, Mrs. Chips was hardly up-to-date on her technology.

"That's the second time you've asked about twine," Sheila said. "Does it have something to do with her accident?"

Fool, fool, fool, why don't you just stop asking questions? Liam was going to blow like a kettle if he got wind that she was once again badgering people about the case. What on earth could she say now? "No, no, sorry. I'm totally mixing it up with another story I heard. It's all this sunshine, I think it's scrambling me brain, ya know? Oh, look! That kite is shaped like a seagull." Siobhán pointed.

Sheila squinted. "That's because it is a seagull."

"Is it?" Siobhán cupped her hands over her eyes. "Right, right. 'Tis. Isn't that something."

"In case you were asking about this case, the answer is no. I didn't drop any twine, because I had an appointment at the bank prior to stopping in at Mrs. Chips and I was all dressed up."

Leave it be. Nothing to do with her. Let Sargeant Healy sort this all out. "The bank? McGee's bank?" Siobhán just couldn't help herself. But who could blame her? Mike McGee and his discretionary loans had something to do with Mrs. Chips's murder. At the very least, his method of deciding who was approved and who was not had enraged Vera enough to place Mike McGee at the very top of her Vendetta List. Speaking of that list, the killer had to be on it. Somehow, Vera had taken her rage out on the wrong person. She'd taken it out on someone who struck back. Someone who wanted to win the back and forth— *permanently.*

"Yes, McGee's bank," Sheila said. "I suppose ever since he gave John Healy a loan to fix up the inn, we've all put our hats in the ring."

If Healy had renovated that inn, Siobhán would hate to see what it looked like before. He still had a rotary phone. "What would you do with the loan, if you don't mind me asking."

"I'd buy a brand-new trawler and new equipment. It would cut hours off me days."

"How did that appointment go?" Sheila cocked her head. Siobhán was asking too many questions. "And no, it's nothing to do with this case or some other random case, I'm just having a chat, shooting the breeze." Siobhán smiled, probably showed too much teeth, for Sheila looked away.

"Right," Sheila said. "It wasn't a go at all. Mike McGee didn't show up."

"That sounds odd," Siobhán said. "You should be able to count on a banker to be prompt."

Sheila shrugged. "Too many late-night poker games, if you ask me." From her tone, she didn't approve. Maybe she would make a good match for James. "I know why you asked if she canceled on me," Sheila said. She spoke as she purchased a kite that looked like a fish. "Isn't it gas?" she said, holding it up. It was the most hideous thing Siobhán had ever seen.

"It's class." Siobhán waited while Sheila paid for it. As they walked toward the beach, Sheila was enrapt with her fish-kite. "Why do you think I was asking you whether Mrs. Chips canceled the appointment?" Siobhán asked.

It took Sheila a minute to answer. Perhaps the question wasn't clear. Just as Siobhán was about to ask it again in a different way, Sheila spoke. "Because I had to listen to Tom Dowd rant about how Mrs. Chips had canceled on him and then had called him that morning in a fit when he didn't show up."

"Do you think it's possible that Tom didn't show up?" This was always a possibility.

Sheila chewed on her lip. "That wouldn't be the Tom Dowd I know," she said. "But I wouldn't put anything past Mrs. Chips."

"I don't follow."

"I just wonder whether she was negotiating prices with Tom the way she was with Daniel."

"Daniel O'Grady?" This was the first Siobhán had heard of this.

"Yes. The whole switching to vegetable oil mess, ya know? He wanted to raise his price over what they'd verbally agreed on and she had an absolute fit, according to Daniel. Maybe that started her off on some kind of mental breakdown."

"Mental breakdown?"

"She was already so stressed from the divorce, and the betrayal from her best friend. And Daniel! Don't get me started on Daniel. He's so mean he'd mind mice at crossroads. But you didn't hear it from me, like."

He was frugal. That wasn't a shocker, but had an argument over pricing snowballed into something else? Siobhán didn't want to forget any of this, so she took a notepad out of her handbag (even a woman on holiday needed a biro and a notepad) and began to jot ideas down. Suddenly Sheila yanked the pad out of her hands and began reading it.

"Are you writing down what I'm saying?" She tore out the sheet, ripped it up, and let the pieces fall to the ground.

Stealing property and littering. Every second Siobhán changed her mind about Sheila Bisby. "That was private property," Siobhán said as she tried to retrieve the little bits the wind hadn't taken away.

"The words out of me mouth are private property too," Sheila said. Murderer or not, there was that temper. She was firmly back in the "not good for James" category. But given how smitten he looked around her, Siobhán knew she'd have no sway over that whatsoever.

"Look," Sheila said, following Siobhán as she retrieved the scraps, "I'm sorry but I have to live in this town. I can't have any of them thinking I was talking out of school. I mean, it's not like Daniel did anything to her. He's not violent. At least, he hasn't been in a while."

Siobhán dropped all the little pieces of litter into her handbag and whirled around. "What do you mean 'in a while'?"

Sheila tugged on her fish-kite and stared at it instead of Siobhán. "He used to be a scrapper alright. Bar fights and whatnot. But I'm sure those days are long behind him." At that, Sheila walked away without another word. Siobhán, still browned off about her notes being ripped up, spent a few moments watching the fish-kite bob above the heads in the crowd. But even as she followed the fish, it was really the fisherwoman that had Siobhán's thoughts churning, this time over Daniel O'Grady. *He's not violent. At least, he hasn't been in a while.*

Chapter 16

Back at the inn, Eoin was happily ensconced in the kitchen while John Healy played with Trigger. They had planned on taking turns caring for their beloved Jack Russell, but John was so thrilled with him that he had been tucked in his arm or at his side practically the entire time. He clipped the leash to his collar and turned to Siobhán. "Do you mind if we have a walk-about?" he asked.

"Do I mind?" she said. "Keep this up and I'm going to have to squeeze you into our luggage and take you home with us."

John chuckled, then turned back to cooing at Trigger as the two went outside. "Make yourselves at home," he called out before the front door shut.

"Something smells incredible," Siobhán said, setting her handbag down on a dining chair. "Are you making curried chips?"

"I'm making curry sauce," Eoin said. "I think I'm getting close to replicating Vera's. And she was right. It's a winner."

"I don't understand, how are you able to replicate it?"

From the expression on Eoin's face he had a juicy secret to impart. "The recipe is from John Healy's mother." He held up an old book. "He said I could have this—he doesn't cook himself—and she was a true artist. I mean, I have loads of new recipes I can try in the restaurant."

"Brilliant," Siobhán said. "But are you saying the recipe is similar to the one Mrs. Chips was working on?"

He nodded. "All curry recipes are somewhat similar, but I think Mrs. Chips based her new recipe off this one." Siobhán glanced at the old book in his hand. If Vera hadn't been in possession of the book but she indeed used it for her recipe, that likely meant she wrote it down. And given the book was still here at the inn, it meant she probably copied it here. Was this where she had been staying? Siobhán flashed back to the dirty towels and sheets on the floor when she'd mistakenly scolded Ciarán. John had been cleaning a room. Vera's room? If so, why hadn't he said anything? Then again, if he was going to tell anyone about it, he would tell Liam, and if Liam was keeping evidence in this case close to his chest, she didn't blame him. She would have done the same thing.

James strode in as she was lost in thought. He was grinning ear to ear and whistling.

"I know that sound," Eoin teased. "You're in love."

"I won't lie," James said. "At the least, I'm a bit

smitten, alright." Siobhán was actively keeping her piehole shut. James zeroed in on her as if he could read her thoughts, and given how close they all were he probably could. "I have some intel on the case if you'd like to hear it," he said with a lazy smile.

"Intel?" Siobhán said. "Why would I need intel?" She sounded believable if she did say so herself. Eoin and James roared with laughter, and before she knew it she had popped out of her chair and her hands went reflexively to her hips. When they finally clocked her expression, their laughter came to an abrupt halt. She could still pull off a stern Irish mammy when pressed.

James put his hands up. "Don't get your knickers in a twist. It's probably nothing." He scanned the room. "Apparently, John Healy got a big loan to remodel the inn."

"I already know that," Siobhán said. "From your *girlfriend*." But as she looked around, it reminded her that nothing appeared to have been remodeled. Had he done something else with the money? Was he waiting for bids? Waiting for contractors? It was true that lately it was challenging to get materials and that construction was taking twice the time it used to. And even if he was spending the money on something else, it was hardly any of her business.

Except now she also knew that Vera had possibly been staying at the inn, and Vera was extremely jealous of anyone who had been getting loans from McGee.

"I can beat your intel," Eoin said, as if they were playing poker.

"The curry sauce?" Siobhán asked.

Eoin shook his head. "John told me that his ladder was missing and he thinks it was Mrs. Chips who 'borrowed' it."

"Borrowed a ladder without asking?" Siobhán said.

"Exactly."

Siobhán frowned. The morning of the murder, John Healy claimed to have found an abandoned ladder near Bisby Fishery. How plausible was it that he was missing a ladder as well? "Did John say whether Vera had been living here at the inn?"

Eoin shook his head. "Nope."

Siobhán chewed her lip. "You don't think he'd mind if we just come out and ask him, do you?"

"To what end?" Eoin said. "His grandson is a detective sargeant. If Vera was staying here, he already knows about it and I'm not sure what difference it would make."

"You never know when a small detail might crack a case open," Siobhán said. "She was using her upstairs flat as a place to stake out her neighbors, but if she was living here, maybe John knows something that could be helpful."

James stepped forward wagging his finger. "And as Eoin said, he would point it out to his grandson, who is the one actually investigating the case."

Unless John didn't want his grandson to know about it. What was she doing? Eoin was right. They were guests at this inn, and John had done nothing but roll out the red carpet. He was walking Trigger right now, for heaven's sakes. "I just worry they're all too close to each other to be objective."

"And maybe you're too interested in a case that isn't even yours," James said.

"It would be nice if you would just be on holiday," Eoin said. "How many more chances are you going to get?"

"Are ye putting me out to pasture?"

"You never go on holiday," James said. "You don't even know *how* to holiday."

"I know how to holiday," Siobhán said. Didn't she? Wasn't it subjective?

James shook his head. "Eoin is right. You're sticking your nose in where it doesn't belong."

"You just don't want me discovering that your new love is a murderer," Siobhán said before she could think it through.

Instead of getting angry, James roared with laughter. He wiped tears out of his eyes as he exited the inn. "A murderer," she heard him say before he shut the door. "Deadly."

Siobhán sunk into a chair. "Would you like a cuppa?" Eoin asked softly.

"Yes." As Eoin set about wetting the tea, Siobhán chewed on everything she knew so far. The one thing she hadn't mentioned—because, truthfully, she shouldn't be discussing the case with them at all—was that John Healy had been on Vera's Vendetta List. Then again, so were most people in town. And folks seemed to be on the list for one of two reasons. Either they had procured a loan from McGee or they had the audacity to eat at Mr. Chips. Siobhán had to speak with Mike McGee herself. And as far as their gracious host was concerned, Siobhán would do this the proper way. When John Healy returned, she would come right out and ask him whether Vera had been staying here. Perhaps his reaction would tell her everything she needed to know. He was such a nice man. But nice men could be killers too.

Hours later, Eoin was still experimenting with his curry sauce and he seemed as if he was on a mission. "I don't understand why you have to make this now," Siobhán said.

"Madeline Plunkett put a bug in my ear," Eoin said. "She suggested I try to replicate the curry sauce that Mrs. Chips made."

"Yes, you mentioned that, but to what end?"

"In honor of Mrs. Chips," Eoin said, as if honoring a woman he'd never met made complete sense. "Madeline said she'd write a nice tribute article for her on the website. For me, if I pull this off I think she could be persuaded to come to my restaurant."

"Why would you want that?" Siobhán persisted. "I thought she wrote hit pieces."

"She does," Eoin said. "But she has an honor code. If she likes what she tastes, she gives an honest opinion."

"Then why do people pay her to write negative reviews?"

Eoin sighed as if Siobhán just wasn't getting it. "They pay her to write honest reviews. But she has a wicked tongue when she doesn't like something."

"I don't think you should trust her. The O'Sullivan

Six restaurant will be mostly for locals, so why take the chance?"

"Why does it have to be for locals? Why can't we draw people from all over, like?" Desperation shone on his face.

"I wasn't trying to say you're not good enough," Siobhán said. "You're absolutely good enough. I see Michelin stars in your future. I just think you should start small and then grow."

"Speak for yourself," Eoin said. "I have an opportunity here and I'm going to take it."

The front door opened and John Healy entered holding a knackered Trigger under his left arm. "He was chasing pigeons. Poor thing wore himself out." He set Trigger down, and the terrier looked up at him longingly.

"He's over the moon about ya," Siobhán said.

"He's a wee dote," John replied. "Makes me think of having another one meself."

"Cup of tea?" Eoin said, turning to John.

John's face lit up. "You're spoiling me in me own inn." He chuckled as he took a seat. "Don't mind if I do."

Eoin brought him a cup of tea and a tin of biscuits.

"That's very kind of you to let Eoin have your mother's recipes," Siobhán said.

John waved his hand as if brushing her compliment away. "It would be a waste not to let someone have them. I have no use for them, and neither does Liam."

"I understand Vera used your mother's curry recipe to make her own," Siobhán said casually. Maybe this would get him chin-wagging about her; maybe he'd admit she stayed at the inn. Siobhán had yet to figure out how to work the strange inconsistencies about the ladder into conversation.

John nodded and crossed himself. "She was going to let me have a proper taste of it but . . . Sure lookit. You know yourself."

"Was Vera staying here recently?" Siobhán asked. He seemed open to talking about her, so Siobhán went for it.

John's expression immediately changed to one of distrust. He pushed his tea away. She'd clearly put him on edge. Behind him, Eoin scowled at her. "What are ya on about?" he asked. On top of the table his hands were balled into fists.

It was too late to back out now, the damage was done. Siobhán sat across from him and kept her voice calm. "The room James is staying in. The one you cleaned out when you learned he was coming to stay with us."

John looked at Eoin. "Is there something wrong with the room?"

"Not at all." Eoin gave her an I-told-ya-so look.

John turned back to Siobhán, and there was no trace of his usual smile. "I don't understand. If there's no problem with the room, what exactly are ya asking me?"

"I was simply wondering whether Vera Cowley might have been staying here recently."

"Who told you that?" He was not a happy man. "What are you trying to say?" He uncurled his fists and slapped his palms on the table. This was not the reaction she'd been expecting. He was obviously defensive, but why?

Trigger, sensing unhappiness, whined at Siobhán's feet. She was upsetting everyone. James was right. She did not know how to holiday. John stood, headed for his kitchen sink, and stared out the little window above it. Siobhán awkwardly came to her feet but didn't approach. "I'm just trying to figure out her movements before she died, or maybe she said something to you. Even if it was small talk—you never know when something might break a case wide open. You gave her your mother's recipes. It sounds as if the two of you were close."

"You'd say that, would ya? You're only here a few days and you think you know everything. You think you could do a better job solving this case then me own grandson, is that it?" He turned around and glared at her, fury in his eyes.

Siobhán shook her head. "No. I don't think that at all. I'm very impressed with Liam."

"Are *you* a detective sargeant?" He pointed at her.

"Easy now," Eoin said to John. He may be angry at Siobhán for starting this, but she knew he didn't like the way John was treating her.

"No. I am not a detective sargeant." *Not yet.* But John Healy was clearly not interested in her career goals.

"Your husband is, is that right?" John crossed his arms and waited for her answer.

He was getting on her nerves now. If he didn't want to answer her questions, he could have just said so politely. Siobhán's jaw clenched. "Yes. Macdara is a detective sargeant."

"And yet he's not here accusing me of things in me own home."

"Siobhán was just being Siobhán," Eoin said. "She asks questions all the time. She meant no offense."

"Accusing me of things in me own home?" John said. "I take offense to that."

"I'm not accusing you of anything." Maybe she needed to give him more information. He obviously had the wrong end of the stick. "The truth is, I think Vera was angry with anyone who received a loan from Mike McGee."

Eoin put his hand on his forehead as if he was trying to take his own temperature. The more she talked, the further she was digging herself into a hole.

"Why would ya think that?" John barked. His breathing had increased and sweat broke out on the side of his face. Trigger barked. Siobhán hadn't thought this through. She couldn't let him know about the Vendetta List, because *she* wasn't supposed to know about the Vendetta List. If Liam found out she knew, both she and Jeanie Brady would be in trouble. And Siobhán could not let that happen. Everyone had warned her to stay out of it. Why didn't she ever listen?

"People talk," Siobhán said. "It's just something I heard." She tried to exit the kitchen. She needed to give him space to calm down.

"What people?" John advanced on her. "What exactly did you hear?"

"Whoa." Eoin stepped in front of Siobhán. "Why don't you take a breath and a step back."

John made a sound that very much mimicked a

growl. He looked at the clock. "I want all of you out of here in thirty minutes. Pack your things and go."

Siobhán's mouth dropped open. Eoin hung his head. "You can't be serious," Siobhán said.

"I'm deadly serious. And no refunds."

Eoin was holding the recipe book in his hands, looking at it with a touch of worry. John walked over and snatched it away from him. "And you won't be taking this now, will ya?"

Eoin and Siobhán were standing on the footpath surrounded by all their luggage when Macdara, Gráinne, Ann, and Ciarán returned. Happy from a day of fun, they were so busy laughing and nattering on that it took them a while to process what they were seeing.

Gráinne was the first to put it together. "What on earth did you do," she said, looking straight at Siobhán.

"I'm beginning to think," Siobhán said, "I don't know how to holiday."

"I've called every place of lodging in Lahinch," Macdara said. They were camped out at a local pub, pondering their next move. "Either John Healy called them all and warned them not to house us, or they're telling the truth and they're booked up. Looks like we'll be ending our holiday early." Siobhán looked at all the disappointed faces around her and could not stand that it was her fault. They couldn't leave now.

Their last memory of this holiday could not be that she ruined their fun.

"Jeanie Brady!" Siobhán said. "She just left her room. And knowing Jeanie, she booked the room for longer than she needed." It was true. One never knew if a case was going to take a long time or be resolved quickly. And although this case was far from resolved, Jeanie had wanted to get back to start the postmortem. "Maybe we can stay there. At least for the wake." Before anyone could talk her out of it, she texted Jeanie.

"Why would you want to go to the wake of a woman we didn't even know?" Macdara pressed.

"You said it yourself. That I'd combust if I didn't get to follow me instincts on this case."

"Once we're on the road, you'll have no choice but to put it behind you," Macdara said.

"Don't you find it odd that all I did was ask a simple question about whether Mrs. Chips had been staying at his inn recently and John Healy threw an absolute fit over it?" She looked to Eoin for backup.

"It was a bit odd," Eoin said, twirling his pint. "She asked a pretty simple question."

Siobhán nodded. "And what about his shady stories about the ladders?"

Macdara covered his eyes with his hand as if the sun streaming in through the pub windows was bothering him, but Siobhán suspected she was the one giving him a pain in the head.

"Do we have to go home?" Ciarán said. "Can't we just go someplace else?"

The windows of the pub rattled. The wind had picked up outside. "I wouldn't mind staying for the wake either," Eoin surprised her by saying. "Despite the fact that he took the recipe book that I was very keen on keeping, I know the curry sauce well enough now to pull it off. I wanted to make it for her wake. As a tribute." He glanced at Siobhán. "And an apology."

Thank heavens, Siobhán thought. He was supporting her. Apart from the apology bit—that was clearly aimed at her. "That's a lovely idea," she said.

"I'm not doing it for you," Eoin replied.

Siobhán sighed. "I only asked him whether Vera had been staying there. Had I known he was going to have a fit over it, I would have kept me gob shut."

"It does sound a bit out of proportion," James said. "I mean, Eoin and I told her not to ask him, like, but ah sure, lookit."

"He's an innkeeper, not a priest," Siobhán said. "What's with all the secrecy?"

"You're a garda and an out-of-towner," Macdara said. "And this is a murder inquiry." He stared into his pint. "Have you spoken to Liam since we were chucked out?"

Siobhán felt a twist in her stomach. *Liam.* How was he going to react to all of this? She really had ruined everything. "I'm sure John has done that," Siobhán said. "I've been watching me phone ever since." She'd had enough of a rapport with Liam that she had no doubt he'd call her the minute he heard.

"You upset his grandfather," Macdara said. "I wouldn't expect him to be happy."

"But *why* did he get so upset? I didn't personally attack him or accuse him of anything." Was John Healy hiding something? Something he was afraid of her finding out? "Maybe he has some kind of mood disorder we don't know about," Siobhán said.

"I was thinking the same about you," Gráinne said.

"I thought he was nice," Ann said. "Trigger liked him."

"And Trigger likes only good people," Ciarán said.

Siobhán's phone pinged. It was a text from Jeanie Brady. "We have a room for tonight," Siobhán said.

"*One* room?" Ciarán said. "For like all of us?"

Siobhán swallowed hard. "It's just for one night," she said. "Think of it as an adventure."

Chapter 17

After checking into their single room at the nearby hotel, the O'Sullivans (all but Eoin, who stayed behind to find a kitchen so he could make another batch of his curry sauce) took a drive, had a spot of lunch outside of town, and then returned to the hotel room, where they took turns using the jax to get ready for Vera Cowley's unofficial wake. Once they were ready, they returned to the same local pub where they'd camped out that morning. But this time the pub was jammers. Eoin had spent the day using Sheila Bisby's kitchen to make the curry sauce, and from the look on his face he was extremely proud of what he'd accomplished. He set the large bowl on the food table with a notice.

About this Curry Sauce
I put a few clues together and came up with what
I believe is a curry sauce nearly identical to the

one Mrs. Chips was about to unveil. If you enjoy it, 'tis her you need to thank. Credit also due to John Healy's mam and her recipe book, which inspired Vera Chips to put her own spin on it. In their honor, we have named this curry sauce Healy-Cowley Curry.
Eoin O'Sullivan
Owner: The O'Sullivan Six farm-to-table restaurant
Kilbane, County Cork, Ireland

"Healy-Cowley Curry?" Gráinne said. She clearly did not approve. It was a mouthful. "People are going to call it Holy Cow Curry."

"Or Holy Cowley Curry," James chimed in.

"Holy Cowley Curry," Ciarán said loudly. "That's gas."

Ann looked as if she was holding in a laugh, but then it came out in a fit.

Eoin grinned. "That wouldn't be so bad, now would it?" Gráinne shrugged. She grabbed a spoon and went in for a taste. Eoin slapped her hand away. "John Healy said he wanted to do the honors first."

"He spoke to you?" Siobhán said, glancing around the pub.

"He did," Eoin said. "I gave him a bell and apologized. He accepted it." He glanced at Siobhán. *"Mostly."*

"The man who chucked us out?" Ciarán shook his head. "He's dead to me."

"Now, pet," Siobhán said. "That's not nice."

"He wasn't nice!" Ciarán said. "I had me own room!"

"He was good to Trigger," Ann said.

"He was good to us too, like. Before . . . he wasn't," Eoin said. "A little kindness can go a long way." Eoin searched the crowd until he spotted John Healy. He was standing at the bar with Liam. Siobhán still hadn't heard from Liam, which wasn't a great sign. She'd rather he give out to her and get it over with. This slow build to whatever she had coming was excruciating. Macdara was right; after the wake they needed to leave Lahinch for good. Maybe she'd join some kind of support group for people who don't know how to holiday. "I'm going to see if I can get him to do the honors," Eoin said, wiping his hands on his trousers. "Wish me luck."

Ciarán looked as if he was going to sneak in a taste of the curry sauce, so Siobhán corralled her brood to the other side of the pub. John Healy was more likely to be amicable if he didn't see her face. She watched Eoin step up to John and Liam and speak with them. Liam raised his head and searched the bar. He made eye contact with Siobhán and gave a quick nod. Maybe he wasn't browned off with her after all. She smiled, and he looked away. Or maybe he wanted nothing more to do with her.

Eoin cleared his throat to get everyone's attention, and when that didn't work Gráinne put two fingers between her lips and whistled. The place fell silent and all heads turned their way.

"Thank you," Eoin said. "I wanted to say a few words." He cleared his throat and shifted his feet. "I did not get to meet Mrs. Chips, but I did have the pleasure of meeting two other folks. One knew her well—John Healy." Eoin looked around until he spotted John and they nodded at each other. "John has shown us great hospitality at the Healy Inn, and I wanted to personally thank him. I am a chef, will soon open my own restaurant in Kilbane. That's County Cork, if you want to have a wander. The O'Sullivan Six—it's a farm-to-table theme . . ." People were getting fidgety, so Eoin moved away from his self-promotion. "Anyhoo. John was kind enough to let me have a glance at a recipe book handwritten by his mam. Mrs. Chips had also had a gander at this recipe book, and from it she was inspired to create a brand-new curry sauce, which I've learned she was very excited to share with all of you." He glanced at Madeline Plunkett, who smiled and then waved to the crowd as if she were in a parade. "Madeline Plunkett is in town because she saw the same article about the chipper as we did—'Save the Chipper'—and when Madeline arranged to pay Mrs. Chips a visit, she wanted Madeline to try this new curry sauce and write a review on her online blog."

That may not have been true, as Eoin had found out, learning about Madeline's hit pieces. Had Liam followed up on this yet with Mr. Chips? What if Madeline Plunkett had *pretended* to be responding to the newspaper article on Mrs. Chips but secretly had been hired by Mr. Chips to write a hit piece? If things hadn't gone downhill already, this would have been a perfect time to confront the pair about this possibility.

Madeline stepped forward, the smile never leaving her face as if it were a fixed feature. "One hundred thousand followers and counting. MadelinePlunkett EatsIt.Com. Be sure to give me a like and a follow."

"A what and a what?" said an elderly woman behind Siobhán.

Eoin gave Madeline's self-promotion a little beat and then continued. "It's really because of Mrs. Chips that my family and I are here and having an absolutely brilliant holiday. As a fellow restaurant owner, I must admit I identified with Mrs. Chips. She was good at what she did. It may have been a small chipper, but it was mighty and it was proud." He waited as a few people clapped and cheered. When he spoke again, his voice had picked up new confidence. "It is in her honor, and in John Healy's late mother's honor, that I have done me best to create a curry sauce that I believe comes close to the one she wanted to unveil that fateful day." Eoin picked up a spoon and gestured to John Healy. "Mr. Healy, would you like to do the honors?"

Madeline took the spoon and made a production of waving John Healy over from across the room.

"I would be honored, so," John said, stepping up. On his way to the table he clapped Eoin on the back. "No hard feelings, lad. You personally are welcome back to me inn any time." He snatched the spoon from Madeline with a bit more force than anyone expected, and Madeline stumbled back a few steps. John turned to the crowd. "What can I say about Mrs. Chips? Me last handyman act for Mrs. Chips was to build her a new bookcase. It was her pride and joy, let me tell ya. And she was no stranger to me inn. She was not a perfect woman, but who among us is perfect?" He looked up to the ceiling. "Vera Cowley . . . May you rest in peace, and may the past be forgotten." He looked around the room. "Liam. Where are you, lad?"

Liam stepped forward. "Here, Pappy."

"Mrs. Chips is lucky to have you on her case," he said. "Er . . . you know what I mean."

Liam held up his pint. "May she rest in peace."

Everyone else raised theirs. "May she rest in peace."

John held up his spoon and grinned. "Here goes nothing." He dipped it into the curry sauce, then tasted a spoonful. His face looked apprehensive as if he were tasting a fine wine and trying to detect all the notes. He smacked his lips and held up a finger. He took another taste. Then another, and another, and another. Finally, as the room filled with laughter, he picked up the bowl and held it to his chest. "I'm sorry this lad didn't make enough for everyone to have a taste," he said, this time bringing the bowl itself up to his lips and drinking as another wave of laughter rolled through. "Jokes aside, it's the worse thing I've ever tasted." From the tone of his voice he meant every word. The laughter stopped and a few gasps were heard.

"That's unkind," Siobhán said, stepping up. "If you want to be angry with me, be angry with me. But me brother was only trying to pay his respects."

"Well, then," John said. "Paid in full with that bitter-tasting nonsense!"

"You've ruined it for everyone," Madeline said.

Eoin's face was truly pained. He hadn't seen the betrayal coming, and John's criticisms had left him stunned. No hard feelings, her arse. John was a sneaky one. Eoin grabbed the empty bowl of curry and disappeared into the kitchen. Siobhán followed. His shoulders shook as he rinsed the bowl.

"He's a small man," Siobhán said. "And I'm truly sorry for all the trouble I caused. This is all my fault." Eoin stopped rinsing but he didn't turn around. "You are a fabulous chef. And no one in Kilbane is going to know or care that a bitter old man disparaged your curry sauce. And I hope you make it again, because I was really looking forward to tasting it."

Eoin let the bowl clatter into the sink. "I was trying to make amends."

"You didn't need to make amends, you'd done nothing wrong."

"Why is he so angry? All because you asked if Mrs. Chips had stayed in that room?"

"It's very odd," Siobhán said. "Very odd indeed."

"What now?"

"Now? We leave. We've definitely overstayed our welcome."

"That's the best idea I've heard all day." Eoin dried his hands on a towel and headed back toward the pub. Once again Siobhán followed. "Let's hope we can get James away from the love of his life."

"He's a grown man. If he wants to stay, he can stay."

Eoin nodded. They merged into the pub. Siobhán really wanted to speak to Liam before she left town, but every time she approached, he suddenly had somewhere else to be. *Let it go.* They remained for an hour just to be polite, but soon Siobhán, Macdara, and her brood were ready to leave.

"Don't let the door hit your arses on your way out," John said. "Out of town, that is." John had gravitated toward them, with Liam standing by his side.

"Pappy," Liam said sternly. "What is the matter with you?" He looked at Siobhán. "What am I missing?"

Had he really not said a word about it to Liam? "He's browned off with me," Siobhán admitted. "I asked a question I shouldn't have."

Liam frowned. It was obvious he was in the dark. "What question?" When Siobhán didn't answer, he turned to his grandfather. Instead of answering him, John Healy started to convulse. "Come on, Pappy, stop messing," Liam said.

John grabbed his stomach and doubled over. The moan that came out of him was real. He moaned again, then hit the floor, as he continued to groan and thrash. Several people screamed as they caught sight of what was happening. Others shouted for someone to call 999. Liam and Macdara knelt next to him, preparing to do CPR. But it was too late. His eyes were open and still, his mouth frozen midscream. Sixty minutes after drinking Eoin's curry sauce, John Healy was dead.

Chapter 18

Liam and Macdara were quick to evacuate the pub and call in the forensic team. The rest of them were all gathered on the footpath and in the street, as close to the crime scene as they were allowed. Madeline Plunkett wasted no time in accusing Eoin. Notebook and biro in hand, she turned to him with penetrating eyes.

"You made the curry sauce, and only you, is that right?"

Before Eoin could answer, Siobhán nosed her way in. "It was sitting on the table. Anyone could have poisoned it *if* that's what happened."

"How convenient he poured it down the drain," Madeline said, scribbling a note.

"He was only rinsing out the bowl and that was *before* John collapsed." Siobhán knew better than to get engaged in this petty bickering, but when it came to her siblings her Mother Bear took over.

"Siobhán," Eoin said. "It's alright."

Siobhán turned to her brother, then gently pulled him aside. She could see Madeline straining to listen. "It's not alright. You cannot say a word to anyone right now. Not a single word. Tell me you understand."

Eoin's eyes flashed wide with fear. "You know I didn't put anything in the curry sauce."

"Of course I know that. But it seems as if someone did. How long was it unattended on the table?"

Eoin shook his head. "It was in the warmer maybe half an hour. I was never far from the table."

"Someone could have been quick."

"But . . . what kind of poison even kills that fast?"

"Cyanide for one." Eoin buried his face in his hands. "Eoin. Look at me." Eventually, he did. "Do you trust me?"

"With me life, Siobhán. You know that."

"Then stay calm. We are going to get through this."

Eoin glanced at Madeline, then jerked his head and walked farther away. Siobhán followed. "You don't understand," he said. "It was Madeline Plunkett who encouraged me to make the curry sauce for the wake."

"You're joking me."

"She practically begged me." He lifted his head as if searching for her in the crowd. "Did she set me up?"

Siobhán felt a wave of rage. "Somebody certainly did," she said. "And she is on the list."

Eoin frowned. "What list?"

"I shouldn't have said anything." The list wasn't really helpful given nearly all of their suspects were on it.

"But you did mention it. What list?"

"Something Doctor Jeanie Brady found in Vera Cowley's upstairs flat. She was keeping a Vendetta List."

Eoin stared at his feet. "Maybe I shouldn't have honored her at all, then."

Siobhán put her hand on his shoulder. "No one is perfect," she said. "Life events simply pushed Vera Cowley over the edge. It doesn't mean she didn't deserve it, and it was a beautiful tribute."

"A tribute that ended in another death."

"We don't know yet what caused John Healy's death. Please don't let your thoughts go rogue until we have an official finding from Doctor Brady." Jeanie Brady would know Eoin had nothing to do with this, and like Siobhán she would be determined to prove that.

Siobhán finally clocked Madeline Plunkett in the crowd. She was standing alone, her face buried in her smartphone as she typed away. Was she already concocting a salacious article for a website? Maybe her hit pieces brought in more money than Siobhán had realized. Maybe she thrived on drama and chaos. Did she also *cause* it? Was this glamorous young woman a cold-blooded killer?

There was no use all of them hanging around a crime scene, so after making sure they didn't see anything that would be useful, Siobhán set Gráinne, Ann, and Ciarán free. They promised to stay together, and Gráinne agreed to keep her phone on in case Siobhán needed them back straight away. James was sticking with Eoin, which was necessary given he looked as if he was going to collapse from the stress. They needed one another. Family was the rock you leaned on in times like this. Siobhán was relieved when Macdara emerged from the pub and joined her. She brought him up to speed on the Madeline Plunkett development, how she was instrumental in getting Eoin to make the curry sauce. "That will be important to tell someone," Macdara said.

"Someone?"

"Liam cannot investigate this case. It's possible that they'll have me take over."

"Even if..." Siobhán hated to say it in front of Eoin. "Even if Eoin is peripherally involved?" She couldn't bring herself to say *person of interest*. Technically he was, but they all knew he had absolutely nothing to do with this.

"I'll have to disclose my relationship to Eoin of course, but given there's no motive on his part and given this death is highly likely tied to Vera Cowley's case, I don't think I'll be removed from the investigation." He hesitated. "And that's if his death is ruled as a murder. We don't even know if this was poison."

"All of this has something to do with his changing ladder story. I just know it."

"Talk it through," Macdara said. This was their process. Even when they both knew the details, often saying them out loud could be the key that sprung open the lock.

"Remember when we first arrived and he pulled up to the chipper with that ladder in his lorry?"

Macdara nodded. "That feels like ages ago."

"It was his first 'ladder explanation.' He said he'd found it discarded next to the Bisby fishery."

"I remember."

"But then recently he told Eoin that he thought Vera 'borrowed' his ladder without permission, for his was missing."

"And?"

"What if he was trying to give himself cover? What if it's his ladder that was greased up?"

"Let's say that's true. He also supposedly found a ladder that morning, so how would that fit in if he's concocting a story?"

"I don't quite know. But I also don't know if Liam has even tried to figure out the ladder. I think he just assumed it was Vera's ladder from the shed. But if the killer brought the ladder . . ."

"Follow the ladder," Macdara said.

"And all ladders lead to John Healy," Siobhán said.

"I'll check to see that the ladder from John's lorry is in the evidence room. Then we can ask Sheila Bisby if it belongs to her." He paused. "But even if it's John's ladder, it doesn't mean he greased it up."

Proving who owned what ladder would not be enough to solve the case. Anyone could have taken someone else's ladder. But still, John's changing stories bothered her. "I know. It's just . . . it doesn't sit well with me."

"What exactly are you saying?"

"I haven't worked it all out yet." She was thinking about the evening John had been invited to dinner at the fancy restaurant by the ocean. How he canceled because he wasn't feeling well. She was thinking about all the meals he'd fixed them at the inn and how she couldn't remember him eating with them ever.

Macdara's gaze was focused on Madeline. She was still immersed in her mobile phone. "Right now I'm more interested in the fact that the curry sauce was her idea."

"Eoin also spent yesterday in Sheila Bisby's kitchen," Siobhán pointed out. James, who had just walked back toward them with Eoin, caught the comment and stiffened. Siobhán placed her hand on his arm. "I'm not accusing her of anything. But maybe someone at her fishery messed with the curry sauce."

Siobhán was thinking back to John's overreaction when she asked him about Vera staying there. Something was definitely off. She was still stewing on it when Liam made his way over. Sirens grew louder as the vehicles approached.

"The coroner is on the way," Liam said. "Jeanie Brady has given permission for him to oversee transporting Pappy to the hospital morgue." His voice caught and he lowered his head.

"I'm so sorry," Siobhán said. "This is such a shock."

Liam nodded. "I'm likely to be removed from the case," he said. "And before you say anything, I'm fine with you investigating," he said, looking between Siobhán and Macdara. "More than fine."

"Full disclosure," Siobhán said. "Both Macdara and I know Eoin had nothing to do with your grandfather's death, and before he died your grandfather was browned off with me."

"I know," Liam said.

"Do you understand why?" Siobhán said. "I think it might have something to do with this case."

"What do you mean?" Liam asked.

"Did he tell you why he was upset with me?"

Liam grimaced. "Apologies, but he just said you were the nosy sort and he'd had enough of it."

Siobhán didn't dare look at Macdara, as she had a feeling he was working overtime to keep a laugh bottled in. "It wasn't that I was nosy. I asked him one question."

"And that was?"

"Whether Vera Cowley had recently been staying at his inn."

Liam frowned. "If she had . . . that would be news to me. But why would that upset him?"

"I think that's what we need to find out."

"He also said something about Mrs. Chips borrowing his ladder without asking," Macdara said. "Have you determined if the greased ladder belonged to Mrs. Chips?"

Liam shook his head. "The ladder is in the evidence room, but I wouldn't know one ladder from another, to be honest with ye. I mean, I know my grandfather had a ladder, and I know Vera had a ladder, but I never paid close attention to either of them. The door to Vera's shed was open, so I assumed it was her ladder."

"And then there's the ladder your grandfather said

he found the same morning we found Mrs. Chips dead," Siobhán snuck in.

Liam stiffened. "What exactly are you trying to say?"

"I'm saying it's too much of a coincidence to me, and it would be worth sorting it out."

Liam seemed to ponder it, then shrugged.

"We'll need you to bring us up to date on everything you've learned about the case so far," Macdara said.

"If you're okay with it, I plan to be as involved as I can be, including bringing you up to date," Liam said. "Even if I'm not officially the one in charge, I don't intend to fade into the background."

"Of course," Macdara said. "We'll do this by the book and can vouch for each other as far as our biases in this case."

Liam nodded. "I know the people in this town. I can be of help."

"Tremendously," Macdara agreed.

"There's something else we just learned, although I'm trying not to jump to any conclusions," Siobhán said.

She had Liam's attention. "Go on."

"Please don't turn around and look, but Madeline Plunkett is the one who encouraged Eoin to make the curry sauce."

Liam looked to Eoin. "I'm not accusing her of anything," Eoin said. "But she was telling me how excited Mrs. Chips was about the new sauce and she thought it might be a fitting tribute."

"Interesting," Liam said. And although he tried to play it cool by swiveling his head in slow motion, Siobhán was still mortified when he stared directly at Madeline. His gaze was so intense she stopped scrolling through her phone and looked up. Liam lowered his voice even though she wasn't within earshot. "But why would she kill Mrs. Chips?"

They fell silent. No one had any clue. Once again Siobhán was dying to say something about the Vendetta List, but she was going to have to wait until Liam brought it up. Otherwise it might compromise Doctor Brady, and all of them would be chucked off the case. All these years later and Sir Walter Scott's words still rang true: *"Oh, what a tangled web we weave . . ."*

"I think we're looking at one killer," Liam said. "My grandfather was everyone's handyman. That's probably why he was making an issue out of his ladder not being returned. Maybe he saw or heard something on a recent job. He definitely wanted to tell me something troubling."

"What do you mean?" Siobhán asked.

"He'd tried to call me before the wake," Liam said. "I was working and couldn't answer. But from the amount of times he called me, he was definitely worried about something."

"He didn't tell you what it was when you saw him at the wake?" Macdara asked.

"We were never alone," Liam said. "I should have taken him aside and insisted he tell me."

"You couldn't have known," Macdara said. "Did

your grandfather have any allergies or any kind of medical condition that you know about?"

Siobhán knew where Macdara was going with this. There was a chance it didn't have anything to do with the curry sauce at all. Siobhán felt guilty for hoping he had a medical condition or a life-threatening allergy to some everyday substance, but it would make things so much easier.

"No," Liam said. "He did not."

"Do you have a local plumber you trust?" Siobhán asked.

"We do," Liam said. "Why do you ask?"

"We washed the evidence down the drain," Siobhán said. "We need to see if some of it is still in the pea trap."

"I'll inform the Technical Bureau," Liam said.

"Why don't you take a few days off," Macdara said to Liam. "You need time to grieve."

Liam pursed his lips. "I know you're right," he said. "I suppose if I have anything to do with looking into my pappy's death the higher-ups will have cause to refute it."

"We'd better do it by the book, then," Macdara said. "Let me give headquarters a bell."

"I don't know what I'll do with meself," Liam said. "I'm always working."

"I like to go for a run when I have a lot on my mind," Siobhán said.

Liam perked up slightly. "You're right, you're right. I should hit the gym, work off a bit of this tension."

"There you go," Siobhán said.

"But you will keep me abreast of everything, will you not?"

"I don't see that's a problem," Siobhán said. But if it was, they'd deal with it then.

"I do have one request," Liam said. "My interview with Mr. Chips is in the morning. I'll let Detective Sargeant Flannery lead the questioning, but I would like to watch from the observation room."

"I think that is a brilliant idea," Siobhán said, given she wanted to be in on that one too. "What time is the interview?"

"Half eleven," he said. "Sharp."

Macdara returned with news. "I'm officially co-assigned to the case," he said. "I'll be working it with Detective Sargeant Healy, but I will be the lead on his grandfather's inquiry—if in fact there is one."

"I'm telling you, my grandfather's sudden death was not natural. You saw how he was convulsing."

"Yes," Macdara said. "But you know the protocol. We'll have to see how Doctor Jeanie Brady rules the cause of death."

"Understood," Liam said. "Will you excuse me?" He headed back into the crowd.

Siobhán turned to Macdara. "Am I right in assuming I'm on the team as well?"

Macdara nodded. "I wouldn't have it any other way."

"But don't worry," she said. "We'll fit in loads of holiday activities—even a few before the interview, just cram it all in there."

"How romantic," Macdara said.

"Exactly," Siobhán said. "And I'd say we start

tomorrow with a little shopping. A very holiday thing to do."

Macdara tilted his head. "And by shopping do you mean the gift shop owned by Tara Flaherty, the best friend of our first victim; the oil and vinegar shop owned by Daniel O'Grady; and the bakery and flour mill owned by Natalie O'Brien?"

"Don't forget the restaurant supply store owned by Tom Dowd, and we'll have to return to the fishery—"

Macdara held up his hand. "Be still me heart."

Siobhán grinned. "I love that you get me."

Chapter 19

The next morning after a walk on the beach, Siobhán and Macdara stopped for coffee and scones and then headed for Tom Dowd's restaurant supply warehouse, mainly because he opened the earliest. Most of the six were still sleeping in; Eoin had been up walking the beach at least an hour before Siobhán and Macdara went out. Understandably, he was still stressing over John Healy's death. The sooner they caught this killer, the better. Eoin had worked so hard to open this restaurant, and Siobhán was infuriated that someone deliberately set him up. His name would be cleared, of that she had no doubt, but in the meantime this event stood to ruin his time of joy. He would never have this exact experience again—anticipating the opening of his restaurant. No one was going to continue to interfere with that if she had anything to do about it.

And in the end, whether John Healy liked her or not, she wanted justice for him. If only he had entrusted her with whatever had been bothering him, he might still be alive. She was anxious for Jeanie Brady's findings. It was unusual for a poison to kill a person that quickly. Was it coincidence that John had been feeling ill on a few other occasions, or had someone been poisoning him over time? Who would do such a thing?

Liam had informed the O'Sullivans that they could return to their rooms at the inn—unless they were uncomfortable with that idea. Given they were going to be in town quite a while longer, they took him up on it, although there was no denying it felt very strange and somber to be back in the inn without John's hospitality. Siobhán couldn't help the questions that were swirling around her mind. Had John Healy known who the killer was? He obviously knew or did *something* to make the killer strike again. She wasn't blaming John, not at all, but if they could figure out his connection, it could be the key to solving the entire case.

The warehouse was only a twenty minute drive from town. Set back behind a large parking lot, the square gray building was devoid of warmth. The blinds were shut and only one car was in the parking lot, but a light shone from within, so someone was here. They had purposefully not given any notice about their visit—often it was best to catch people off guard.

The door was locked, but after they pushed a small buzzer next to it, they heard the telltale sound of the door being unlocked. They entered a small waiting room with a reception desk, and behind it sat a large woman with cropped black hair and a bright smile.

"How ya," she said. "I'm afraid you've missed Tom and we don't officially open for another few hours, but if you'd like to leave a message I'd be happy to scribble it down." She began searching a messy desk, lifting reams of paper and peering underneath. "I had me message pad around here somewhere."

"That won't be necessary," Macdara said as they came closer. "I'm Detective Sargeant Flannery, and this is Garda Siobhán O'Sullivan."

"Please to meet you, Detective. Garda." She turned a placard around: CAITLIN KELLY.

"Beautiful name," Siobhán said.

"Thank you." Her cheeks flushed red. "I've always liked Siobhán meself. Does anyone call you Shiv?"

"Not if I can help it."

Caitlin threw her head back and laughed. It was a hearty and warming sound.

"I usually call her boss," Macdara said.

Confusion came across her face. "We're married," Siobhán said.

Caitlin erupted into laughter once more. She wagged her finger at Macdara. "Happy wife, happy life. Now." She wiped tears away from her eyes. "Would either of you like a cuppa? I have a kettle in the back." She was already rising. Siobhán could sense Macdara was about to decline, but she placed her hand on his arm.

"We'd love one," Siobhán said. "Thank you."

Caitlin grinned, then gestured to chairs lined up against the wall. "You can pull those closer to the desk, or I can do it if you'd like?"

"Not at all," Macdara said. "I'll do it."

As Macdara arranged their chairs, Caitlin hurried to

the front of the desk and shoved papers away, making enough room for their cups of tea, and then she headed for the back room.

"You read her right," Macdara said. "She likes the company."

Siobhán gazed at the mountains of papers on her desk. "Who wouldn't want a sanctioned break from that?"

She returned minutes later with two cups of tea, milk, and sugar on a tray. She placed their teacups on the cleared-off spots, then set the tray on a stack of papers, giving it a jiggle to make sure it wouldn't fall over. Then she held up a finger and disappeared again. When she returned, she was holding a teacup for herself and a tin of biscuits. She took her time sitting down, then stared at her desk in dismay as if trying to decide where to put her tea. Finally, she gave up and sat it down on a pile and placed the tin of biscuits on another. She opened the lid and gestured for Siobhán and Macdara to take one. Siobhán was stuffed from the scone, but Macdara was more than happy to pick up the slack. After a few minutes of sipping tea, complimenting the tea and biscuits, and making small talk, Macdara pulled out a notebook and biro.

"We'd like to ask you a few questions," Macdara began.

Caitlin was eyeing the notebook. "That's the way to do it now," she said. "I should get me a blazer to keep a notepad and biro handy."

Macdara nodded and smiled. "We'd like to ask you a few questions about Vera Cowley."

"Fire away." She sat back in her chair as if steadying herself for a heavy conversation.

"We're investigating her murder," Macdara said.

Caitlin nodded, her face somber. "Poor pet." She leaned in. "I promise I won't say a word. But why do you think it's murder? People fall off ladders all the time, do they not?"

"I'm afraid we're only here to ask the questions," Macdara said with a grin.

She backed off, nodding again and mumbling apologies. "How can I be of help?"

"We understand that Vera Cowley called Tom Dowd several times the morning before she died."

Caitlin was already nodding. "Did she ever. The woman was crazed. Enraged, when she was the one who canceled the appointment in the first place."

"Who took the cancelation call?" Macdara asked.

"I did." Caitlin held up a finger, rummaged around her desk some more, and finally unearthed a schedule book. She opened it up and ran her index finger down a page, then tapped an entry. "Tuesday afternoon, the day before she died, she called at 3 p.m."

"You spoke with her?" Siobhán said.

"I tried." She didn't offer anything more.

Macdara leaned in. "What does that mean, you tried?"

"There was some kind of interference on the phone. I asked if she was calling me from a helicopter."

"A helicopter?" Siobhán and Macdara asked in stereo.

Caitlin nodded. "It was all warbled and high-pitched as if she was yelling at me from a helicopter."

Siobhán and Macdara exchanged a glance. What did

this mean? Was it simply bad reception? "Did you ask her about this interference?" Siobhán asked.

"I tried," Caitlin said yet again. "If she heard me she didn't offer an explanation, she just said she was canceling tomorrow's appointment and then she hung up."

"Is it possible it wasn't her?" Macdara said.

Caitlin tilted her head. "Why would someone else call and cancel her appointment?"

Why indeed. Macdara's phone buzzed. "Headquarters wants me to give them a bell," he said. "We should get our legs out from under us."

They thanked Caitlin and stood to go. Caitlin rose as well. When they were almost to the door, she stopped them. "I don't want to gossip . . ."

Siobhán stopped. "Go on, so."

"Vera's wasn't the only strange phone call I answered that week. The next morning, before Vera started calling nonstop, I took another call from yet another woman in an absolute panic."

"Oh?" Macdara said. "And who might that be?"

"Natalie O'Brien. She owns a bakery in town?"

"We're aware," Macdara said.

"I swear I thought she was going to have a heart attack she was so worked up."

Siohan felt a tingle up her spine. "Worked up over what?"

Caitlin held her hands out palms up and shrugged. "I tried me best to find out, but she only wanted to talk to Tom, so of course I had to transfer her." She stared at them as if waiting to see if she did the right thing.

"Of course," Siobhán said.

Relief flooded Caitlin's face as she continued. "Right after she called, he was out the door in a flash."

"Wasn't he off to see Vera?" Siobhán asked.

"He was going to make it there as soon as he could, but it was after Natalie's call that he flew out of here. I can't tell you where he went, I can only tell you that's the order in which things happened."

"Thank you," Macdara said. "We'll follow up on that."

"Don't forget, you didn't hear it from me," Caitlin called after them.

Macdara was due at the garda station for a teleconference with headquarters to discuss teaming this murder probe with Detective Sargeant Healy and to air out any possible conflicts of interest on both sides, then get everyone caught up on the status of the two separate murder inquiries. But first he dropped Siobhán off at Natalie's bakery.

Although normally the delightful sugar smells that wrapped around Siobhán when she entered a bakery would make her swoon, between the breakfast scone and Caitlin's biscuits, she was not able for it. It was a small but delightful space with a peek-a-book view of the bay and trendy bistro tables. The color white dominated the space, which made all the pastries in the case (especially the colorful assortment of delectable macaroons) pop like colorful art on a gallery wall. On second thought, even though she wasn't hungry now, it wouldn't hurt to buy a couple boxes of assorted macaroons. It was much easier to ask questions of a person if that person thought of you as a customer as well as a guard. It would also endear her to her sweet-toothed husband and siblings.

She ordered two assorted boxes, agonizing over her choices, then deciding on a variety. They were so expensive, so French. It was Macdara's dream to eat their way through Paris one day (eating was his love language), but in the meantime they had establishments like this, and of course Eoin was more than capable of making a French meal. After receiving a bag of the little boxes by the petite young employee at the counter, she ordered a cappuccino and then squeezed into a small table by the window. It was early enough that the bakery was only half full. Siobhán knew that if she lived in a seaside town she would be up as early as possible to take in the quiet before the hustle and bustle of the day began. It took a while for Natalie to emerge from the kitchen, and when she did she didn't even glance Siobhán's way. Siobhán waited until a customer left and wandered over to the counter.

"How ya," Natalie said. "What will it be?" Up close Siobhán was surprised to see that Natalie's eyes were a gorgeous shade of green. She remembered her walking on the beach in her yellow hat and bikini. She was a looker. Siobhán never liked walking around in public in a bathing suit, not because she didn't have a good figure—she was blessed to be tall and running kept her thin, and everyone mentioned her long auburn hair—but because she was so pale that she knew any prolonged time in the sun would burn her to a crisp.

"Do you mind joining me?" Siobhán gestured to her table. "I would like to ask you a few questions about the morning Vera Cowley died."

Natalie looked stricken and glanced around to see if any of her customers had big ears. "You're investigating now, is that it?"

"That's it," Siobhán said.

"So, this is official, like?"

"Right now it's a friendly inquiry. If you'd like to make it official and take it to the garda station instead, that can be arranged."

"I'll make a cup of tea and be right over. Do you need a refill?"

"No, thank you, I'm grand."

When Natalie finally settled across from her, Siobhán ditched the small talk and got right to it. "Did you ring Tom Dowd the day before Vera Cowley was killed?"

Natalie's jaw dropped. "Who told you that?" Siobhán put down her biro and took a sip of her cappuccino. She looked out the window and made eye contact with a fat seagull. Natalie squirmed. "I suppose if he says I rang him, then I rang him."

"What did you ring him about?"

Natalie slumped. "What does any of this have to do with her death?"

"I don't know," Siobhán said. "You tell me."

"There's nothing to tell."

"After you rang Tom, did he pay you a visit?" Natalie chewed her lip. Siobhán leaned in. "If he did, I'd be very willing to tell a guard if I were you."

Natalie frowned. "Why is that now?"

"It's a pretty good alibi."

"Alibi? Why do I need an alibi?"

"Because we're investigating a murder, and if you have an alibi and you can prove it, then we can eliminate you as a suspect and spend our valuable time looking in all the right places."

Natalie straightened her spine and her demeanor brightened. "Now. There's something I can do." She stood. "Follow me."

Siobhán grabbed her cup and had to hustle as Natalie was already halfway across the shop. They crossed behind the counter and through the swinging doors to the kitchen. Once back there, Natalie guided them into a little office on the right. She went straight to a computer monitor and began typing. "I had a camera installed last year. They were having a special and, well, the locals I trust but the tourists can get a bit . . ." She stopped as if suddenly remembering Siobhán was a tourist.

"Say no more," Siobhán said.

Natalie began shifting through dates on the screen. "There." She pulled up a video. "This was when Tom visited me. It's time stamped, it was ten forty-five in the morning." She squealed as if she'd just won the lotto. The screen played images of Natalie meeting Tom on the footpath in front of her bakery. They appeared to be having an intense conversation—the pair of them gesticulating, glancing around, and stopping the conversation whenever anyone was in earshot. They spoke for approximately ten minutes, and then Tom moved out of the frame, most likely going to his lorry, and Natalie popped back into the bistro. Natalie went to shut off the footage.

"Let it play," Siobhán said.

"Why? That's it."

"I just want to see the part where you come back out and the two of you head to the chipper together."

Natalie cried out in frustration but let the tape play. She crossed her arms as the two of them watched her come back out a few minutes later and disappear off camera in the same direction as Tom. "Satisfied?"

"I'm a bit closer to being satisfied," Siobhán said. "But I'm not quite there yet." It was true that this made it highly unlikely that either of them had murdered Mrs. Chips. The phone call, the arrival at the bakery, the conversation—all of that was most likely at the same time the killer was waiting for Mrs. Chips to march across the street with black spray paint just so the killer could set up the greased ladder. The black spray paint still bothered Siobhán. If the killer had brought it, didn't Mrs. Chips find it odd that suddenly a can of black spray paint materialized just when she needed it? More likely, Mrs. Chips had seen the brown paper being placed over the mural, and she may even have been spying on Tara Flaherty as she painted it. She must have known she wasn't going to like it— whatever it was. Natalie, arms still crossed, sat on the edge of her desk and waited. Siobhán directed her attention back to the footage. "It seems as if you and Tom were in a passionate conversation."

"Passionate?" This propelled Natalie to a standing position. "There's nothing passionate between meself and Tom Dowd."

"Pardon me. I didn't mean to imply you had a romantic relationship. We wouldn't want Daniel O'Grady getting wind of that rumor now, would we?"

Natalie's eyes narrowed and she crossed her arms. "I have no idea what you're on about."

"Your cheeks do."

"What?"

"Your cheeks just flushed red, so I have a feeling they know exactly what I'm on about."

"You have no right to come in here and accuse me of all sorts of things you can't prove."

Interesting. "What were you and Tom Dowd discussing?"

Natalie bit her lip. "Mrs. Chips," Natalie finally said.

Siobhán felt the hairs on the back of her neck tingle. "You were discussing Mrs. Chips?"

"Yes," Natalie said, reaching for a pack of cigarettes. "And the evil things she was up to."

Chapter 20

Siobhán eagerly waited for Natalie to say more. Instead Natalie clutched her pack of cigarettes and stared at Siobhán with leery eyes.

"You do realize I'm not leaving here until you explain that last statement," Siobhán said. "What nefarious activities do you believe Vera Cowley was up to?"

"It's strange to hear someone call her by her proper name," Natalie said. She held up her pack of cigarettes. "Don't judge. But if I'm going to be spilling secrets, I need a smoke." She held out her hand, showing fingernails bitten to the quick. "I'm wrecked."

Siobhán glanced at her bag of macaroons and hoped cigarette smoke wouldn't seep into the cookies. "I'll follow you."

Natalie pushed open a back door and they exited onto the alleyway. Here more seagulls waited, all lined up like folks out for Sunday brunch. "I forgot the scraps to toss them," Natalie said. Siobhán got the feeling she was looking for any excuse to avoid this conversation.

"They can wait," Siobhán said, blocking access to the door. She'd been patient enough and would not play second fiddle to a flock of seagulls.

Natalie lit her cigarette, inhaled deeply, and then let out a long trail of smoke. A seagull let out an indignant cry, and Siobhán felt a solidarity with the yoke.

"I can't help thinking of poor John Healy," Natalie said. "I bet me life she was doing it to him too."

"Doing what?"

"Coercing money out of him. She was threatening everyone. She wanted me to vow I would never step foot in Mr. Chips." She took another puff while shaking her head. "I told her to get bent. Maybe that's what set her off."

"What did she do?"

"She demanded I lower her flour prices while raising his."

"And by 'his' you're referring to Corman Cowley?" Siobhán purposefully used his real name, normally she went out of her way not to irritate people if she could help it, but there was something about Natalie's demeanor that set her on edge.

"Yes, Corman Cowley," Natalie said. "Mr. Chips. I wouldn't be surprised if he got wind of it and lost the plot altogether." Before Siobhán could interject, Natalie continued. "Then again, why on earth would he want John dead? Do you think there's more than one killer in Lahinch?"

"We're keeping an open inquiry," Siobhán said. But she believed they were looking for one killer. There had to be a connection between the two deaths.

"Mrs. Chips was a bitter pill to swallow, but everyone loved John Healy. You know yourself. He was everyone's handyman, you know? And his prices were fair. We all appreciated him."

"What leverage did Vera have over you?"

Natalie tossed her cigarette down and smashed it with the tip of her kitten mules. "I said nothing about leverage now, did I?"

"If she didn't have any leverage I don't see why you would be calling Tom Dowd in a panic the morning she was murdered."

Natalie swallowed hard. "Honestly it's nothing."

Siobhán took a step forward. "The only crime we're investigating here is murder. If you've done anything else improper, even illegal, I swear to ya, it's of no interest to me."

Natalie pursed her lips. "But you'll write it down and hand it off to someone who is interested, like."

"This is not how you should play this. We will find out. And believe me, it will be much better for you if you come clean now."

"You're an outsider. You'll go away and never think of us again. I have to live here. I have a business here."

"Just because Mrs. Chips accused you of doing something doesn't mean it's true, and it doesn't mean her suspicions have to go any further."

"What about other people?"

"What do you mean?"

"I don't want to get anyone else in trouble."

Interesting. "Natalie, if you don't start talking I'm going to take you into the station right now for formal questioning."

"You wouldn't dare."

"Try me."

"Mike McGee, alright. Are you happy now?"

"What about Mike McGee?"

"He granted me a loan, that's all. But he turned Mrs. Chips down and she was furious about it." There was more to the story. Siobhán waited for it. If Natalie wanted to play the waiting game, she'd quickly discover that Siobhán was very very good at it. "I won the loan in a poker game. There you have it. I had four queens." Her eyes lit up at the memory. "Four queens!"

"He traded loans at poker games?" In this job, a garda saw it all. But this was something Siobhán had never even considered. What was McGee playing at?

"Don't say it like that. It was a proper loan. With interest and everything. But he couldn't pay me what he owed, so yes. Maybe he processed my application a little bit quicker. That's all. Everything else about the loan was done proper, like. I swear to ya."

Playing favorites. There was nothing proper about that. "And Tom Dowd? Did he also win his loan?"

Natalie nodded. "He had a royal flush. He was approved for a larger amount."

This was insane. No wonder Mrs. Chips was furious. Even if Mike McGee was not a murderer, at the least he was going to lose his job. "How did she find out?"

"She snooped, that's how. Binoculars out her window. Then she started nosing around our shops asking questions of anyone who was doing improvements. Where did we get the money, was it a loan, was it from Mike McGee, did we happen to play late-night poker? I mean, she considered herself an armchair detective." Natalie gestured down the alley. "Shall we walk to the water? I'm upset now and it calms me."

Siobhán was thrilled to get out of the smoky alley. Seagulls soared above them, crying out for bits of dropped pastries. "The last time I spoke with Mrs. Chips was at me bakery. She threatened to tell Liam—pardon me, Detective Sargeant Healy—about McGee's proclivity to pay off his poker debts with loans. I don't know whether or not she did. Three days later she was dead."

And if McGee got busted, then everyone's loan would most likely be canceled, and the balance would be due immediately. "But something must have happened the morning she died. Why else would you call Tom in a panic?"

"Would ya stop saying I was in a panic? I'm emotional, that is all."

"My question stands."

"She rang me. Over and over. I didn't answer. But there were a dozen raging messages on me voice mail."

"What were the messages?"

"She demanded immediate cash and Tom Dowd's head on a platter." Natalie scoffed. "Or in a fish and chips basket." She chuckled to herself. They'd reached the promenade. For a moment, they lost themselves in the sights and sounds of the bay. The sun shone on the rippling water and the scent of the ocean clung to the air. Siobhán briefly lost herself in the waves. She wondered what it would be like to live here year-round. Would she still have the same awestruck feeling when looking out at the bay, or would it fade into the background? Given she was still enamored with her medieval walled town even after spending her entire life there, she assumed there were at least a handful of folks who never lost their sense of wonder. That was the only way to go through this life. It was so short. Which was why Siobhán was a guard. For someone to take a life, which had such limited time to begin with, was a crime that could not go unpunished. "I wasn't trying to be cruel just now," Natalie said softly. "I used to like Mrs. Chips. I don't know how things got to this point. But sometimes a bit of humor keeps me sane, even if it's gallows humor."

"When Tom Dowd met with you that morning, did the two of you come up with some sort of plan?"

"Listen." Natalie turned to face Siobhán. "I know this sounds crazy, but maybe she did all of this to herself."

"Come again?"

"Maybe she threw herself off the ladder just to stick it to Tara Flaherty and Mr. Chips. They're together, you know? *Romantically.* Maybe she wanted to frame him for her murder. She was that out of her mind over this whole loan thing, and she was that spiteful."

"I'm sure you can understand why she was upset," Siobhán said. "McGee has no right to hand out loans on the basis of gambling."

Natalie shook her head. "I told you! I knew you were going to use this against me."

"I'm doing nothing of the sort." *McGee was another matter. He was definitely in hot water.* "Did you tell Mike McGee about her threats?"

"I didn't have to. She'd been ringing him too. And he saw her peeking out her window with those binoculars."

"Do you know if she was making the same threats to Daniel O'Grady? Have you spoken with him?" Siobhán tried to keep her tone casual, wanting to see if Natalie would admit she was involved in a romantic relationship with him. Not that it was any of Siobhán's business, but Natalie's reaction would at least give her some idea of the nature of their relationship.

"I can't imagine that she wouldn't have. I already told you she was threatening everyone. I did feel bad for her. Divorce at their age! I'm not saying Mr. Chips is a bad person. But he is a stubborn fool. It couldn't have been easy being married to a man like him all these years. All that and then he dumps her for her best friend? I would have gone mental too." With that Natalie turned and walked away. This time Siobhán did not follow. She breathed in the fresh air as she mulled it over. There were too many secrets in this holiday town. It appeared that backroom poker wasn't the only clandestine game they were playing. Vera, it seemed, had been threatening everyone, watching everyone, and unraveling day by day. She was playing her own game of poker and most likely exaggerating her hand. The question wasn't *if* but *who* felt threatened enough to call her bluff.

Chapter 21

Tacky was the only way to describe Tara Flaherty's shop. It was filled with hideous beach accessories and outfits in jarring colors, images, and patterns. Seagulls with sunglasses drinking cocktails with tiny umbrellas and whatnot.

"Ciarán would have loved this," Siobhán said. "But Gráinne would have needed smelling salts."

Just then Tara Flaherty emerged from behind a rack of said hideous clothing. Unlike the clothing she peddled, she was stylishly dressed in a white flowing dress. She tucked a strand of white hair behind her ear and adjusted her blue tortoiseshell glasses as she stared at them. Siobhán immediately felt a wash of shame come over her. Had Tara heard her disparaging the shop? Her face gave nothing away. Was she also a local poker player? If she had received a loan from Mike McGee, she certainly hadn't spent it dolling up the shop. It was crammed and hot. Siobhán suddenly wished she had gone to the Cliffs of Moher with the rest of the O'Sullivan Six. They'd be gone for the day, and it was perfect timing. Eoin needed to get his mind off what had happened to John Healy.

"How may I help you?" Tara said as if she had no idea who they were.

Macdara was busy holding a beach shirt up to his chest. It was black and showcased yellow suns with faces. They were all wearing black sunglasses and sticking their tongues out. "That suits you, Detective," Tara said, perking up. "And I have the match right here." She strode to the rack near Macdara and riffled through until she found what she wanted. Soon she was holding up a matching pair of shorts. She held it out until Macdara finally took it. Siobhán knew instantly he'd been about to make a joke about the shirt, and now he was stuck.

"You know what," Siobhán said. "That does suit you. You must get it."

Macdara raised an eyebrow. "Must I?"

"I insist."

"Don't forget these," Tara said, whipping out a pair of sunglasses framed in the same yellow sun.

"Brilliant," Siobhán said. "You should wear these out of the store."

"Only if you do the same, boss." Macdara turned to another rack and plucked out a neon-pink shirt with flamingos holding cocktails and looking as if they'd already had one too many. "And look," he said, snatching the matching shorts. "Perfect!"

Tara was quick to produce pink flamingo sunglasses

as well. Before Siobhán could protest, Tara herded them toward a cramped pair of dressing rooms in the back.

"We actually have a few questions for you," Macdara said.

"I'll answer them as soon as you suit up and pay," Tara said. "I'm sure you understand—this is me workplace, and work comes first."

"I was only messing about actually trying these on," Siobhán said. "I'm sure they'll fit." She would pay for them but she'd be tossing them into the nearest bin as soon as they were out of the shop.

"We must be sure they fit," Macdara said. "Are you not brave enough?" He grinned as he waited for her answer. She could feel Tara's gaze on her as Tara also waited for her answer.

Siobhán clenched her jaw. If only she'd kept her gob shut. There was no going back now. From the way Tara was behaving, if they didn't change into these outfits and pay, they wouldn't get a thing out of her. It would be helpful to glean what they could before the interview with Mr. Chips. This was the mistress, and she was no small player in the drama. Resigned, Siobhán went into one dressing room while Macdara went into the other. Moments later they emerged and stared at each other. They looked as if Halloween and Easter had had a baby. And hated that baby.

"Aren't you two the most adorable!" Tara said with a glint in her eye. "I must get a photo." She whipped out her mobile phone. Before Siobhán and Macdara could duck into the dressing rooms to hide, she had already snapped a picture. "I'll blow this up nice and big and put it up on our visitor wall, where everyone can see."

In that moment, Siobhán knew that killer or not, this woman was diabolical. Tara pointed, and sure enough there was a wall filled with photos of other victims in color-clashing, in-your-face beach costumes.

Macdara paid for their torment. Tara handed them bags in which to place their normal clothes. Siobhán leaned in to Macdara. "We're going to change out of these costumes, right?"

Macdara glanced at a clock on the wall. The center was a martini glass and the hands were made to resemble olive sticks. It glowed neon green. "No time." He turned to Tara, but before he even asked a single question, she started speaking.

"I know this is about the mural," she said. "I have to make a living. Did I feel bad?" She shrugged. "Vera would have done the same thing to me. If she had any artistic talent, that is. But if she had, I'll tell you one thing. I certainly wouldn't have taken a can of black spray paint and added horns, and did you see the fish getting sick all over the chips? Well . . . you saw it." She shuddered, then set her mouth in a hard line. "That mural took me *days* to finish."

"How do you know Vera was the one who defaced it?" Siobhán asked. Given they had found a can of black spray paint in the chipper, and most likely Liam had pulled CCTV footage by now, there was no doubt that she had, but Siobhán still wanted to see how Tara would respond.

"Are you joking me?" Tara shook her head. "Who else would it have been?"

"That's not proof," Siobhán said. "It's only a guess."

Tara sighed and began messing with a jar of pens on the counter. "Corman has it on video. It's her, alright. And believe me, she had quite a good time doing it."

Macdara jotted down a note, no doubt about the video. They'd both want to see it as soon as possible. "I'm glad she had a good time doing it," Siobhán couldn't help but say. "Because less than an hour later your once-upon-a-time best friend was dead."

Tara crumpled, laying her head on the counter as she began to sob. Macdara gave Siobhán a look. She'd gone too far. But how could she help it? Up until now she hadn't seen an ounce of empathy out of the woman. And this outfit was irking her. She would swear to it the flamingos were mocking her. Tara lifted her head, and her eyes were clear of any genuine tears. "Why did she climb that ladder all alone?" Tara wailed. "Everyone knows you never climb a ladder alone." Cold or not, there was some truth to that. Even with the treads greased, Vera might have lived if someone had been there to catch her. Then again, if Vera fell on someone hard enough they could have been dealing with three dead bodies. When neither Siobhán nor Macdara replied, Tara changed tactics. "And why didn't Tom Dowd show up on time? I blame him."

"I heard she canceled that appointment," Siobhán said. *Or someone did.* Was it the mercurial woman before them?

"Do you think the same person who killed Vera also murdered John Healy?" Tara looked between them, her eyes wide.

"We're looking into all possibilities," Macdara said.

"Do you know anyone who would wish to harm John Healy?"

Tara shook her head. "Far from it. Everyone relies on him as a handyman. He's quick and he gets the job done to perfection."

"He did some work for Mrs. Chips recently, I believe," Siobhán said. "A bookcase?"

Tara nodded. "She was over the moon about that bookcase. Don't ask me why."

"Do you know if Vera and John had any kind of falling out?" Given Siobhán knew there was some connection between their deaths, she figured she'd start there.

"Falling out?" Tara frowned. "Not that I'm aware." She glanced at her clock, then at the front door. "Is there anything else?" Tara said. "I happen to know that you're due to interview Mr. Chips and I have work to do."

"I'd like to ask you about your timing," Siobhán said. "Why did you pick those exact days to paint the mural?"

"The weather," Tara said without hesitation. "They were slotted to be sunny and warm. You can't paint if the rain is just going to wash away your efforts." She waited, and when Siobhán didn't have a follow-up, she smirked. "Anything else?"

"Just one more question," Macdara said. "When did you start sleeping with your best friend's husband? Was it before or after they divorced?"

Tara's mouth twitched. They had their answer.

Chapter 22

Liam idled in his garda car at the curb, but when Siobhán and Macdara approached, it took him ages to recognize them. Outfits with glaring yellow suns and neon-pink drunk flamingos turned out to be excellent camouflage. To make it worse, they'd been forced to buy flip-flops to go with the clothes. Siobhán had gone for a pedicure before the holiday, but she'd chosen a bright shade of red. Normally, she was fine with red and pink together—what could she say, it was the rebel in her—but neon-pink and bright red were not the best complements. Liam stared at her feet as he finally rolled down his window. "Detective Sargeant Flannery? Garda O'Sullivan?" It was as if he knew who they were but he just couldn't believe it.

"Detective Healy?" Macdara said. "It's us."

Siobhán held up her bag from the shop. "My uniform is in here."

It was almost worth the price of the outfits to see Liam's jaw drop. He then grinned and wagged his finger at them. "Brilliant," he said. "It's a tactic, isn't it?"

"Of course," Macdara said. He raised an eyebrow at Siobhán.

"Absolutely," Siobhán said. "It's a tactic, alright. Spot-on."

Liam slapped the outside of his car door with his hand. "You plan on wearing those hideous costumes during the interview just to completely disarm and distract Mr. Chips!"

"Right you are," Macdara said. Before they could get into the car, a familiar woman came out of a nearby hair salon. *Gráinne*. She was supposed to be at the Cliffs of Moher. Her hair was perfection, her outfit new and expensive. She walked right past them, a scent of flowery perfume trailing after her.

"Gráinne?" Siobhán called.

Gráinne stopped, then slowly turned around, cupping her hand over her eyes and squinting. When she recognized them, she gasped. "Heaven help us," she said. "It's you." She clocked Macdara. "And you." She looked them over and shook her head as she approached. "You poor things. I knew this would happen to ye sooner than later, I was just really praying for later." She sighed and gave Liam a what-are-you-gonna-do look. "I suppose there's no stopping time."

"We're perfectly fine," Siobhán said. "These are for charity." Charity for Tara Flaherty, but Siobhán left that bit out.

"Ah, pet," Gráinne said, shaking her head. "Do *not*

give those outfits to charity. Even those in need do not need"—she gave them another once-over and waved her hand vaguely around them—"whatever you're supposed to be, like."

"These outfits aren't just for charity, they're a tactic," Macdara quickly chimed in with a head nod to Liam. Liam pointed a finger gun at him, winked, and cocked it.

But Gráinne had already moved on. She swiveled her pretty head toward Liam, and a seductive grin took over her face. Mystery of why she was not at the cliffs solved. Had James stayed back as well to chase the one woman who knew exactly how many fish were in the sea?

Liam's face looked just as bright as he emerged from the car, and if Siobhán wasn't mistaken he set his shoulders back. "You are gorgeous," he said to Gráinne, as if Siobhán and Macdara weren't standing right there. "The sun, the moon, and the stars have nothing on you."

Macdara cleared his throat. "I like to start my interviews on time," he said.

"Right, right," Liam said. He nodded at Gráinne. "I hope I see you around later."

"Not if I see you around earlier," Gráinne said. She walked away, with a bit more sass than usual, and Liam ate up every second of it.

"Come on, Detective Romeo," Siobhán said, as she and Macdara piled into the squad car. "Drive it like you stole it."

* * *

Mr. Chips appeared knackered but eager to be helpful. He had trouble making eye contact as he tried to smooth down bits of white hair standing at attention. Every once in a while he'd stare at their outfits and frown.

"We bought these at your girlfriend's shop," Siobhán said.

Mr. Chips nodded, although he did not look impressed. "I hope they were on sale," he finally muttered.

"Take us through everything you remember the days before your wife was murdered," Macdara started out.

"Ex-wife," Mr. Chips said. "Are we here to talk about Vera or John Healy?"

Pick a murder, any murder. "We're here to talk about whatever or whomever we want to talk about," Siobhán said. The flamingos were mocking her once again, and she could feel the tension building up in her.

"Are you sure it was murder, like? Vera was always impulsive. Her temper would get the best of her and before you know it she would be doing something foolish. You know?" He licked his lips and waited to see if they would agree. "Do you want to know what I think?"

"No," Siobhán said. "We want to know what you know."

"But you see. I think she fell off that ladder. Because she wasn't familiar with it."

Macdara, who had been writing notes, looked up. "How do you mean?"

"She borrowed that ladder from John Healy." He leaned in. "And when I say borrowed, I mean stole." He sat back, crossed his arms, and waited.

"We're going to need more than that," Siobhán said.

"I saw her meself. John Healy's lorry had been parked out front of her chipper and I saw her take the ladder right out of it and drag it around the side. She must have been putting it in the shed."

"What day was this?" Macdara asked.

"Dunno. A few days before her accident, I believe."

"How do you know she didn't have John Healy's permission to borrow the ladder?"

Mr. Chips shrugged. "You could be right. I don't know. And I would have said all you have to do is ask him, but you can't now, can you?"

And once again they were back to ladders. Now that they were officially on the case, Siobhán wanted to have a look at that shed not to mention the upstairs flat. Mr. Chips was right. They could not ask John. But what Mr. Chips didn't know was that John had already mentioned that Vera took his ladder. But why? "Did Vera not have a ladder of her own?"

"We had one, alright," Mr. Chips said. "She won it in the divorce."

Siobhán had a hard time stifling a laugh. He wasn't taking the piss.

"You should know that we've already spoken with Tara Flaherty," Macdara said.

"I assumed as much," Mr. Chips replied, once again looking between them at their outfits. He suddenly leaned in, shaking his head. "Sure, lookit. I won't report ye, but if I may be so bold as to make a suggestion?" Macdara crossed his arms and waited. "You're not really convincing as guards dressed like that. I don't know how you do things in Kilbane, but we're a bit more professional here in Lahinch, like."

How you do things in Kilbane. He'd been looking into them. Was it an attempt to know thy enemy? Was it a killer trying to be prepared?

This time Macdara did laugh. He leaned in. "Are ya more professional here now?"

"We are."

"Normally, I would agree with you," Siobhán said. "But in this case, we have a very good reason for dressing like this." Macdara's gaze shifted to her. She knew he couldn't wait to see where she was going with this. "You see, as you so adeptly realized, we've just paid a visit to your mistress, Tara Flaherty." Siobhán leaned in. "We find people bloom open like spring flowers when we support their businesses." She glanced at her flamingos and Macdara's suns. "No matter what it takes."

Mr. Chips swallowed hard.

"That's right," Macdara said. "She was very forthcoming."

"I couldn't believe how forthcoming," Siobhán said.

"Then again, her ex–best friend is dead," Macdara said. "That's enough to shake the truth out of most anyone."

"The affair?" Mr. Chips said. "Is that what you're on about? It's no secret. Everyone in town knows."

"Do they know it began *before* you were divorced?" Macdara said.

"Way before," Siobhán said, taking a guess. From the look on Mr. Chips's face, they were bang on.

"No matter what you think of me, I had me reasons," Mr. Chips said. "Vera was not an easy woman to live with."

"Because she put unreasonable demands on you?" Siobhán said. "Wanting her name added to a sign on a chipper in which she had an equal stake?"

"Stake?" Mr. Chips said. "It was my chipper. She had no stake."

"Marriage means an equal partnership," Siobhán said. "From everything we've heard, she was very invested in making a go of that chipper."

"It was my idea. My shop. You don't change a sign after forty years! It was a brand. The brand was Mr. Chips. Not Mr. and Mrs. Chips. *Mister.*" He made a noise akin to a growl. "And why are you sticking your nose into my marital business? I know me rights. It's not illegal to refuse to change the sign in me own shop, is it?" He poked the table with his fingertip. "If it's illegal I'd like you to cite the law right here and now."

"It's not illegal to be a stubborn husband," Siobhán said. "But it speaks volumes about your character."

Mr. Chips pushed back from the table and stood. His jaw trembled. He pointed at Siobhán. "How dare you attack my character. How dare you."

Macdara stood. "Sit back down or you'll be spending a night in custody, and before you say another word, I do *not* give second chances."

Mr. Chips sat. Macdara remained standing for a moment. "I believe you owe Garda Siobhán O'Sullivan an apology."

"I don't need one," Siobhán said. "You see, I *was* attacking his character. I find his actions despicable."

Macdara continued to stare at Mr. Chips until the man squirmed. "Garda O'Sullivan, I apologize."

"For what?" Macdara said.

Mr. Chips struggled with his anger. "For raising my voice, and pointing," he said.

"And for disrespecting the best garda you'll ever have the pleasure of meeting?" Macdara added.

Mr. Chips crossed his arms. "That's taking it a bit far, like." He glanced at Macdara, who wasn't messing. "But if I disrespected you, I apologize."

"Try that again," Macdara said.

"I said if I—"

"There's no if. Again."

"I apologize for disrespecting you."

"I do not accept," Siobhán said. Mr. Chips's mouth dropped open. He then shut his gob. Macdara sat. They hadn't planned on this tack, but given it was probably the opposite dynamic that Mr. Chips had in his marriage, it was working. This was a man who needed to be in full control and they were thoroughly getting under his skin. And murderer or not, he needed to be shaken out of his ways. Siobhán had a new empathy for Vera Cowley. The fact that his late wife had hung in there for forty years was a testament to her character. Or a sign of mental illness.

"Are you the beneficiary of your late wife's will?" Macdara asked casually.

Mr. Chips sat up straight. "Where did you hear that?"

There was a knock on the one-way glass that separated them from the observation room where Liam stood. His voice suddenly came over a speaker. "Answer the question."

Mr. Chips glanced at the glass. He jerked his thumb toward it. "Why is he hiding back there?"

"I'm not hiding," Liam said. "I'm observing."

"We need a verbal answer." Siobhán pushed the recording device toward him.

Mr. Chips stared at the one-way glass, waiting.

"From you," Siobhán said to him. "We need a verbal answer from you."

Startled, he looked at the recorder and then sat up straight. "Yes," he said. "I'm the beneficiary of her will. But before you jump to any conclusions, believe you me I was more surprised than anyone that she'd never officially changed it after our divorce. Are you going to punish me because she was a master procrastinator?"

Siobhán scoffed. "From what I know of your wife, she was anything but a procrastinator."

"You didn't know her." Mr. Chips slumped in his chair. "Sure, lookit. She would have left the chipper to a seagull over me had she known she was going to die. I'm sure that's exactly what she would have done. But you cannot blame me." He straightened up and leaned in. "I did not know she hadn't changed her will until a solicitor notified me soon after she died. Who thinks about these things?"

Siobhán jumped on this. "Did you change your will?"

He gulped. Then shrugged. Then nodded. "I did, so."

"Then I guess *you* think about these things," Siobhán said. She was starting to feel confident. Maybe the flamingos were her friend. "Who is the beneficiary of your will now?"

"I have a brother, a sister, nieces, nephews," Corman said loudly as he lifted his chin.

"Did you leave everything to your brother, sister, nieces, nephews?" Macdara asked.

Mr. Chips crossed his arms and leaned back. "I don't see how that has anything to do with this case whatsoever."

"Are you refusing to answer the question?"

He sighed. "I left some of it to them and some to various friends."

Macdara nodded. "Is Mike McGee one of those friends?"

Mr. Chips wagged his finger. "You're not fooling me twice. If he didn't say anything about it, then neither will I."

"You realize you just told us?" Siobhán asked.

Mr. Chips slumped in his chair. "He doesn't want that going around."

Siobhán leaned in. "Why would you leave money to Mike McGee? Was it in exchange for that loan?"

"I wouldn't say in exchange. It was a friendly gesture given that in turn he'd helped me get through the loan process." Siobhán and Macdara looked at each other. "What?" Mr. Chips said. "You're not accusing Mike of killing her, are you?"

"I didn't say that and I didn't hear Garda O'Sullivan say that, so why are you jumping to that conclusion?"

Macdara was now leaning in to the unfriendly approach.

"What motive could Mike possibly have?" Mr. Chips's gaze bounced between them, his eyes wide with alarm.

"As Detective Sargeant Flannery just told you, we aren't accusing anyone of anything. We're simply gathering information. However, you've just told us that Vera left everything to you and in exchange you're leaving some of her hard-earned money to Mike."

"Oh," Mr. Chips said. "*Oh.*" He rubbed his chin. His shoulders relaxed. He sat back and folded his hands over his stomach. "So, you do think he did this, like?"

"We ask all sorts of questions," Macdara said. "But we don't get paid to think." Siobhán slid him a look. "You know what I mean." He held up a pair of binoculars and shook them in Mr. Chips's direction. "Do these look familiar?"

"If you mean did I see me wife—me ex-wife—peeping at me through them nearly every day, like?"

"Is that a yes?" Macdara asked.

"Yes." He shook his head. "I reported her, but you know a certain person was too lenient with her." Mr. Chips pointed at the glass and mouthed *Detective Healy*.

"He can see you," Macdara pointed out.

Mr. Chips looked at his finger, then quickly put it down and returned to sulking.

"How could you hire your ex-wife's ex–best friend to paint the mural on the new chipper you opened directly across from her chipper?" Siobhán asked. "Was it all just to torment her?"

"All's fair in love and war, and fish and chips," Mr. Chips mumbled.

"You're saying you and Mrs. Chips were at war?" Macdara asked.

Mr. Chips frowned, then he sat up straight. "I'll admit. Tara and I got carried away. But it's not illegal."

"It could be seen as motive," Macdara said. "You were desperately trying to drive her out of business."

"I'd say it certainly doesn't look good," Siobhán said. "And one could argue it's cruel to boot."

Mr. Chips shook his head and leaned forward. "Tara and Vera were on the outs before this whole thing started. I swear to ye. Their quarrels had nothing to do with me."

Macdara took notes. "What did they fall out over?"

"I haven't a clue. Neither of them would tell me what it was. Funny, isn't it? They fall out and yet they both keep the secret. Women!" He didn't dare look at Siobhán. "No offense."

"I can see there's no offense given you're on defense," Siobhán shot back.

Macdara covered a laugh with a cough while Corman Cowley squirmed in his hard chair. "Having an affair is not a crime. I tried to save me marriage. Vera wanted full control of the chipper. It was my chipper! My chipper!" He was working himself up into a tantrum. "There was a long queue of folks waiting in front of Vera's that morning. Are you treating all of them like murderers?"

"The door was locked," Siobhán said. "How do you suppose the killer got in?" Siobhán already knew that Vera had left the door open while she stormed across the street to spray-paint the mural. And she knew from Tara Flaherty that Corman had it on videotape. She wanted to see how big of a liar they were dealing with here. Would he cop to the video?

"Vera recently changed the locks," Corman said. "I don't know how many keys she had made. If only you could ask the locksmith."

"What do you mean 'if only'?" Macdara asked.

"I bet you anything that John Healy changed her locks." He crossed himself. "May he rest in peace."

Chapter 23

The next morning, back at the inn, Siobhán's brood had returned from the Cliffs of Moher, and they were a welcome relief to the tensions of the previous day. John Healy had a refrigerator stocked with food, and Liam had encouraged them to use it. "It's what he would have wanted. Eat, drink, enjoy the inn. You'll need fuel to keep the long hours on this case."

Doctor Jeanie Brady had been keeping in close touch, and she was doing everything she could to speed up John Healy's toxicology results, but it was still going to take time. Too much time. But it wasn't until Eoin's version of a full Irish breakfast—eggs, rashers, black and white pudding, potatoes, brown bread—was laid out in front of them and they were about to dig in that Siobhán stopped everyone.

"Wait," she yelled. "I don't know what we were thinking. We can't eat anything from this kitchen."

"Siobhán," Eoin said. "If you're trying to insult me cooking, you could at least do it after tasting it."

Gráinne, seated to Siobhán's right, raised a fork to her lips. Siobhán grabbed Gráinne's wrist and wrestled the fork down as her sister actively resisted. "Get off me," Gráinne said. "You have a plate of your own, like."

"John Healy was poisoned," Siobhán said, finally yanking the fork out of her sister's hand and jabbing it in her direction. "How do we know the curry sauce was the first time he'd been poisoned?"

"I've been around him nearly every time he cooked at the inn," Eoin said. "I would have known if anyone poisoned him." His face morphed into terror. "That won't look good for me, will it?"

"I'm willing to be a test subject," Macdara said, longingly staring at his brekkie.

"We're going to the breakfast cafe, and that's that," Siobhán said. She began to mull it over. "Most poisons take time to kill a person. It needs to build up in the body."

"What are you saying?" James asked.

"What if it wasn't the curry sauce that killed him? Or rather, what if it wasn't just one incident of poisoning. What if someone had been slowly poisoning him for weeks? Months, even."

The group stared at her, then uneasily made eye contact with one another. "His diary!" Siobhán said, jumping up. "We need to find his diary."

"His ledger," Eoin corrected.

Siobhán ignored the correction. "Where did he keep it?"

Eoin shrugged. "Dunno. He always had it with him."

Siobhán began opening cupboards just in case. She was on the lookout for the diary and/or anything that looked suspicious—any type of poisoning.

Macdara cleared his throat. "I should probably tell you that Detective Sargeant Healy is—" As if this were a movie and he'd been waiting for his cue, the door opened and Liam Healy strode in. His eyes lit up when he saw the table of food, and he went straight to the chair that had been Siobhán's.

"You waited for me? What a polite lot. Now." As everyone stared at him he took his fork and dug in, oblivious. They all watched him as he shoveled forkfuls of food into his mouth. "Top-notch," Liam said in between bites.

Macdara gave Siobhán a half shrug, then dug in. Soon everyone was eating but Siobhán. *Typical.* Personally, she wanted to go to the cafe, but if they were all going to drop from food poisoning, someone had to be here to pick up the pieces.

After breakfast, and once they finished cleaning up after themselves, everyone announced their intentions for the day. Ciarán and Ann were going surfing, Eoin agreed to tag along with them, James was headed to the fishery to see Sheila, Gráinne was lingering until Liam left, Macdara and Liam were due for a virtual meeting with the higher-ups in Dublin, and Siobhán planned on paying a visit to Daniel O'Grady's oil and vinegar shop. It was a cool day with the first layer of gray she'd seen in ages. Surprisingly, she welcomed it, like an old friend. She hoped Ciarán and Ann would change their minds about surfing, as a strong wind had also kicked up. Situated along the promenade were half a dozen easels with aspiring painters staring out at the sea, brushes in hand. Leading the class was none other than Tara Flaherty. Siobhán had no intention of interrupting the class. Their next visit with Tara would be at the garda station. Siobhán carried on to Daniel's shop, trying to ignore the hunger pangs prodding at her.

She reached the end of the promenade and took a right. The shop was a few stops down. Her timing was perfect; just as she arrived, Daniel O'Grady was flipping his bespoke wooden sign to OPEN.

"Garda," he said when she stepped in. "I've been expecting you." His blond hair was slicked back, and he looked sharp in a white suit with a peach-colored dress shirt.

"You have?"

He nodded as he straightened a white apron bearing a bottle of olive oil. It read, OLIVE YOU. He saw her staring at it. "I love you, Olive you," he said with a grin.

"I see," Siobhán said.

"Perhaps you'd like my *Planet of the Grapes* better, but it's being laundered. They sport an adorable rendering of ape-grapes, running after a bottle of oil intent on demolishing it."

"I'm so sorry I missed that," Siobhán said.

He seemed to be eagerly awaiting a laugh. When she remained silent, he sighed and headed for a cardboard box on his counter. "I heard you've been making the rounds. Do you mind if I attend to opening me shop while we chat?"

"Not a bother," Siobhán said.

He thanked her as he began lifting out bottles of oil and placing them on the shelves. "I specialize in all varieties of oil," he said. "Olive oil, grape seed oil, vegetable oil. Mrs. Chips was smart enough to see the writing on the wall, but the same cannot be said for the mister."

"Did Vera recently try to convince you to lower your prices?"

"She did, so. But I stood my ground. She finally gave up. I don't rattle easily."

Perhaps she had nothing to hold over him. His shop was tidy and looked up-to-date but showed no signs of being renovated. Siobhán had a feeling that Daniel O'Grady was not in need of any loans from Mike McGee. She thought of his speedboat, and although she had no idea what it cost, it seemed something only the well-off would purchase. It also seemed something that a younger person would gravitate toward, but who was she to judge? If he wanted to tool his dates around on a giant ocean in a tiny speedboat like a carefree teenager, it was his right to do so.

"What time did you arrive at Mrs. Chips the morning she was found dead?"

He continued to stock his items as he answered. "I was early. Given she had recently switched to vegetable oil, she had a large pallet being delivered and I wanted to see if she had any questions as well as see how the change was going over. I also understood she had a food critic arriving that day—whom I've now met—I'm sure you have too. Madeline Plunkett?"

Siobhán nodded. "When I saw you in line it was after eleven. I don't call that early."

"I was there hours earlier. As a matter of fact, I arrived to see her spray-painting over the mural." He stopped and shook his head. "I suppose I should have called Detective Sargeant Liam to report the vandalism, but to be fair, Mr. Chips did have it coming, like."

"Did she see you?"

He shook his head. "I don't think she would have noticed a parade going by. She was intent on her activities."

"Was anyone else around?"

He hesitated, just enough for her to know he had seen someone or someones. "It doesn't mean you're accusing anyone of anything. It's not illegal to be out and about early. I like to go for a run in the mornings."

He was still debating how much he should reveal. "I saw Mike McGee briefly. He was peeking out the window of the building next to the bank. It's been every shop you can imagine over the ages. It's abandoned now, but McGee owns it, alright. I saw him peeking out the window. I thought maybe he was interested in the shenanigans Mrs. Chips was up to."

"Did he see you?"

"I don't believe so, but you'd have to ask him."

"Who else did you see?"

"I saw a woman in a floppy hat."

Siobhán stood up straight. "What color was it?"

He frowned. "Yellow? Or maybe it was so bright

out I thought it was yellow. I don't really pay attention to the color of ladies' hats."

"Describe this woman, if you wouldn't mind."

"I'm afraid that's not possible. I saw her walking away from me."

"On Mrs. Chips's side of the street or Mr. Chips's?"

"Mrs. Chips's. But she was several shops past it."

"What else was she wearing. Was she short? Tall? Thin? Heavyset?"

"She was tall and thin, and she was wearing a long tan coat. Like a man's trench coat." He shook his head. "An odd assortment of clothing, you know?"

"Were there many vehicles parked on the street?"

"There are always vehicles parked on both sides of the street. I didn't notice anything unusual."

"Did you notice whether the door to Vera's chipper was open or closed?"

He concentrated as if trying to visualize the moment. "I'm sorry. I don't think I even looked." He removed the now-empty box from his counter and began to break it down. "Listen. I heard the ladder was greased with something. I've been waiting to hear— with what exactly? If you tell me it's vegetable oil, I'm going to be in bits."

"Where did you hear that?" Siobhán kept her voice light as if she were hearing it for the first time. But inwardly she groaned. Key evidence in the case had been leaked. By whom? Then again, she knew that keeping secrets in a small town was par for the course, but keeping secrets *from* a small town was nearly impossible.

Daniel waved his hand like it was nothing. "People talk. I've already told you she had ordered a large quantity of vegetable oil. I hope no one wasted it by greasing the ladder." He stopped as he took in Siobhán's expression. "Right," he said. "That's not the important bit, is it?"

"No. It isn't."

Daniel clasped his hands in prayer position and bowed his head. "I was truly shocked and saddened by her death. She could be a bit crusty, like a good French bread! It's wonderful dipped in olive oil." He stopped to imagine it, then shook his head as if to toss away the minidaydream. "I had a soft spot for her. She didn't have it easy, with all that nasty business with Mr. Chips." He shuddered. "Beef fat drippings! In this day and age. Killing people one heart attack at a time." He clenched his fists. It was obvious this was his mission—save mankind from high cholesterol.

Siobhán knew that Daniel O'Grady wasn't happy that he hadn't been able to convince Mr. Chips to switch to vegetable oil, so she reminded herself to take everything he said with the proverbial grain of salt. Or grape seed. "You saw Mike McGee, Vera, and a lady in a yellow hat."

"And trench coat," he added.

"And that's it?"

He shrugged. "I did see Madeline Plunkett, but it was later at the breakfast cafe. That's where I went as soon as I realized Mrs. Chips was going to be at that mural for quite a while. And given the mood I assumed she was in, I decided it was best I be on me way. I had planned on stopping by later, which is exactly what I did. When I returned at eleven, there was already a queue on the footpath in front of her shop." He held up a finger. "But as I said, I did see Madeline Plunkett at the cafe. And, given you've already stated you want every detail, she was arguing with someone over the phone. Quite loudly."

This was a turn Siobhán had not been expecting. "What was the argument about?"

He grimaced. "I'm sure it was all work related, but to the best of my recollection she said something like, 'She'll never see it coming.'"

She'll never see it coming. What did it mean? To whom was Madeline speaking and about whom?

"Perhaps it was her editor," Daniel offered. The bell dinged as a few customers strode in—an older woman with a younger one. Given their identical curly brown hair, she pegged them as mother and daughter. Daniel gave them a wave and a smile. "Let me know if you have any questions or want to taste any of the oils or vinegars. You'll find delectable bread and sample cups in the back right of the shop." He glanced at his watch.

"Is the bread from Natalie O'Brien's bakery?" Siobhán asked.

For a moment, his face lit up. "I like to support local businesses, especially the ones that support me."

Siobhán nodded. "One last thing," she said. She was inclined to rule out Daniel as a suspect. Even though one could not rely completely on instinct, hers was strongly pointing toward Daniel as being on the periphery of whatever drama had led up to the two murders. Then again, there was a matter of the one last thing. She set the crime scene photo of the bottle of vinegar down on his counter. The bottle was being kept at the hospital morgue. "Does this look familiar?"

"Yes," he said straightaway. "It looks like the one I gifted Mrs. Chips." He tilted his head as he stared at the photo. "Where did the yoke wind up, like?"

Siobhán removed the photo without answering. "Why did you give it to her?"

"Given she was using me vegetable oil, I was trying to entice her to purchase our vinegar too. The warehouse sends me those bottles to display or give out to customers who spend a dear amount." He pointed to a nearby shelf, where six identical bottles sat filled with vinegar. "Those are my display copies only." They were interrupted by the deafening sound of smashing glass. The front window imploded, and a dark object sailed toward them.

"Duck," Siobhán yelled to all of them as she hit the ground. Luckily the mother and daughter reacted quickly by diving to the floor, but Daniel was rooted to the spot. The projectile barely missed his head and crashed into a row of bottles on the shelf behind him. Siobhán's ears were ringing, but she could still hear the screams of the two women inside, not to mention a few who had been walking by outside. She lifted her head to see Daniel headed for the object.

"Don't!" she yelled as she scrambled to her feet. "Don't touch it." She made eye contact until he nodded. "Nobody touch anything, but check yourself for cuts, glass, sprains, fractures. I'll be right back." Siobhán dashed outside, where a crowd had gathered. They were staring at the jagged hole where the front shop window used to be, mouths open in shock.

"Where did he go?" Siobhán yelled. It could have been a female, but Siobhán had no time to stop for pronouns.

"He was dressed all in black, even a ski mask," a few people shouted.

"He went that way." Everyone pointed to the left. She dashed left. As she ran, she managed to pull out her mobile and call Macdara, whose number was on speed dial. By the time she reached the promenade, several artist easels were knocked down and a clump of people were blocking the path. "Move!" Siobhán yelled as she pushed and maneuvered around them. In the distance the figure wearing black took a left. Siobhán pushed harder, her adrenaline pumping. She had to catch him (or her); this could be the killer, and they had so little else to go on. "Stop the man in black," she shouted, just in case someone was around the corner and able to pounce. It felt like forever before she reached the street and took a left, but she could see right away she was too late. A few people were standing around, looking down the street as if the runner had already streaked by. Had the person ducked into a nearby shop?

She wanted to keep going. She imagined scouring every establishment until she found the culprit, but in the meantime there was real evidence back at Daniel's shop and she couldn't afford to let anyone mess with it. She turned and, keeping the same fast pace, ran back to the oil and vinegar shop. Panicked folks were standing outside chatting about the incident. Siobhán pushed her way inside and was relieved to see that the large black stone hadn't been touched. Daniel was gathered in the front of his shop around his customers, trying to comfort them. "May I sweep up the glass?" he asked Siobhán.

"Not yet," she said. "I'm going to need you to escort all of your customers outside."

"Right away," Daniel said. "I take it you didn't catch him?"

"That person is in good shape," Siobhán said. "I'll give 'em that."

Siobhán finally reached the projectile. It was indeed a fat black rock, about the size of a brick. She'd seen a rock just like it—many rocks just like it, that is—at Sheila Bisby's fishery. This rock had words painted in black. She leaned down to read it: Dún do bhéal! The message was clear, for there was only one translation: *Shut your mouth.*

Chapter 24

"Why didn't anyone see who threw it?" Liam stood in front of Daniel's shop, addressing the gawpers who were still clumping around the area.

"We saw him, but he was in disguise," a man said. "Dressed all in black like a cat burglar."

As Liam interviewed individuals on the footpath, Siobhán found Macdara standing over the rock, which was still on the floor where it had eventually landed. "That could have killed you," he said without turning around.

"Sure, lookit. Me head is probably hard enough to take it."

"That's not funny." He turned around. "It could have killed you."

"Did your meeting with headquarters just finish?" Siobhán asked.

Macdara shook his head. "It was postponed. I was

going through the inventory in the evidence locker when I heard about this."

"Anything of interest?"

"Don't change the subject," Macdara said. "But no, nothing dramatic in the evidence locker so far. Siobhán." He pointed to the rock. "This could have easily killed you."

"I don't think the person was trying to kill anyone. In fact, I think this person had excellent aim."

"It could have killed you."

He was relentless. "Or Daniel, or the two other customers in the shop. And given the message written on it, I'd say it was intended to scare Daniel O'Grady. He insists there isn't any incriminating information he's sitting on, but someone obviously thinks there is."

"From now on, we're not separating," Macdara said. "Where you go, I go."

She sighed. At times her husband had a hard time separating their personal life from their professional. "Well I do know one place where you can accompany me," she said, pointing at the projectile. "I've seen that type of stone before. A pile of them. At Sheila Bisby's fishery."

Macdara's face gave away what he was thinking. "We'll have to tread carefully."

"I know," Siobhán said with a sigh. "If his new girlfriend is a killer, James is not going to be a happy lad."

When they arrived at the fishery, they found Sheila dressed in overalls and wellies, carrying crates of fish to and fro. Tailing her, dressed in identical overalls and wellies, complete with a crate of his own, was James.

"Are you here to take away me best helper?" Sheila said with a grin and a head nod to James. "You might have to fight me for him."

"Can you please put the crates down?" Macdara said. "We need to have a brief chat."

A flicker of worry crossed her pretty face. "Not a bother." She set the crate down. "Him too?" she asked, looking at James.

"No," Siobhán said. "This doesn't involve him."

"You sound so serious," Sheila said.

James set his crate down with force. "What's the story?"

"Someone just tried to kill your sister," Macdara said. "With a rock." He glanced around, no doubt trying to spot the pile of rocks Siobhán had seen here on their last visit.

"Now, now," Siobhán said to Macdara. "I already told ya I wasn't the target. Just possible collateral damage."

"What?" Sheila said. "What are you on about?" They told them about the large stone thrown through Daniel's window. "Absolutely horrific," Sheila said. "How can I help?"

Macdara turned his mobile phone toward her, showing her the photo of the stone.

"Shut your mouth," Sheila said. "That's not nice."

"Do you not recognize the stone?" Siobhán said, pointing to the distance where she'd seen them piled up.

"Those black stones are all over the place," Sheila said. "Bigger ones too." She peered at the photo closer.

"It's not wet," she said. "Which means they didn't take from the pile close to the water." She made eye contact with Siobhán. "I bet that any rock like this you find around me fishery is going to be wet. They're all near the water, like."

Which meant either these rocks were found in multiple locations around Lahinch or someone had had it long enough for it to dry. Given this killer seemed to be a planner, she wasn't surprised. That still didn't leave Sheila in the clear.

"Aren't these type of stones all over Lahinch?" James asked.

"No," Sheila said. "Mostly around this section." She gestured around her property. "But as you can see, we're not a fortress. There's no locked gate, or fence. Anyone could have slipped in and taken it. And not necessarily recently. Someone could have taken that stone ages ago."

It was as if she'd reached into Siobhán's poor head and plucked out her thoughts. Was it because she was the one who had taken it ages ago? "Well, just in case it was recent, have you seen anyone lurking about who doesn't belong here?" Macdara asked.

"I assume you're excluding the handsome lad behind me," Sheila said.

"Handsome?" James said as a grin took over his face. "Did she just call me handsome?"

"Settle down, Romeo," Siobhán said. "But she's right. You are handsome."

James frowned and shook his head. "Not the person I want to hear it from," he said.

"Too bad." Siobhán turned to Sheila. "I'm afraid

I'm going to have to ask you where you were the morning Vera was killed."

"Siobhán," James said. "Are you joking me?"

"We have a job to do," Macdara said to James. "You know that."

James clenched his jaw and didn't respond.

Sheila placed her hand on his arm, calming him before turning back to Siobhán. "You saw me in line for the chipper," Sheila said. "Before that, I was here, and before that I was out at sea."

"Do you have any kind of system where you log in when you come and go?" Siobhán said.

"No. But the harbormaster does. And we have security cameras around the docks. I'm sure I can dig one up if you're interested. I have nothing to hide."

"I'd appreciate a call to the garda station when you have that footage ready," Macdara said.

Sheila nodded. "I'll have them pull it right away."

"The day you took us out on the trawler, why did you punch the wall down in the cabin and then slug back whiskey?" Siobhán asked.

James's expression turned dark, and Sheila's mouth dropped open. "You saw that?"

"We both did," Siobhán said, squaring up to James. "What was that about?"

Sheila bit her lip. "It's rather embarrassing."

"You don't have to say anything more," James said.

"Yes, she does," Siobhán countered. "Unless she wants to remain at the top of my suspect list."

James started to speak again, but Sheila held up her

hand. "It's okay. You might as well know." She glanced toward the water as she spoke. "I fall in love too easily and often with the wrong man. I was starting to have feelings for someone, and I was worried it was all happening too fast, so I was trying to tell meself to slow down. But I didn't want to. When me thoughts get too loud, it helps to hit something. But I'm terribly ashamed that you were there to witness it."

"There's nothing to be ashamed of," James said. No doubt he was the one she was falling for. But was she calling James "the wrong man"? From the look on his face he didn't mind a single bit. "But I hate the thought of you hurting your hand." He walked up to her, took her hand, and kissed the back of it. Siobhán tilted her head back and sent a little prayer to the heavens before she found something to punch.

"Are we done here?" James asked.

"You'll know when we're done," Macdara said. "Our mouths will stop moving and our feet will start walking." James glowered but looked at his feet.

"Do you own a floppy yellow hat?" Siobhán asked.

Sheila laughed. "Sounds more like Tara Flaherty than me."

"Did you see anyone in a floppy yellow hat the day Vera was murdered?" Siobhán pressed. "Or a tan trench coat?"

"A tan trench coat? In this heat? Are you mental?"

"She is not," Macdara said. "Answer the question."

"Hey," James said.

"James, I think you should walk away," Siobhán

said. "I don't want a war with ya, but we have a job to do." A murderer to catch, even if it was a pretty one who was in love with her brother. Siobhán was starting to understand why couples did not bring their entire family on their honeymoon.

"It's alright. I've already told them I have nothing to hide, and I meant it." Sheila shook her head. "I did not see anyone in a floppy yellow hat or a trench coat."

"Thank you," Siobhán said. "If you speak with your employees, please ask them if anyone saw someone—employee or not—pluck a stone like this from the pile."

Sheila shrugged. "Children too? I can't count the number of young ones who come here to nick stones."

"Do you mind if I have a nose around that rock pile?" Macdara asked.

"Knock yourself out," Sheila said. "But is it alright if I get back to work? Fish don't stay fresh all on their own."

"Of course," Siobhán said.

"Are you going to mention the other thing?" James said just as Siobhán was set to walk away.

Sheila nodded. "Listen," she said. "I know your sister has a little crush on Liam. I just want you to know that even though I did go on about his crush on me, I don't think she should worry about that."

"Gráinne?" Siobhán said. "Worrying is not her style. Besides, Liam seems a bit smitten with her as well."

"Men are like taxis," Sheila said. "When their light comes on, they're ready. I think he's looking to settle down. I hope she doesn't break his heart." She shuddered. "Especially after what happened to his grandfather." Her face turned serious. "I don't know who's doing this. But please. You need to stop him."

"Or her," Siobhán and Macdara said in stereo.

On their drive back to town, Siobhán reviewed the case with Macdara. "Daniel O'Grady said that he and Madeline Plunkett were in the breakfast cafe at the time of the murder. If we could have someone verify that, then I'd say we can eliminate them."

"And if Sheila comes up with corroborators for her movements, we may be able to eliminate her as well," Macdara added. "It would probably be best for family relations to do that."

Siobhán sighed and gazed out at the magnificent bay that made this coastal drive so spectacular. "You're right, you're right," she said. "But I wouldn't go to his job site and try to shut him down."

"He's smitten," Macdara said. "It's a powerful drug."

"Even more so when you're not allowed to do any other kind of drug," Siobhán agreed. "But that's also a red flag—he's not using any common sense at all."

"Mike McGee is high on my list," Macdara said. "Let's hope for love's sake that she has nothing to do with it."

"Even if she doesn't, she's still a woman with a temper."

Macdara chuckled. "Maybe you could teach her to whittle."

"Har har." If he wasn't driving she would have given him a little shove. "We're lucky that Mike McGee's interests are so obvious," Siobhán said.

"Golf and poker," Macdara said.

"Sounds like it's another perfect day for a lad's day out," Siobhán said.

Siobhán was using Macdara's temporary office at the garda station, and it was there that she took the video call from Jeanie Brady. She had an update on John Healy.

"I don't have the toxicology yet. However, he did not die of natural causes. It was definitely some kind of poison. Signs point to a slow-burn poison, something that took a week or longer to build up in his system."

"He did bow out of a dinner one night because he wasn't feeling well," Siobhán said. "Do you have any idea if it's an organic or inorganic poison we're looking at here?"

Jeanie Brady nodded and fussed with her hair on camera before focusing again. "I spoke with Liam. He said his grandfather had recently purchased quite a few plants. I asked him to suss out if one of them is a castor plant."

"Beans?"

"No beans about it," Jeanie said with a hearty laugh. "I'm only messing. You're right, you're right. Beans!"

"What did Liam say?"

"He wasn't up-to-date on his grandfather's recent purchases, but he said John regularly bought new plants for the back garden."

"I remember John mentioned something of the sort," Siobhán said. "What exactly about castor seeds intrigues you?"

Jeanie held up a finger. "Castor seeds contain ricin. Ricin can kill within three days if the dose is big enough, or it can build up for a week or more. But he would have shown food poisoning symptoms in the days before his death." Jeanie tilted her head. "And as you said, he wasn't feeling well before he died."

"Do you mean anything he ate with castor beans in it may have poisoned him?"

Jeanie shook her head. "No, pet. The bean is simply used to extract the ricin. It can then be added to anything, no beans about it." Jeanie stopped to laugh at her own joke. "Sorry, but sometimes humor helps."

"That it does," Siobhán said.

"What do you think?" Jeanie asked. "Is it possible?"

"I never saw him eat at all," Siobhán said. "He bowed out of dinner and did look ghastly when I saw him at the pub, and that was before he tasted the curry sauce." She nodded. "I believe it's possible."

"I'd say Bob's your uncle," Jeanie said.

"We need to see if there are castor plants in his garden," Siobhán said.

"You're staying at his inn again, are you not?"

"How do you know?" Siobhán asked.

Jeanie grinned. "I have eyes and ears everywhere."

"I haven't been out to his back garden. I got the feeling that gardening was his private escape and I didn't want us to intrude on that."

"Liam sent guards out to check the plants. One guard is an amateur horticulturalist."

"He never mentioned it."

"Sorry, I called him first. I didn't realize the two of you were leading the charge now."

"Totally fine, it's an interesting development."

"I wish there was more I could tell you. What's next on your agenda?"

"He had a diary—he called it a ledger—and I'm hoping to find it. And before you warn us about cooking at the inn, Eoin made everyone a big breakfast using food from the kitchen there and I told them not to chance it, but they did and everyone is fine."

"Caution is always advised. However, this was a deliberate poisoning. Someone had to have been visiting him the few days prior, perhaps on a pretense of helping him, but they'd actually been poisoning him."

"I wonder. Could someone have purposefully timed it so that he would die at Vera's memorial gathering? Or is that just the way things worked out?"

"I don't see how anyone could have planned it that precisely. Except for John himself, that is. How long it takes to die from a poisoning has many factors. If only he'd gone to the hospital when he first started falling ill."

"What do you mean, except for John himself?"

"I was only being literal. If he were poisoning himself, it's possible he knew when things were progressing, that death was near."

"Why didn't he go to the hospital?" People could be so foolish about doctors. He might be alive today if he hadn't ignored his pain.

"If I knew why people did half the things they did, I'd be a whole lot wiser," Jeanie said.

"Does this mean there was or wasn't poison in the curry sauce?" Eoin would be thrilled if there wasn't a trace in it.

"As I said, I'm still waiting on the report. We'll have an answer relatively soon, but I know in your line of work it's never soon enough."

"How much ricin does it take to poison someone?" Siobhán asked.

Jeanie shivered. "The tiniest amount can do the trick."

"How tiny?"

"Seventy micrograms. The weight of a grain of salt." Siobhán let that sink in. "It's one thousand times more poisonous than cyanide," Jeanie continued. "Colorless, tasteless, and soluble in water. It can be delivered as an aerosol spray, injected, or swallowed. It's stable, so storage isn't an issue, and it's not volatile, so transport isn't an issue."

"The perfect poison," Siobhán said.

Jeanie nodded. "And if we are dealing with ricin here, and it wasn't sourced straight from a castor plant, I suppose with a bit of planning someone could have laid their hands on it and brought it in."

Like Madeline Plunkett from London? Perhaps that wasn't fair, and too much of a stretch. Evidence rooms in garda stations all over Ireland were filled with a variety of confiscated drugs. This was the world they lived in.

Siobhán and Macdara stood outside of Mr. Chips discussing Jeanie Brady's video call. Macdara shook his head. "What kind of lunatic are we dealing with here?"

"A planner," Siobhán said. "Someone who flies under the radar."

"Not for long," Macdara said. "I don't care how small the blip is, I'm finding this killer—on or off the radar." He frowned.

"What's wrong?"

"When did Jeanie Brady speak to Liam about this?"

"I don't know exactly," Siobhán said. "But she insinuated it had been a fast-moving development."

"He hasn't mentioned it." Even though it was subtle, Siobhán could tell from Macdara's tone that he was furious about it. They'd agreed to work together, but was Liam going rogue? One could get overheated when one's family member was involved. Siobhán and Macdara understood that, but there were limits.

"Maybe he hasn't had time to tell us," Siobhán said.

"Or maybe he resents that we're heading this case and he's intentionally cutting us out."

"He seemed fine with it," Siobhán said.

"Maybe too fine," Macdara replied. "Maybe it was all an act."

It was a profession of big egos, especially at the detective sargeant rank. And the victim was his grandfather. Still, they would not get anywhere if they were all working at odds.

"If you see him before I do, don't mention it," Macdara said. "I want to be the one to clear the air."

"Not a bother. But we also need to have a look at John's back garden."

"Pronto," Macdara agreed.

Siobhán's mobile phone rang, making her jump. She glanced at the screen. *Eoin.* "Hey, pet," she answered. "Where are ye off to now?" She consoled herself that they were having a proper holiday. Well, at least the young ones.

"We need help," Eoin said. "It's Trigger."

"Trigger? What's he up to now?"

"I don't know," Eoin said. "That's just the thing."

"I don't follow."

"He's missing," Eoin said. "We can't find him anywhere."

Chapter 25

To the credit of the townspeople, once word spread that Trigger was missing, everyone came out to look for him. Siobhán volunteered to search the inn again, while others spread out from the front door of the inn, the back of the house, and the street in both directions. Siobhán didn't have much time to suss out plants, but she didn't immediately see anything that looked suspicious—although they may have been, because a guard was already there to check it out. He was poking around, jotting down notes. Trigger was last seen that morning, but after breakfast one of them must have left the door open, and precious minutes had been taken up arguing over which one might have done it. They were all to blame, including Siobhán. John Healy had been the one giving Trigger the most attention on this holiday, and the poor thing probably missed him. Perhaps

Trigger even went out on the same walks that he'd been on with John. Volunteers were searching the beach and the promenade.

Siobhán was about to search the premises when Liam stepped in. His fingernails were black with dirt. He noticed her gaze. "We've been searching Pap's garden," he said. "I have news from the pathologist, but I was saving it for a more formal meeting."

"We look forward to it," Siobhán said. She wouldn't go into it now. She needed to find Trigger. He was a member of the family.

"Let me wash me hands and search the inn," he said. "I know all the hiding places."

Siobhán hesitated. On one hand, she had a feeling Trigger had indeed slipped out the door, given it was ajar when her siblings returned and realized he was missing. On the other hand, she'd been hoping to use the search to look for John Healy's diary. A wave of shame came over her. Trigger deserved better. And she was dying to ask Liam if his garda had found any castor bean plants in the back garden. She wanted to read him the riot act for keeping them in the dark, but she'd already promised Macdara he could have that satisfaction.

"Did you know your grandfather kept a ledger?" she said instead, careful not to use the word *diary*.

"Of course," Liam said. "He was always scribbling in it. Why?"

"I was thinking, maybe there's something in it that might give us a clue."

"How so?"

"Vera was staying here. It's possible someone visited her, or he heard or saw something. There has to be a reason he was targeted."

"Why are you assuming he was targeted? Wasn't it random? Anyone who tasted the curry sauce?"

She hesitated. She hadn't filled him in on everything she'd learned from her recent call with Jeanie Brady and everything she'd been thinking since then. Maybe now was not the time. "I'll save it for a briefing," she said. "But I think it's strange his ledger hasn't been seen since . . ."

Liam nodded, and he turned away. "You're right, you're right," he said, his voice thick with emotion. "It has to be here somewhere."

"Thank you." Siobhán slipped out the door, leaving Liam to his grief. Outside, the air felt fresh and it was hard to believe there was anything but positivity on this grand day. Siobhán was headed toward the beach when her mobile rang. *Macdara.* "Tell me you found him," Siobhán answered.

"He's been spotted inside the arcade," Macdara said. "We're all headed there now. Apparently the lights and noises are so terrifying he's not letting anyone get close to him."

Siobhán's heart squeezed. "Poor thing. I'm on me way." She texted Liam, letting him know they'd found Trigger but that he might want to keep searching for the ledger. She couldn't help thinking there was something in it they would find useful. She finished the text, then began to run. *I'm coming, Trigger. Hold on.*

* * *

It had been ages since she'd been in an arcade. Instantly it went from a sunny day to a dark one, bar the occasional flashing lights, and her ears were assaulted with bings and chirps and video gunfire. *Nightmare.* Trigger would have never run into a place like this. Never. If he was in here, someone had deliberately brought him inside. The question was, Why? The room was large, and from the entrance she couldn't even see to the back door. The poor thing could be anywhere. Couldn't they get the manager to turn everything off for a few minutes? But given the intense faces of the young people glued to the games, Siobhán worried that a shutdown could cause a revolt. Where would Trigger hide? It all depended on where someone had set him down.

"You're here," Macdara said, sneaking up behind her. She let out a yelp, which was drowned out by the chaotic noise around her.

"Any luck?" she shouted.

"No, but we have quite a team of volunteers—Daniel O'Grady, Natalie O'Brien, Sheila Bisby, Mike McGee, Madeline Plunkett—"

"In other words, all of our suspects?"

"Ironic, isn't it?"

"Someone must have brought him in here. He'd never come in on his own."

"I agree, but come with me. I'll show you our search quadrant."

"How will we even hear if he's found?"

"Everyone agreed to a text chain," Macdara said. "Come on, we're the left and back."

Siobhán followed Macdara to the back section of

the arcade, and they began looking behind games and around the legs of the children playing them. Siobhán approached a photo booth. Visible below the curtain was a pair of high heels. Soon a familiar voice filtered out. *Madeline Plunkett*. Given there were no other shoes next to hers on the floor, she must have been talking to someone on the phone.

"Disaster!" she said. "If anyone finds out, it's going to be a total disaster! I need to leave this place as soon as possible, but if I run now they're going to find it suspicious. Why did I let you drag me into this mess? I don't even *like* fish and chips. You know I'm too good for this. I don't care how much you pay me next time. No more hit jobs!"

Just then a click and whir and photographs came spitting out of the side of the booth. Exactly where Siobhán was standing. She leaned down and tore them off, then brought them up to her eyes, squinting in the dim light. In the photographs, Madeline was posing a variety of ways—smiling, serious with a tilt of her head, mouth open in surprise—but she wasn't alone. Next to her, with pretty much the same expression but his tongue hanging out, was Trigger.

Siobhán threw open the curtain. Madeline, holding her phone in her right hand and Trigger in her left, screamed.

Siobhán ignored her and snatched Trigger out of her arms. The poor thing was shaking uncontrollably, and Siobhán planted a million kisses on his wee head as she held him. Madeline scurried out of the booth and tried to run past Siobhán. "Stop," Siobhán yelled. "Dara!"

Macdara, who had been a few arcade games away, was there in a flash, blocking Madeline Plunkett's exit. Her shoulders slumped.

"It's not what you think," she said.

Macdara shook his head. "It never is," he said. "It never is."

Seated in the interview room at the garda station, Madeline Plunkett continued to toe the line. "Yes," she insisted. "I was hired to write a hit job against Vera. And I asked Eoin to make her curry sauce because I felt guilty about that. You know. Given she was dead and all. But I certainly did *not* poison anyone or push anyone off a ladder!"

"Who hired you?" Macdara asked, using his stern voice.

She sighed. "Who do you think?"

Macdara glanced at the tape recorder. "Answer that again please, and leave me out of this."

Madeline folded her arms. "Mr. Chips," she said. "Mr. Chips hired me to write the hit piece."

Just as they'd heard. It wasn't new information, but it was confirmation of the truth. And the closer they came to verifying everyone's version of the truth, the closer they came to the killer.

Now that they'd extended their holiday so they could officially help investigate, Siobhán wanted to dedicate each morning to a swim. Although for her first morning, a float was going to have to suffice. She suited up and spent some time walking the beach before wading in. The cold water gave her a jolt, but as she went farther in, it began to revitalize her. When she was acclimated to the temperature, she floated on her back and stared up at the clouds. They were puffy and white; one looked like a potted plant. It reminded her of the castor bean plant, and she wondered if the guard Liam assigned had found anything in John's garden. The stress of losing Trigger had driven it right out of her mind. She was doing it again, forgetting how to holiday.

She forced her thoughts off the case and tried to relax. She didn't realize how much stress she'd been holding until she allowed herself to let go. Gráinne, Ciarán, and Ann were a ways down the shore hunting down unique rocks and shells. She could get used to this life, although she'd never want to leave her medieval town or new farmhouse. She missed her morning runs around the abbey, but right now she was in heaven. Trigger was back with them and currently with Eoin. They'd all agreed to take turns being the one in charge of Trigger, which meant carrying him around and plying him with treats. After the recent scare, they were all too happy to do it. Siobhán closed her eyes and started to drift. This was it. This was the life. This was how you did it. She could see why people liked it. The next thing she knew, strong hands were clamping down on her shoulders, and before she could tell one of her siblings to stop messing, she was suddenly deep under the water and being held down.

She wanted to convince herself it would be alright, that it was a harmless prank, but her body was already in panic mode. She thrashed her arms and legs as she tried to push up. Forcing herself to open her eyes, she could make out only something dark hovering above her in the murky waters. She pounded on the gloved hands with her fists while fighting the instinct to breathe. Terror filled her as her lungs began to sear with pain. She did the only thing she could think of—she grabbed the fingers of that glove and with a burst of desperate energy she bent them back as hard as she could.

Just when she thought her life was over, the hand let go. She swam away as far as she could before she surfaced, and sucked in a breath. Her eyes were stinging, so she couldn't see if her attacker was still nearby. "Help!" she screamed as loud as she could. "Help!" She dove back under in case the attacker was coming back. Then she did the only thing she could do. She swam hard. She swam for her life.

Chapter 26

Siobhán sat at the dining table of the inn being fussed over by way too many folks. She had a blanket wrapped around her and was probably on her fourth mug of tea. The chocolate biscuits in the tin had been devoured. Macdara, who had not been able to stand the thought of someone trying to drown her, was out at the beach, most likely pacing and speaking to everyone in sight, inquiring if they saw someone in a wet suit and goggles in the vicinity of where Siobhán had been trying to have a relaxing soak in the sea. Liam was at the inn, worrying nearly as much as Macdara, wondering who this killer might target next and even suggesting it might be better if Siobhán went home with her siblings.

She'd already told him "Not on your life," but there was a part of her that wanted to send her siblings home. However, when she floated the idea they were just as adamant that they weren't going anywhere. Ciarán was once again messing with the antique fan, speaking into it and laughing hysterically at how it made him sound. Lads will be lads, and at times his laugh was irritating, but Siobhán knew there would come a day where she would give anything to have these moments back.

"I'm glad we're staying," Ann said. "I can keep surfing."

"I don't know if you should be doing that. Not after what happened to your sister," Liam said.

Ann shot her a terrified look. Siobhán knew her sister wasn't afraid of being attacked, she was afraid of being told she couldn't surf. And given Ann wouldn't be able to surf in Kilbane, Siobhán wanted her to enjoy every minute here that she could.

"She'll be grand," Siobhán said. "We don't let fear stop us. And we'll always make sure the instructor is with her."

Gráinne's phone rang, and she let out a groan. She picked it up. "Whatever you're selling I'm not buying, so stop wasting me time." She hung up and shook her head. "That's the third call this morning."

"Maybe it's an admirer," Liam said, with the tone of a man who hoped it wasn't but was fishing to find out.

"I do have a lot of admirers," Gráinne said. "But none of them live up to the hype." She treated him to a full-beam smile, and he seemed lost in it.

"Can I call the surf school?" Ann said. "Set up more lessons?"

"We'll go by there today, pet," Siobhán said. She wanted to speak with them in person, make sure that

Ann would be looked after. Siobhán reminded herself that there was a whole world waiting for Ann and Ciarán, filled with activities they once might have never imagined. Then again, Ciarán might have a simpler life, if his fascination with the fan was any sort of prediction. "Ciarán, would you move away from that fan before you lose your tongue in a rusty blade?"

Ciarán backed away, then turned around. "I still have it." He stuck it out once again, and déjà vu washed over Siobhán. Sometimes she felt they would have the same conversations the rest of their lives.

"Good for you. But enough. Are you wanting to sign up for more surf lessons as well?"

He shook his head. "I'd rather hang out in the arcade."

"He fancies a colleen who works there," Ann said with a grin. "She's older."

"Wrong," Ciarán said as his face turned the color of a beet. "She plays the fiddle, and she wants me to join her and some friends for a session."

"Lovely," Siobhán said. Ciarán was the only musical one of the lot, and he was quite good at the fiddle. She wished she could hear him play more, but he usually snuck off to do it. From the look on his face, Ann had been spot-on. He had a little crush. This holiday was turning out to be filled with romance. Poor Eoin, he was odd man out. Perhaps he couldn't get his mind off Aretta, or Garda Dabiri, as Siobhán usually referred to her.

A colleen. Siobhán had been waiting for Ciarán (and Ann) to show interest in someone. She had suspected he'd had various crushes on local girls over the years, but he was turning out to be fiercely private. She had a feeling he liked being fussed over and at home clung to a younger version of himself. Apparently, away from home he was Mr. Romeo. He was just as handsome as Eoin and James. They were a good-looking family, little heartbreakers all of them.

"Remember, kindness is your best asset," Siobhán said. She was dying to grill him about this girl, and while she was at it, drill Ann about whether there was a girl for her, but she had enough on her plate without disturbing the family peace.

Ciarán rolled his eyes. "Whatever."

James gave him a shove. "Mr. Romance," he said. "Let me know if you want some tips."

"Learned me lesson last time," Ciarán said. Off Siobhán's quizzical look, he said, "Last time he had a tip for me, he told me to plant me corn early." He frowned. "Makes no sense."

James threw his head back and laughed until tears rolled down his cheeks. Then he wiped them away. "Ah, stop." He gave a satisfied sigh. "I'm thinking of staying even longer than you lot," James said. He was leaning against the kitchen counter, a somewhat dreamy look on his face.

"Me too," Gráinne said. "What do you think, Liam? Is there room for little old me in this seaside town?"

Liam nodded so hard Siobhán thought his head was going to sail off, land with a thud on the floor, and roll to Gráinne's feet. Gráinne must have been having the same thought, for her grin was so large Siobhán could barely see the rest of her pretty face.

Eoin, who had been quiet, approached Liam, wiping

his hands on his trousers. "Listen, mate. I've been giving this a lot of thought. I've been trying to put meself in your shoes, and when it comes to family, you have to do right by them. You may not believe me, because you don't know me, like. But I had great respect for your grandfather. We enjoyed cooking in this kitchen together. I just need to say it—I had absolutely nothing to do with his death, and except for a few minutes in the pub when I set it down on the table, that curry sauce wasn't out of me sight. In fact, your grandfather was right here next to me when I was making it, like."

Liam, who had been listening patiently, put his hand on Eoin's shoulder. "I believe you. This all started with Vera. Somehow me grandfather's death is connected to hers. And given you never even met Mrs. Chips, I promise ya I believe you."

"Thank you." Eoin still seemed stressed. "The thought of anyone thinking I'm a killer, the thought of Madeline writing about it in her blog . . ."

"Her hit job," Siobhán said. "We'll make sure she doesn't." Siobhán didn't know how to do that, but given that Madeline seemed equally worried about being considered a murder suspect, they ought to be able to drive the point home. Unless of course she was their killer, in which case Siobhán hoped Madeline would be put away before she could type a single disparaging word. Not only was Eoin stressed about his new restaurant opening, he also had been quite fond of John Healy. It was going to take some time to heal from this trauma.

It wasn't long after Liam made his exit that Gráinne stared out the window twirling a strand of hair around her finger. "I'm going to do it," she said. "I'm going to ask Liam out."

"Not until this case is solved," Siobhán said. "We need to focus."

Gráinne sighed. "Murder before love," she said. "It's always murder before love."

The day flew by and Siobhán didn't see Macdara until he walked into the inn late that evening hauling golf bags. He'd run into Mike McGee in town and had finessed another invitation to join him.

"Did you learn anything this time?" Siobhán asked the minute he set the golf bags down.

"Well, hello, gorgeous. Why yes, I played a fantastic round, thank you for asking." Macdara planted a kiss on her, and Siobhán gave him a playful shove.

"We need to solve this case before Gráinne drags Liam off to elope."

Macdara groaned. "I did clock one thing. Mike McGee was rather chipper," he said, heading for the kitchen.

"Pun intended?"

Macdara grinned. "Forgive me. When men gather on the golf course, there will be puns."

"Why was he so chipper?"

"He said he was coming into an inheritance."

This stopped Siobhán cold. "An inheritance?"

Macdara nodded. "And then he clammed up."

"We need to learn more about him, his family, any recent deaths, that sort of thing."

"Let's start with Liam," Macdara said. "We might be able to catch him at the station."

"Now?" Siobhán said. "It's getting late."

"Were you hoping for some romantic holiday time?" Macdara teased.

"Murder before love," Siobhán said, grabbing her handbag. "Murder before love."

"You just missed him," said the clerk at the front desk of the garda station, pushing up the oversized black-rimmed glasses that had slipped down his long nose. "Shall I ring him?"

"No," Macdara said. "We'll catch up with him in the morning."

"I was about to leave as well, like," the clerk said. "And I'm the last hen in the house. Shall I stay late?" His glasses slid down again, and this time he left them there, peering over them with a look of pure dread.

"Not at all," Macdara said. "We'll lock up."

The clerk grinned and didn't hesitate to grab his things. Before they knew it, they were alone. "What are you thinking?" Siobhán asked.

"I've been meaning to finish checking out the evidence room," Macdara said. "Let's see what they have on the Chips's case."

The evidence room was small but tidy, and it didn't take long to find the section for Vera Cowley. "Her ledger!" Siobhán exclaimed, pointing to the notebook. "I saw a few photos from it when Jeanie was in town." If only John Healy's diary was here as well. Macdara handed her a pair of gloves. Siobhán slid them on and opened the notebook. The last entries were lists of contractors and numbers to purchase equipment. "This is all pricey stuff," she said. "If Mike McGee refused to grant her a loan, how would she have been able to afford it?"

"Hmmm," Macdara said. "Maybe she was just planning for the future?"

"It might be worth ringing some of these contractors," Siobhán said. "This town is like a merry-go-round of suspicious financing." She flipped to the next page. There she found a single name and a phone number. "I wonder who this is," she said, tapping the number. There was a station phone back at her temporary desk. Siobhán hurried over and dialed. It went to voice mail: *This is Jimmy. Leave it all at the beep.*

Siobhán left a message asking for a callback as soon as possible. "We didn't learn much here," Siobhán said as they checked everything else in the evidence locker.

"I have CCTV cued up in the tech room," Macdara said. "Just received footage. We'll be the first to see it."

They set up in the equipment room near the screens, and Macdara cued up the footage. "It starts the day before Vera took the tumble off the greased ladder and continues until just after her death."

He pushed play. They watched the day before. People came in and out of the frame, including Vera, who ferried in and out of her chipper. Mike McGee was often standing in front of the bank on a cigarette break, and John Healy was seen going into a building toward the end of the street that was barely visible. "We need to know what that building is," Siobhán said.

"Hold on," Macdara said. He turned to a second monitor and pulled up a view from Google Earth. Soon they located the building. "It's a solicitor's office," Macdara said.

"Interesting," Siobhán said. "Name?"

"Kevin Casey," Macdara said.

"Let's pay him a visit in the morning."

"Should we loop in Liam?"

Siobhán hesitated. "Given the personal nature of visiting a solicitor and the fact that they're family, he probably already knows. But let's wait and see what we're dealing with."

"Agreed."

On the tape, dusk was approaching and the streets were thrumming. Tara Flaherty was painting the mural on Mr. Chips. Several folks were going into the abandoned building next to the bank where they played their poker games. As they watched, Liam pulled up in his squad car, emerged from the vehicle, and had a chat with Mike McGee, who had simply moved over a little to the abandoned building but was still standing outside smoking. Liam and McGee chatted, and then Liam left. The entire encounter was less than ten minutes. "I believe that's when he was following up on Vera's complaints," Macdara said. "But I'll double-check with him."

Macdara cued up to the next morning. This was it. Siobhán leaned in eagerly. The footage began with Vera pacing the footpath in front of her chipper and McGee opening the bank. Then at the far end of the street, Siobhán saw her—a tall, thin woman with a floppy yellow hat and a long tan coat. "There!" Siobhán said. She leaned even closer to the screen.

"Who is she?"

"No clue," Siobhán said. "Daniel O'Grady mentioned seeing her that morning as well."

Just as Siobhán and Macdara were doing right then, Vera on tape carefully watched the woman in the yellow hat. A few minutes later, Vera disappeared into her chipper, but just as quickly she came out with an object in her hand.

"What is that?" Macdara squinted.

"Black spray paint," Siobhán said. After looking both ways, Vera marched across the street.

"See?" Siobhán said, pointing to the Mrs. Chips door. "She left it unlocked."

"I can see why," Macdara said. "She's just across the street and she doesn't intend on being there long."

They leaned in, waiting to see whether someone—perhaps the tall woman in the floppy yellow hat—would enter Mrs. Chips. Their excitement grew as indeed the yellow hat came back into the frame.

"Is this our killer?" Macdara asked. "Will she go in?" This time they both leaned forward. And then, as they eagerly watched, the tape cut off and the screen went black.

Right then they couldn't do anything about the ruined tape. "Maybe we can pull tape from another business on the street," Macdara said. "But it will have to wait. Let's get some shut-eye." Macdara had use of a squad car while they were on the case, so they were able to drive back to the inn.

"It has to be her," Siobhán said as Macdara parked the car in the small lot designated for the inn. "This woman in the floppy yellow hat has to be the killer. I wonder if she somehow tampered with the tape as well, like."

"That sounds like a bit of a stretch," Macdara said. "How would she sneak into the garda station to mess with the tape?"

Siobhán chewed on it. "Maybe she flirted with Liam," she said. "He is rather vulnerable to pretty females."

Macdara shook his head. "He knows when to be a detective and turn off distractions. And those tapes malfunction all the time. And we've no proof that she's our killer. But I do agree we need to figure out her identity."

It was a cool evening, and in the distance she could hear waves lapping against the shore. Somewhere out there was the killer. Was it the woman in the floppy yellow hat, and was that woman Tara Flaherty? Was it Sheila Bisby? Sheila also had access to the type of stone thrown into Daniel O'Grady's shop. Or was it Natalie O'Brien? Was she only pretending to be romantically involved with Daniel? Was it an effort to cover up her involvement?

"Stop it," Macdara said, looping his arm around her. "I can hear ya thinking. What do you say we spend the rest of the evening in holiday mode?"

"I'd say that's why there's champagne in the fridge and a box of chocolates on the counter."

Macdara chuckled. "You never miss a trick."

"When it comes to chocolate?" Siobhán said. "Never."

"I'll take that as a win."

"Remember this night," Siobhán said. "Just this once I'm allowing it to be love before murder."

"Be still my heart," Macdara said. "We could have worked that into our wedding vows."

Chapter 27

The O'Sullivan-Flannerys were up bright and early the next morning. First, they took a family stroll to the beach, where they watched the sun rise over the glistening water. Then they all went to the breakfast cafe, but instead of settling in, everyone placed take-away orders. They all had their day somewhat planned out and were eager to get to it. When Siobhán and Macdara received their coffee and pastries, they said their good-byes, which never failed to make Siobhán's heart squeeze. Then she and Macdara ate their breakfast baps on the promenade before walking to the solicitor's office. Luckily, Kevin Casey was an early bird. They watched him approach the front door, briefcase in hand, and they intercepted before he could enter.

"I'm Detective Sargeant Flannery, and this is Garda O'Sullivan," Macdara began.

"O'Sullivan?" Kevin Casey raised an eyebrow.

"Yes," Siobhán said.

"I see, I see," he said. "You're in town with your siblings, are you not?"

This was the last thing Siobhán had expected to come out of his gob. "I am, so," Siobhán said. "Why do you ask?"

"Come in, come in," he said as he held open the door. "Will they be joining us?"

Once again Siobhán was taken aback. "Why would they be joining us?"

Kevin Casey looked startled for a moment as he stared at Siobhán. "I see," he said. "I see."

Siobhán, on the other hand, was totally in the dark. She and Macdara exchanged quizzical looks. They followed Mr. Casey through two sets of doors and into a large office. He sat down behind an enormous desk and gestured to a pair of leather chairs facing him. Siobhán and Macdara remained standing, but they pulled out their notepads and biros. Casey looked up at them, and suddenly he seemed reluctant to talk. He began to drum his fingers on the desk. "I'm afraid I don't have much time," he said. "How can I be of service?"

"We're here to speak with you about John Healy," Macdara began.

Casey raised his hand to stop them. "Given the circumstances surrounding John Healy's death, Mr. Healy's estate is in limbo . . ." He cleared his throat. "I haven't even been able to notify the beneficiary as of yet."

"You mean you cannot implement his will until his murder is solved?" Siobhán asked.

"Not exactly," Casey said. "But I am waiting to hear from Detective Sargeant Healy, as well as the beneficiary. These are delicate matters indeed." Casey removed a handkerchief from his suit pocket and wiped his brow. "I'm sorry. But you have to understand I operate under a strict code of ethics." He placed the handkerchief back in his pocket, opened the center drawer of his desk, and brought out a prescription bottle. He opened it, tapped two white pills into his palm, shoved the pills into his mouth, and swallowed them dry.

"I am officially in charge of this investigation now," Macdara said. "And I will need questions answered."

"I need to speak with Liam Healy first. Not as a detective sargeant but as a grandson," Casey pleaded. "I want to know if John had been suffering from any health concerns." He cleared his throat. "Mental health, that is."

"I'm assuming by all of this that John Healy was a client?" Macdara asked.

"Yes. I believe I can tell you that much. John Healy was my client."

"And did he visit you the day before Vera Cowley was murdered?" Siobhán asked.

Casey's mouth dropped open. "Are you trying to say there's a connection between my appointment with a client and a murder the next day?"

"If I were you, I wouldn't try to interpret the questions, I'd just answer them," Macdara said.

"Is this because I said I was concerned about Healy's mental health?" Casey continued. "Believe me it's not because I was worried he would hurt anyone— it wasn't that kind of concern. Not at all. Not at all."

He slapped his desk. "But he was an elderly man you know, and some people like to prey on the elderly—the worst kind of person, in my opinion—but John Healy is not a murderer. You're not going to suggest to Liam that I insinuated his grandfather was a murderer, are ye?"

"Mr. Casey, I assure you—" Macdara tried to respond, but Casey wasn't listening.

"This is why I don't like speaking with the guards. They twist everything you say!" He glanced at his prescription bottle as if he were thinking of taking more.

"What exactly were your concerns about John Healy's mental health?" Siobhán jumped in. She was surprised to hear the lawyer bring this up. She'd found John very stable and coherent.

"I find John's actions the weeks before his death to be very troubling."

They'd yet to mention they were simply following up on the CCTV footage, trying to ascertain what brought him to Casey's building at such an early hour, but it sounded as if Casey had a lot more to offer, so Siobhán and Macdara lowered themselves into oversized leather chairs across from the desk.

"Please tell us everything you can about these troubling actions," Macdara said.

"He changed his will multiple times," Casey said. "He was rambling about his new plants. He looked ghastly as well. Like a man with demons, ye know that kind of way? That's about as specific as I can get right now."

"New plants?" Siobhán came to attention. "Castor bean plants?"

Casey slapped the desk again. "If ye know this already, why are ye asking me? Is it a test?" He licked his lips. "Am I passing?"

"No," Macdara said.

Casey pulled at his collar as if he wanted to rip off his shirt. "I'm doing me best."

"Tell us everything you know about his sudden interest in castor bean plants," Siobhán said.

"You want to ask about the plants?" Casey said. "Of everything I'm telling ye it's the plants that start your engines?"

"Mr. Casey," Macdara said, raising his voice. "It's none of your concern what starts our engines. Let me be very clear. We ask the questions, you answer them. End of story."

Casey leaned in. "But what about the last change to his will? Surely that's way more interesting than a hill of beans." He chuckled at his own joke. "But if you want to talk about plants, by all means let's talk about plants. He bought castor bean plants. What for? I dunno. I suppose he likes beans. Next question?"

Macdara stiffened as if he were about to yank Casey from his chair and choke him. Siobhán placed her hand on Macdara's arm.

"Last change to his will?" she said. "Would you please elaborate?"

The handkerchief came back out, but this time Casey simply waved it around. "He left everything to a total stranger! His entire estate. I don't even know whether Liam realizes it. It's not something I want to tell Liam over the phone and he's yet to pay me a visit." He shook his head. "I've tried calling this *other* person numerous times, but every time she hangs up on me!" Casey's gaze landed firmly on Siobhán, and it almost felt as if he was accusing her of something.

A total stranger. Who was she? Could it be the woman in the floppy yellow hat?

"We're going to need the name of that beneficiary," Macdara said.

Casey nodded. "Perhaps you can help me locate her," he said. "When I asked John who this woman was and why on earth he was leaving everything to her, he was very cagey."

"How so?" Siobhán asked.

"He told me it was personal and he didn't need to explain himself."

Siobhán retrieved a notepad and biro. "Name," she said.

Casey cleared his throat and then opened a folder. "I don't know if this is a test. Is it?" His eyebrows arched up.

Macdara leaned in. "Why would we be testing you?"

"Your name is O'Sullivan, is it not?"

"It is," Siobhán said. She was ready to throttle him herself.

"And you are related to a Gráinne O'Sullivan?"

Siobhán felt as if she'd been slapped. "What does me sister have to do with any of this?"

"I'm surprised you asked me about John's visit before Vera Cowley was murdered," Casey said. "I thought you were asking about his second visit."

"Mr. Casey, I'm about to grab you by the shirt collar

and haul you into the station for questioning," Macdara said, coming to his feet. He leaned over the desk. "Now stop dodging every question we ask and start making some sense!"

Casey swallowed hard and nodded. He gestured for Macdara to sit back down. "Please." After a moment, Macdara lowered himself. Kevin cleared his throat. "The day before Vera's murder, John wanted to know how long it would take to change his will. I tried getting more out of him, but he refused to explain himself. He simply wanted to know how long it *would* take if he decided to change it. I explained it would be a relatively quick process, and he left." He twiddled his thumbs. "I asked if he and Liam had had a falling out."

He was implying that prior to the change, Liam was the sole beneficiary. This made sense. "And did they?" Siobhán asked. "Have a falling out?"

"Not at all," Casey said. "According to John, that is. Which makes this change very suspect!"

"You said he paid you a visit in the days before he died?" Macdara asked. "Why did he visit you then?"

"He had given it some thought and he said he was ready to change his will," Casey said. "He was ready to make a complete stranger the beneficiary." Once again, his gaze slid to Siobhán.

She screeched back her chair and stood. "Why do you keep looking at me?"

"You really don't have any idea?"

Siobhán planted her hands on his desk. "Believe you me, Mr. Casey, I have plenty of ideas. And you wouldn't like a single one of them."

Casey seemed to shrink under her gaze. "The beneficiary," he said. "The day before Vera Cowley was murdered, John Healy changed the beneficiary."

"We gathered that," Macdara said. "Can you give us a name?"

"Gráinne O'Sullivan," Casey said. "The beneficiary of John Healy's entire estate is Gráinne O'Sullivan."

Chapter 28

They found Gráinne racewalking in the exact area where Liam happened to be conducting a house-to-house inquiry. *What a coincidence.* She was wearing a light pink tracksuit and new white runners. "That's her," Siobhán said, pointing at the back of her sister. "I'd know that wiggle anywhere."

"Is she . . ." Macdara squinted. *"Exercising?"*

"If you weren't here to witness it, I'd think I was hallucinating," Siobhán said. "She might even be sweating."

Macdara parked the car, and they hoofed it over to her. Gráinne let out a squeal, then a yell when she realized who it was, then gave out to them for putting her heart in crossways, and then she was finally ready to listen.

"I think we'd all better sit down for this news," Siobhán said. "Can we go to the cafe?" She for one could do with another cappuccino. They hadn't found out from the solicitor exactly how much John Healy's estate was worth, but there was the more pressing question in Siobhán's mind: Why didn't he leave it to Liam? And how was Liam going to react when he found out?

"I'm having a bit of exercise and you want to drag me to a cafe?" Gráinne managed to get out between taking gulps of air. "Typical."

"Believe me, you're going to want to be sitting down with a treat for this," Macdara said.

"What?" Gráinne said, her eyes wide. "Who *else* died?"

"No," Gráinne repeated, after she'd heard the news. "That's not possible."

"Did you do something special for him? Did you say anything to him about money or . . . ?" Siobhán had already asked this question, but they were having a second go at it.

"I told you—no, no, and no. Eoin talked to him more than me. I don't understand why he would leave anything to me at all." She chewed her lip. "What does Liam think about it?"

"I don't believe he knows," Macdara said. "The solicitor hasn't notified anyone because of the current investigation."

"How much did he leave me? Like, the entire inn?"

"Do not start thinking that any of it is actually going to be yours," Siobhán said. "There's something fishy going on."

"It would be fishy if he left me a chipper," Gráinne said. "But there's nothing fishy about an inn." She couldn't help but grin.

"He was poisoned," Siobhán said. "And he cut his grandson off cold. You know. The grandson you fancy." Gráinne's smile disappeared. Siobhán turned to Macdara. "We need to bring Mike McGee into the station—enough golfing for him—we need to tell Liam about this development before he finds out from someone else and loses all trust in us. And we must uncover the identity of the woman in the floppy yellow hat."

"Floppy yellow hat?" Gráinne said. "I feel like I've seen one of those somewhere." She frowned. "I think I saw one at the inn."

Siobhán sat up straight. "At the inn? What would a floppy yellow hat be doing there?"

"Maybe it was Mrs. Chips's hat," Gráinne said. "She was staying there, wasn't she?"

"If it was her hat, then someone else was wearing it the morning she died," Siobhán said. Had that been the goal? To distract Mrs. Chips by strolling past wearing her hat? The video had clearly showed them in the frame at the same time—Mrs. Chips marching across the street as the woman strolled by. Then the woman in the floppy hat turned around and headed back toward the door that Vera had left unlocked. It wasn't a coincidence that the tape had cut off. Someone had messed with the tape. They were going to have to ask Liam about its chain of command. If he left it vulnerable somehow, he would be at fault. None of these conversations were going to be easy.

"Why don't you go back to the inn and have a look

for that hat?" Siobhán asked Gráinne. "We have too much on our plates, and it would really help us out."

"You're going to tell Liam about this?" Gráinne asked. "Today?" She swallowed hard.

"We are, so," Siobhán said. "Don't worry—we'll make sure he knows that you were completely blindsided by this."

"And while you're looking, let us know if you come across John's ledger," Macdara added.

Siobhán's phone rang, and she glanced at the screen. "Speaking of John Healy."

Gráinne's mouth dropped open. "Someone's calling you from his phone?"

"No, pet. It's a call about John." It was the contractor whose number they'd found among John's things in the evidence room. "I'll take this outside."

The contractor wasted no time in spilling the beans. Siobhán didn't even have to meet with him in person. "John Healy hired me to remodel the inn. We spent months on the planning and the sourcing materials, and I hired extra laborers—it was a no-expense-spared type of situation, like. He started off as a dream client!"

"And then?"

"And then he canceled everything with one phone call. Like a blade to the back of the head, it was. Quick and lethal. Left me holding the bill for the materials too—said he'd have to owe me, that an unexpected emergency came up."

"An unexpected emergency," Siobhán repeated. "Did he say what it was?"

"His lips were sealed," the contractor said. "But you know, I didn't pry. I mind me own business."

"Of course." She paused. "If you could categorize his demeanor . . ."

"Desperate," the contractor said without hesitation. "He seemed to me like he was on the verge of a breakdown. And sure, lookit. I was waiting for you to call. It's the only reason I haven't come forward yet, I was waiting for ye."

"Go on, so."

"One of my crew said that on our last day of work, John Healy asked him did he know how he could get ahold of a castor bean plant. But not a seedling or a starter one. He wanted the full plant. He wanted it with the beans."

"Did your crew member supply him with any suggestions?"

"There are plenty of nurseries around Lahinch, but supposedly John didn't want to visit any of them. That's when my man told him to buy it on the internet."

Siobhán stared at her phone long after she'd hung up. He hadn't wanted anyone in Lahinch to see him buying a castor plant. *He'd wanted it with the beans . . .* Given the work on his inn had been interrupted for quite some time, that meant he asked about the castor bean plant well *before* Mrs. Chips died. A thought was swirling around Siobhán's poor head. What if? What if? What if? What if John Healy had planned on poisoning someone? Was it Mrs. Chips? Had he changed his mind about the method?

But if John Healy killed Vera, then who killed John Healy? Or what if John Healy wanted to poison someone else? And that someone beat him to the punch? (Or the curry bowl, although she'd never say that in front of Eoin.) And what exactly was this emergency that made him drop his remodeling project, especially when the contractor had already purchased the materials? Had John Healy been suicidal? If so, what drove him to such desperate thoughts? And another little voice was whispering in her ear: What if someone had *pretended* to be John Healy on the phone just like someone pretended to be Vera when calling Tom Dowd to cancel the appointment? There were so many threads to pull on this case, it was maddening. Was she getting closer to the answer or further away?

"I can't believe I was right," Jeanie said. "I mean, I know I'm good at me job, like, but that was partly a wild guess." As soon as Siobhán learned of Healy's request to obtain a castor plant, she just had to video call Jeanie. Jeanie was at work, but luckily she answered the call against a plain wall. Siobhán wasn't squeamish per se but she saw enough bodies in her line of work, and she appreciated Jeanie finding a neutral spot in the morgue from which to take the call.

"How exactly would he have extracted the ricin?" Siobhán asked. She had just searched John Healy's back garden and found nothing but shrubs, herbs, roses, and perennials. She did see a few round indents in the grass, as if large pots had been sitting there. Were they castor bean plants? Where were they now?

"There is a process to soften the outer coat of the bean, and then certain solvents can be added to extract the ricin," Jeanie said. "It's not terribly difficult if one is determined." Siobhán could see Healy learning those steps easily; after all, he was very handy. Jeanie paused and stared at Siobhán through the video app. "Are you actually suggesting that John Healy poisoned himself?"

"I don't know," Siobhán said. "Maybe accidentally?"

"That wouldn't be possible," Jeanie said.

"What if he intended to poison someone else?"

Jeanie raised an eyebrow. "And, what? Someone turned the tables?"

"Exactly. Maybe he was making it for someone else, then changed his mind—and this someone else didn't like that." Someone like Vera Cowley? But why? And if that was the case, what happened? Did Vera catch on and then turn the tables on John Healy? But before she could live to see him die of ricin poison, he found another way to kill her?

A double murder with each suspect planning on killing the other . . . that would be a first. But how could she ever prove it when both of them were dead?

"Siobhán?" Jeanie said. "You're away with the fairies again."

"Sorry," Siobhán said. "I'm wondering if Vera Cowley had planned to poison someone, maybe Mr.

Chips, and asked John Healy to source a castor bean plant for her."

"Where's the connection between her and Healy?"

"She was staying at his inn before she died."

"Hmmm."

"I know. It's weak. But she was also badgering—some might say extorting—money out of literally everyone she could. And John Healy had been enthusiastically planning a remodel of his inn when he suddenly ordered all work to stop. He mentioned an unforeseen emergency." And Mike McGee had mentioned he was going to come into an inheritance. Was there a connection there?

"And you think Vera is the emergency to which John was referring?"

Siobhán nodded. "Unless it's something to do with Liam, that's my best guess."

"But why would he give his money to Vera Cowley?"

"Maybe she was holding something over his head." She paused. "There's more . . . I don't know yet why or how it fits in, but John Healy changed his will in the days before he died. He assigned a new beneficiary of his entire estate."

"That person could be our killer!" Jeanie said. Her face shone with excitement.

"It's Gráinne," Siobhán said.

"*What's* Gráinne?"

"John Healy named Gráinne as his sole beneficiary." Jeanie's mouth dropped open. "I know," Siobhán said. "She's not going to accept it. We'll make sure it goes back to Liam, but first we have to figure out the reason for it, or was he simply out of his mind."

"The poisoning could have affected his mental state," Jeanie said. "It's impossible to think clearly when everything in your body is shutting down."

Siobhán felt a cold chill ripple up the back of her neck. "Poor man."

"I'll leave it to you to sort out," Jeanie said. "But I feel for ya. It might be easy for me to work with the dead, but unfortunately they're not going to help you find any answers."

"You'd be surprised," Siobhán said. "You'd be surprised." They were telling her so much already.

Liam wanted to meet at Mr. Chips. Apparently Mr. Chips was still offering deep lunch discounts in honor of Mrs. Chips. By the time they slid into Liam's booth he was pushing back an empty basket. "Shall we order more?" he asked as they joined him. They both declined. Liam raised an eyebrow. "Has there been a development?"

Macdara nodded. "We have no choice but to look into this angle," he said. "But I'd like to make it very clear that we have not and will not leap to any conclusions."

Liam frowned. "Okay."

"And it's nothing that cannot be reversed," Siobhán added. "It will be reversed, I assure you."

Liam raised an eyebrow. "I'm intrigued."

Macdara took the lead. "Were you aware that your

grandfather was about to remodel his inn but canceled on the contractor at the last minute?"

Liam nodded. "That wasn't surprising. Me grandfather often changed the scope of his projects." He frowned. "Are you saying the contractor might have killed me grandfather? Out of revenge, like?"

"No," Siobhán said. Although truth be told, she should have considered that possibility. "I didn't get that impression when I spoke with him. He was a bit aggravated but didn't seem in a rage." Then again, anyone could seem pleasant while speaking to the guards about a murder.

Liam pondered it. "He probably had an argument with him and decided he could do the work himself. My grandfather had mad skills."

"But he wasn't doing any work," Siobhán pointed out.

"He was probably too busy doing work for everyone else," Liam said.

"Even so," Siobhán said. "We'd like to dig into your grandfather's financial history."

"To what end?" Liam was already sounding defensive.

Macdara delivered the bad news. "We think it's possible that Vera Cowley was extorting him, maybe holding something over his head."

Liam pushed his empty fish and chips basket away and crossed his arms. "What makes you think that?"

"According to the contractor your grandfather hired, he stopped the project quite abruptly. Vera was staying at the inn, and we know she was going after everyone who took a loan from Mike McGee, asking them for money—"

Liam was already shaking his head. "My grandfather never took a loan from Mike McGee." He leaned in. "I promise you that."

"That doesn't mean Vera didn't ask him for money," Siobhán said.

"Even if she did, so what?" Liam asked. "I mean, Vera is dead. She can't have murdered my grandfather." He crossed his arms. "Or are you accusing *him* of something?" He stared at them as they waited for him to work it out. "The castor bean plants," he said. "My grandfather was the one to order them." He stared at his empty basket of chips. "He liked to cook. I didn't see anything alarming about it."

"Castor beans contain ricin," Siobhán said. "Doctor Jeanie Brady, the state pathologist, believes that your grandfather was poisoned by ricin."

Liam swallowed hard. Siobhán could tell he had already worked this out for himself but was struggling to accept it. "Believes or knows?"

"She's still waiting on the toxicology but it's a very good guess. And with this second piece of information about the castor plant—"

"Then why didn't we find the castor bean plants at the inn? What if he ordered them but they never arrived?"

What if someone else received them? Liam was bringing up things that Siobhán should have already worked through. She took a deep breath. Liam was emotional. "I found two indents in your grandfather's back garden where it looked as if a few large pots had been."

Macdara interrupted before Liam could protest yet again. "Remember what I said at the beginning of this conversation. We are simply looking into all possibilities here."

"You're going to have to connect the dots for me, Detective. Are you saying that my grandfather poisoned himself?"

"Is it possible?" Siobhán asked.

Liam shook his head. "It just doesn't make any sense. Why would he want to kill himself?"

"Can you think of any reason?" Siobhán kept her tone light. They were both fully expecting Liam to explode at some point. Given the sensitive nature of the discussion, they couldn't blame him, and they hadn't even yet told him the most shocking bit.

"No. My grandfather loved life. And he didn't let bullies get the best of him. I don't know why you're on this road, but trust me, it's a dead end."

Siobhán couldn't bring herself to throw out the other possibility. That John Healy had ordered the castor bean plants to poison someone else. Someone like Vera Cowley, who most likely was staying at the inn when the plants arrived. She was afraid to make this kind of bold statement without more evidence to back it up.

"Are you familiar with Kevin Casey?" Macdara asked.

Liam nodded. "Of course. He's my grandfather's solicitor."

"Have you spoken with him since your grandfather's death?"

"Briefly. He called to tell me that he wouldn't be able to execute the will until the investigation was concluded."

"Some cases are never solved," Macdara said. "But wills still have to be executed."

"What are you saying?" Liam said. "Are you saying Kevin Casey is being dishonest?"

"Your grandfather recently changed his will," Macdara said.

"Very recently," Siobhán added. "Were you aware?"

"No," Liam said. "I was not." His voice squeaked and sweat beaded on his brow. Siobhán and Macdara hadn't forced him to take any bereavement leave, but now she saw they should have at least strongly suggested it. But doing so at this very moment could make this tense situation even worse. Siobhán should have ordered a basket of curried chips. Or a hundred.

"I must first say that the new beneficiary was completely blindsided by the news as well." Siobhán paused. "She had no idea she was in his will, and she certainly didn't expect to inherit a single thing, let alone the entire estate."

"She," Liam said. He began to blink rapidly. "The entire estate?"

"There's no easy way to say this," Macdara said. "But his new will leaves everything—his inn and all his assets—to Gráinne O'Sullivan."

Liam stared at them for a moment before erupting in laughter. Soon, he was pounding the table with his fist as he tried to control the hysterics. "That's gas." By the time he was finished, he was wiping tears from his eyes. He shook his head. "You had me going there for a spell."

"We're not having a laugh," Macdara said. "You can ask Kevin Casey."

Liam returned to staring at them, open-mouthed.

"Gráinne had no idea," Siobhán said. "And I can say with certainty she has no intention of letting this stand. *We* have no intention of letting this stand. The O'Sullivans don't take what doesn't belong to them."

"Okay," Liam said. "Then it's just a matter of paperwork. Why didn't you lead with that?"

Siobhán shook her head. He wasn't following the trail; yet even more evidence that he was too emotionally involved. "Your grandfather made this bizarre change recently. It has to fit in with this case somehow. It's a thread we have to pull on."

"Are you implying my grandfather and I had a falling out?" Liam slid to the end of the booth and lingered.

"Did you?" Macdara asked.

"No," Liam said. "We did not."

"Can you think of any reason he might have made this change?" Siobhán asked.

"Your sister," Liam said, processing it all over again. "Your sister is the beneficiary of my grandfather's entire estate."

"Yes," Macdara said. "Those are the facts."

"He changed his will shortly before he died. You can get the exact dates from Kevin Casey," Siobhán added. "I think there must be a reason. However, I should point out that if he was being slowly poisoned—

whether he knew it or not—it may have affected his mental capacity."

Liam slid out of the booth. "Don't follow me," he said. "I need a few minutes to think." He exited the chipper, letting the door slam on his way out.

"We didn't even tell him about the interview with Mike," Siobhán said. It was set up for this afternoon at the garda station. She for one was eager to face the man whose fingerprints seemed to be all over this case.

"We couldn't let Liam sit in on the interview anyway," Macdara said. "I'm afraid the ties are getting too close for him."

"You're cutting him from the case?" Siobhán knew it made sense, but it was also going to cause a whole lot of problems. Technically, with Eoin's unfortunate proximity to John Healy, not to mention the poisoned curry sauce, Liam could try to get *them* thrown off the case as well.

Macdara stood, then took Siobhán's hand as she rose from the booth. "I don't see any other choice, do you?"

"No," Siobhán sighed. "I do not."

"Let's get to the station," Macdara said. "The sooner we get Mike McGee talking the better."

Chapter 29

"There's nothing wrong with the loans I've given out, and I welcome—no, I dare you—to find anything." Mike McGee sat in front of them in the interview room in a wrinkled blue suit. He'd asked for a can of Coke, but instead of drinking from it, Mike left it sweating in front of him. For a second, Siobhán wondered whether the can had something to hide. He pulled at the collar of his dress shirt as if it were strangling him.

"We're not accusing you of anything," Siobhán said. "We're trying to find out who killed Vera Cowley and John Healy."

Mike sighed as if he'd rather be anywhere but here. "Vera Cowley was upset with me. I wouldn't give her a loan."

"Why not?" Macdara asked.

"She had no solid credit history. Everything had

been in her husband's name. I told her to wait a year, build some credit of her own, and I would have been happy to loan it to her then."

Siobhán felt her jaw clench. No credit of her own after being married for forty years and co-running the chipper. The arrogance of this small, small man. Her husband's credit should suffice. No wonder Vera lost the plot. She couldn't imagine starting over again after forty years and having to face all this. Had Vera thought about poisoning Mike McGee?

"Did you know that Vera thought you were giving out loans as personal favors, or perhaps granting loans in exchange for personal favors?" Macdara asked.

"It's absolutely ridiculous!" Mike said. "She even sent Liam knocking on me door asking me questions."

"Do you ever receive anything in exchange for the loans you grant?" Siobhán asked. "Or *did* you?"

Mike arched an eyebrow. "Such as?"

"Gifts, money, favors, anything at all," Macdara said.

"Of course not," Mike said. "That would be highly unethical, not to mention illegal."

"It certainly would," Siobhán said. "But if the thought of breaking the law was enough to stop folks, we wouldn't have jobs, now would we?" she said with a nod to Macdara.

"What do you think we'd be doing instead?" Macdara asked.

"You'd probably be golfing," Siobhán said. "You're quite good at it." She glanced at Mike. "As you recently discovered," she added.

Mike's expression turned even more sour.

"And what about John Healy's loan?" Macdara asked.

"What loan?" Mike raised an eyebrow. "I never set up a loan for John Healy."

They knew this to be true, but Macdara wanted to rattle him even further. It seemed to be working. He grabbed the can of Coke and chugged down the soda.

"Do you know who inherits John Healy's estate?" Siobhán said. She hadn't even planned on asking that, but given that John's last-minute decision to bequeath everything to Gráinne had to mean something, she figured she'd throw wet noodles at the wall and see if anything stuck.

McGee crossed his arms. "As a matter of fact, I do. And it has nothing to do with the bank, for as I said, I never set him up with a loan. But if it's gambling you're after, good luck to ye. And in the meantime, I won that inn fair and square."

"Wait," Macdara said. "What do you mean you won the inn?"

Mike chuckled. "Good job, Detective. Making me think you don't know anything more than you let on, is that it?" He leaned in, a grin on his face. "Well, you wouldn't be asking me about his estate unless you already knew." He sat back and tapped his head. "Up here for thinking." He pointed to his legs. "Down there for dancing."

Mike continued to grin as he folded his arms. He seemed to feel at ease now, in control. "Not only that, I happen to know you paid a visit to Kevin Casey yesterday, and lo and behold you called me into the station soon thereafter." He leaned forward. "Is it Liam, is it?

Is he trying to take it back?" He shook his head. "I'm afraid it's too late for that. A bet is a bet."

"No," Siobhán said. "He's not involved in this case any longer."

"I don't care what he says, what he does, what he threatens. I won that inn fair and square."

"In a poker game," Siobhán said slowly, putting it together in the dark.

"Four queens," Mike said with a grin. "Wasn't my fault Liam tossed in the keys to his grandfather's inn. It was his inheritance, so who was I to say what he does with it?"

His inheritance. Which he gambled away. What then? He told his grandfather . . . And John Healy was so livid he turned around and changed the will. He gave the estate to Gráinne. Gráinne, who had been circling Liam's orbit since they'd first arrived. Had he done it to encourage Liam to marry Gráinne? Was it the last wish of a dying man—a man who planned on dying soon?

And there was that nagging three-letter question rearing its head again: *Why?* Siobhán had at least one thread to pull on. There had to be some closer connection between John Healy and Vera Cowley. There had to be a reason for John to want her dead.

"Vera Cowley employed John Healy as a handyman," Siobhán said out loud, still trying to make the pieces fit.

"She did," Mike said. "Had her 'special bookcase' installed."

"What deemed it 'special'?"

Mike shrugged. "I would say to ask John Healy, but

I suppose you'll be waiting a long time for the answer."

Siobhán jotted down a note to Macdara.

He's not our killer.

"Is there anything else you wish to tell us?" Macdara said. "Now is your chance."

"Vera was on a collision course. Without a loan, she only had a few months before she was likely to lose the chipper."

Siobhán couldn't believe this small man sitting across from her. "You knew that and still you told her to reapply in a year?"

"Look," he said, "I don't work in a silo. I have bosses and me bosses have bosses. I couldn't have loaned her the money. It would have never been approved."

"So even though she co-ran that chipper for forty years, in your mind she had nothing to do with its success?" Mike was working Siobhán's last nerve, and she could no longer hold her tongue.

Mike sighed. "I've already told you. She doesn't present well on paper. It was out of me hands."

They stood in Mrs. Chips staring at the bookcase. It looked like a typical bookcase to them. And only a few recipe books stood in it, so technically it was just a tall shelf in the back right-hand corner of the chipper. The books on the shelf had their spines facing out.

"If the case were filled with books, we'd be pulling

them out to see if this hid a secret door," Siobhán said. They had already tried tugging on the bookcase, and the only thing they discovered was that it was fixed securely to the wall. "There has to be something here. We need to feel along the bottom of each shelf and pick up every book."

"That won't take long," Macdara said. "I'll do it." Siobhán stepped back as Macdara went at it. He ran his hands under the shelves and lifted the books, shaking his head as he went. On the next-to-last shelf, as he was running his hands underneath, he called out. "There's a latch! There's a latch!"

Siobhán heard a click, and suddenly the right-hand portion of the shelf swung open.

"You did it," Siobhán said.

"It was your suggestion." They stood peering into the opening, which was shrouded in darkness. Siobhán turned on her mobile phone's flashlight as they entered a room no larger than a closet. Siobhán turned the light on two large potted plants, a floppy yellow hat, and a mason jar of fat.

"Castor plants, our infamous floppy yellow hat, and a jar of beef fat drippings."

"What in the world?" Macdara said.

"This is where the killer hid," Siobhán explained.

Macdara raised an eyebrow. "Why are the castor bean plants here?"

"John Healy, or the killer—and it's possible they're one and the same—hid them here."

"You're going to have to walk me through it," Macdara said.

Siobhán directed the light to the floor. Visible in the

dust was a partial footprint. It looked too large to be a woman's. Then again, it could have been made by a woman wearing man-sized shoes. "Vera marched next door, leaving the chipper open. The woman, or man, in the floppy yellow hat slipped into the shop. The killer knew about this special bookcase. Then he or she set up the ladder, arranged the twine under the bag of flour, climbed down, greased the treads, and hid in this closet. The killer would have been in the closet, maybe even when we were here, just after we discovered the body. That's how he—let's go with *he*—locked the door from the inside. This person could have slipped out unnoticed when the place was crawling with crime scene investigators."

"You think someone would stay in a closet that long?"

"If it meant getting away with murder? I do."

"That means the killer had to know about this special bookcase."

"I've been meaning to fill you in on a theory of mine. It's going to sound a bit far-fetched."

"Try me."

"Scenario one. What if John Healy is our killer?"

Macdara pondered it. "Then who killed John Healy?"

"He did."

Macdara took a step back. "You think he killed himself after killing Vera?"

"I have to at least work through the scenario." She went through everything she'd been piecing together. "I think Vera found out that Liam had gambled away the inn. She used that information to begin her extortion scheme."

Macdara was listening intently. "How would she extort him with that information?"

"If she reported Mike to the authorities, and Liam knowingly participated in illegally gambling away his grandfather's inn in a poker game, Liam could have been in trouble—and maybe even John, if he was aware of it. He could have lost the inn. But my guess is that he wanted to protect Liam. If he changed his will and then he died, there would be no consequences for Liam."

"Other than losing his inheritance."

"Which is why John left everything to Gráinne."

"You're saying he was playing matchmaker?"

Siobhán nodded. "I think John Healy believed Liam would be able to charm Gráinne into either marrying him or simply handing over the inheritance." *Exactly like she was poised to do.* Had they all been played? Or was the deranged mind of a dying man all to blame?

Macdara dropped into a nearby booth as he thought it through. "How do we prove it?"

"I suppose that's the genius of his plan. It's all circumstantial. He hadn't been feeling well, which according to Jeanie is exactly the state he would have been in if he had been poisoning himself little by little. John Healy is the one who ordered the castor bean plants and asked around about them first, wanted one with all the beans—and if you remember Vera's memorial, he snatched that entire bowl of curry for himself. I believe he was trying to prevent anyone else from being poisoned, which means he knew the poison was in there."

"He added beans to the curry sauce?" Macdara sounded horrified.

Siobhán couldn't help but laugh. "No, although I had the same question for Jeanie Brady when the discussion came up. Ricin is extracted from the bean. I think it needs to be softened, and you need a few other bits and bobs to pull it off, but Jeanie said a determined person could do it."

Macdara pondered it. "And it's why he became so irate when you asked him about Vera."

"Exactly. And Gráinne thought she saw the floppy yellow hat at the inn. *And* remember how Tom Dowd's employee, Caitlin, said the caller sounded as if he or she was in a helicopter?"

Macdara nodded. "I remember."

"John Healy has an antique fan. Ciarán's been driving me mental all week talking into it because of how it made his voice sound. I think John Healy placed that call from the inn."

"Because he couldn't risk Tom Dowd or anyone else to walk into Vera's chipper and save her life," Macdara pieced together.

Siobhán nodded. "He's the one who made the bookcase, so he certainly knew how to open it."

Macdara snapped his fingers. "He's also the one who had a ladder in his lorry. I believe he made up the story about finding the ladder at the Bisby fishery. I think it was Vera's ladder. He switched it with the one he had greased up."

Siobhán sank into the bench across from Macdara. How she wished none of this had happened. She imagined they were sitting there about to be served a heavenly basket of fish and chips. She imagined everyone in Lahinch alive and well. "One thing still bothers me," she said.

"Go on."

"The timing of John Healy arriving in his lorry. He must have slipped out of the secret room sooner than I had been thinking. Maybe he even managed to do it while she was spray-painting the mural. In and out."

"Hold on. If that's the case, why would he need to hide in the bookcase room?"

"Maybe he didn't," Siobhán said.

Macdara gestured toward the secret room. "But there's a partial footprint."

"True, but we have no idea when that footprint was left. It's possible it's from when John Healy was building it." She mulled it over. "Or when he snuck the castor plants in." The two spots she saw in his garden at the inn must have been where he'd originally placed them.

Macdara nodded as he drummed his fingers on the booth. "There's one problem with this theory."

"I know," Siobhán said. An image of being held underwater assaulted her. "Dead men don't try to drown you and they can't throw stones."

Macdara sighed. "Are you thinking what I'm thinking?"

"Are you thinking something you really don't want to be thinking?"

"I am."

"Then, yes. I'm thinking what you're thinking."

Macdara sighed. "We're back to square one. How do we prove it?"

Siobhán thought for a moment. Her eyes landed on a funnel hanging on the wall. She thought of everything this killer knew. Everyone the killer knew. She thought about Sheila Bisby's fishery and how Daniel O'Grady kept his speedboat docked at the shore with his keys inside. "We pretend we've solved the case and we anticipated every move the killer might reasonably make, and we funnel this person in the guilty direction."

"Translation please?"

"What do guilty people do when caught?" She paused. "If they can?"

Macdara gave it a beat. "They run."

"They run," Siobhán agreed. "We're going to see if we can make this killer run."

"And then?" Macdara shook his head. "I don't see how we're ever going to prove it."

Siobhán went to the wall and retrieved the funnel. "This," she said. "This is how we're going to prove it."

Macdara laughed. "Go on, so."

"Once we figure out the moves the killer is going to make, we set the trap."

Macdara drummed his fingers on the booth. "That means the only way to pull it off is if we keep everyone in the dark. Including the local guards."

"That goes without saying. Everyone in this town is too close. If we tip our floppy yellow hat to anyone at all, it's game over." She paused. "We're also going to need to get a warrant, find the ledger, arrange a 'good-bye party' at the fishery with all our suspects, and contact the coast guard."

"In other words," Macdara said, "we're going to have to lie to absolutely everyone."

"Unfortunately," Siobhán said. "That is how you catch a killer on holiday."

Chapter 30

The forensic team had arrived, Siobhán and Macdara were suited up, and it wasn't long before Liam joined them in front of the bookcase. "Lads," he said. "What's the story?"

"Your grandfather built it," Siobhán said. "You really don't know?"

"I know he built it," Liam said. "But why are you pointing it out?" He scanned the shelves. "Whatever you're selling, I'm not buying yet," he said with a grin. "But I know Pappy's work was class."

Siobhán pushed on the lever and the door swung open. Liam gasped. "That's a new one." He closed his eyes for a moment. "Please tell me there's not a dead body in there."

"Thankfully, no," Macdara said. "Have a look."

Liam peered in. "Potted plants," he said. "And jars of fat?"

"Beef fat drippings, a partial footprint, and castor bean plants," Siobhán said.

Liam whistled. "You're saying that's what poisoned me grandfather?"

"It's further evidence of that possibility," Macdara said. "But we still have to wait for the toxicology report."

"I don't understand. Does this mean Mrs. Chips was going to poison him?"

"No," Siobhán said. "We believe all of this was stashed here by the killer."

Liam whistled.

Macdara pointed to the jars of fat. "One of these jars was used to grease the ladder treads."

"How did you find this?" Liam shut the shelf, then felt around until he found the mechanism. "I'm gobsmacked."

"We believe this is where the killer hid *after* Mrs. Chips fell off the ladder."

"For how long?"

Siobhán shrugged. "Until the coast was clear."

"Do you think we'll be able to get fingerprints?"

"That's why we have the forensic team here," Siobhán said. "But if we're right, it's not going to matter."

They stepped back to let the forensic team work.

Liam frowned. "What do you mean it's not going to matter?"

"We have a theory as to who our killer was," Siobhán said. "But you're not going to like it."

* * *

They sat in a nearby pub, filling Liam in on the theory that his grandfather had planned on killing Vera and then ultimately killed himself. They said he pretended to find a ladder, but it was *his* ladder. The one Mrs. Chips had borrowed without permission. That he had most likely stolen hers out of her shed in order to grease the treads. That she had dropped a jar of beef fat drippings at his door, just like she'd done with everyone who had dared eat at Mr. Chips. But after setting up the greased ladder in her shop, he'd realized his ladder was in her shed. He didn't want any connection between them, so he threw it in the back of his lorry and pretended he'd found it at Bisby Fishery. Then he disguised himself in Vera's floppy yellow hat that she'd left at his inn.

"I give ye credit for being creative," he said. "But my grandfather had no motive. He had no motive to kill Mrs. Chips, and he certainly had no motive to kill himself."

"That's where we're stuck," Macdara said. "I think we're at a dead-end."

"I understand," Liam said. "You can't stay in Lahinch forever."

"If only we had found John's ledger," Siobhán said. "Maybe we'd find an explanation."

"I highly doubt that," Liam said. "You're barking up the wrong tree. My grandfather wasn't a killer."

"And yet there is a lot of circumstantial evidence," Macdara said.

Siobhán nodded. "It's a puzzler."

"I could make the same case for every one of our suspects. But there's no proof. There's not even a smoking gun. But you tried, lads. That's all that matters."

"Do you have any theories?" Macdara asked. "You know these people better than we do."

"I've always thought it had to be Mr. Chips and Ms. Flaherty."

Siobhán shook her head. "Mrs. Chips built that bookcase after she and Mr. Chips parted. She wanted her secret room to be secret."

"That may well be, but it doesn't mean he didn't find out," Liam said. "I bet Vera stored those castor bean plants in there. I bet she was planning on killing someone with them. Not me grandfather but Mr. Chips."

"The castor bean plants are healthy," Siobhán pointed out.

Liam raised an eyebrow. "Your point?"

"They haven't been sitting in a small dark room for long." She gave it a beat. "And if they belonged to Mrs. Chips, how do you explain the fact that your grandfather asked one of the crew working on his inn about castor bean plants?"

Liam shrugged. "Maybe he was asking for Vera."

"Then why did he quit working on the inn after Vera demanded money?"

"He never said a word to me about Vera demanding money. Do you have any proof that she did?"

"She insisted on cash," Macdara said. "Just like she was trying to squeeze everyone in town. Especially those who took loans from Mike McGee."

"Well, there you have it," Liam said. "My grandfather never took a loan from McGee."

Siobhán and Macdara sighed in unison. "I'll be calling headquarters to let them know we're at a stalemate," Macdara said. "We'll be heading home."

"And Gráinne?" Liam asked.

"We've set up an appointment at nine tomorrow morning for you and her with Kevin Casey," Siobhán said. "To make sure everything is back in your name before we go."

"I appreciate that," Liam said. "Does your sister have any qualms about that?"

"Not at all," Siobhán said. "She knows she has no claim to the estate and that most likely your grandfather wasn't thinking clearly."

"I wish I knew what he'd been thinking," Liam said.

"We'll probably never know," Siobhán said. "But after all the paperwork is taken care of tomorrow, we're having a good-bye picnic at the fishery."

"At the fishery?"

"Sheila offered the area by the dock," Siobhán explained. "She's going to head up a fish fry. We want to have a proper good-bye and make sure everyone in town is feeling okay about the way things stand."

"We're worried we put folks at odds with one another and we want to extend a few olive branches," Macdara added. "We hope you can join us."

"And Gráinne?" Liam asked.

Siobhán nodded. "I'm sure she'll be there with bells on."

"You'll be missed around here," Liam said. "Hopefully next time you can holiday without murder."

"If only we could have solved it," Siobhán said. Her stomach twisted a little as it always did when she practiced deceit. But she couldn't worry about that now. *All is fair in love and murder.*

By the next morning, Macdara had been able to get an expedited warrant. Given this person had already killed twice, the judge saw the urgency. They waited until Gráinne had left for her appointment with Kevin Casey and Liam, and a guard stationed at the fishery said that all the suspects had arrived to set up for the good-bye party, before arriving at their suspect's residence. Guards quickly broke down the door. It took them twenty minutes to find the ledger tucked into a laundry basket of dirty clothes. They flipped through it, and there it was—John Healy's confession. He'd admitted his part, and of course the killer's part as well. "You were right," Macdara said. "You were right."

"I'll admit," Siobhán said, "this time I wish I wasn't."

"We'd better hurry," Macdara said. "We have to find a duplicate ledger, get to the fishery, and set the bait."

Lahinch was granting them a last day filled with sunshine. Tables were set up by the water for the fish fry, Daniel's speedboat was parked at a dock close to where they were to be seated, the coast guard was on standby, and their suspects were all gathered. Two large outdoor grills were fired up, sending a light scent of burning wood into the air. Tom had donated a makeshift outdoor kitchen, Daniel got his way and supplied vegetable oil and vinegar, and Natalie brought the sweets from the bakery. Madeline Plunkett had her notebook ready; she was going to do a write-up about Lahinch in general, and this was Mr. Chips's time to shine. Only Siobhán and Macdara knew that they weren't really there to celebrate or say good-bye. Then again, any time a killer was unmasked was a cause for celebration. Guards had managed to replicate the outside of John Healy's ledger, so at a glance the killer would not be able to tell it was a fake.

And Siobhán had been correct. John Healy used his diary to write down absolutely everything, from the mundane to the finger-pointing. How sad it had all turned out, and how she wished she'd been wrong about the killer. But now she was determined to prove it.

Siobhán had copied down the dedication in the front of the ledger so when she read it aloud, the killer might not know how they got a hold of it but it would ring true. Then she hoped the killer would snatch the ledger in an act of desperation and make their getaway on Daniel's speedboat. Unfortunately for the killer, the coast guard would be waiting to pounce.

It wasn't long before Gráinne and Liam arrived from the solicitor's office.

"Did everything get signed?" Siobhán asked.

Liam shook his head. "Kevin Casey had to cancel. Some kind of personal emergency."

More like an order from Macdara to cancel.

"We'll be back at his office bright and early tomorrow," Gráinne said. Liam treated her to a smile as everyone sat down to eat. For their trap to work, they allowed everyone time to eat, chat, and enjoy. After all, only one of them was a killer; the rest deserved at least a decent feed before everything went sideways. It was well into an hour, when everyone was full and relaxed, before they began to implement the plan.

"That's some speedboat you have there, Daniel," Macdara said, loud enough for everyone to hear.

"Do you want to take it for a spin, Detective?" Daniel asked with a grin. "The keys are in her."

"Isn't it risky to leave the keys in her?" Siobhán asked.

Daniel laughed. "I have two detective sargeants and a garda here," he said. "I've never felt safer."

"Are you really leaving without closing the case?" Sheila asked.

Macdara glanced at Liam, who nodded before speaking up. "We have reason to believe this case is going to go cold quick. It's unsustainable for these two to stay until the case is closed. Headquarters will send another detective, but if I were you, I wouldn't count on the case being solved any time soon."

Ye of little faith, Siobhán couldn't help but think.

"That means you all have to live wondering if you're next?" Madeline Plunkett shuddered. "If I were you, I'd get out of town while you can."

"There's no need for that kind of alarm," Liam said. "We'll look out for each other."

"Actually," Siobhán said, grabbing the copy of John's ledger that they had placed in an evidence bag, "we're gathered here today to arrest the killer."

Shocked faces stared at the evidence bag. "What is that?" Sheila asked, her voice squeaking.

"This is John Healy's ledger," Siobhán said. "It took some doing, but we finally got our hands on it."

"What?" Liam shot out of his chair. "Why do I not know about this?"

"Because you were busy in the solicitor's office," Siobhán said. "And of course, we couldn't tip our hand."

Liam frowned and shifted his weight as he remained standing.

Tara Flaherty raised her hand. "I think you mean tip your hat." She grinned, looking around the table. "I'm having a sale on hats. They're three percent off today."

"Why did you bring the evidence here?" Liam asked. He held out his hand. "I'd like to have a look at that."

"I bet you would," Siobhán said.

"What did you say?" Liam glared at her and finally she could see it, the killer underneath the smiling eyes and dimples. On one hand, this was going to devastate Gráinne. On the other, this was going to save her life.

Siobhán pointed to Mike McGee, who had already been given a good proverbial shakedown by the guards and would most likely be facing charges of his own, not to mention losing his job, but he had cooperated, knowing the legal process would be easier for him.

"Have a seat," Macdara said to Liam. "We're just getting started."

Liam glanced at Gráinne. She had put on huge sunglasses. Ever since they'd broken it to her last night, the poor thing had been crying her eyes out. The fact that she had managed to hold it together during the pretense of the solicitor meeting and throughout this lunch made Siobhán both immensely proud and sad. She would find her soul mate, a partner who liked strong, brilliant women, not to mention a woman whose style was off the charts. She deserved the world, and whoever this love was, it was not Liam Healy.

"That's why you wore those this whole time," he said, gesturing to Gráinne's big sunglasses. "You knew."

Gráinne stared at the table but did not say a word. *Poor chicken.*

"The fake appointment," Siobhán said. "Kevin Casey did not have a personal emergency. We canceled the meeting." They wanted him on edge. They wanted him angry.

"I'm calling headquarters." Liam started to walk toward his squad car. Macdara whistled. A line of guards stepped forward from the warehouses. Liam stopped in his tracks.

"What is going on here?" Sheila Bisby asked.

"Everyone stay where you are," Macdara said. "Everyone is safe." He glanced at Liam. "There's nowhere to run." Then, as discussed, his eyes flicked to the speedboat and away, as if he didn't want Liam to notice it.

"It really all started with those clandestine poker games, didn't it?" Siobhán said.

Liam wasn't listening. He had been watching the line of guards and Macdara. His gaze fell to the speedboat.

"Would you please tell us what's going on?" Natalie asked.

"At first I thought John Healy might have killed Vera Cowley and then himself," Siobhán said.

"You're right, okay?" Liam said. "It was my pappy.

Vera drove him to the edge. I'm sorry I lied. I just . . . couldn't face what he'd done."

"I suppose I'm not surprised that you'd rather stain his memory than admit you're the killer," Siobhán said.

Someone at the table gasped.

"Killer?" Daniel said. All heads turned to Liam.

Macdara joined in before Liam could bolt. "You became addicted to the poker games. Started spending more than you could afford."

"That's not a crime," Liam said.

"Until you felt backed into a corner, and instead of putting cash into the pot, you decided to put your grandfather's inn on the line." She made sure to stare at Mike McGee.

"It's allowed," Mike said. "I don't make the rules."

"Mike!" Liam growled. "What have you done?"

Mike threw open his hands. "She figured it out," he said. "I had no choice."

"You absolutely made the rules, Mr. McGee," Siobhán said. "But Liam wasn't really going to leave you the family inn."

Mike crossed his arms and threw a dirty look to Liam. "I didn't tell him to kill his grandfather. I could have waited. He was old."

"But you see, Vera Cowley found out all about it," Macdara said. "And she threatened to end both of your careers."

"I had no idea," Mike said.

"But Liam did," Siobhán said. "And he was not going to let that happen."

"Surely none of you are believing these lies," Liam said, trying to make eye contact with someone, anyone at the tables. "These two blow-ins are trying to confuse you. They're talking pure nonsense, grasping at straws."

"You confessed your sin to your grandfather," Macdara said. "Was it the same day that Vera left a jar of beef fat drippings at the door to the inn? The same week she also threatened your grandfather?"

"I told her not to do that," Mr. Chips said. "I told her she was going to brown someone off if she kept leaving jars of fat at doors." He shook his head. "It tastes better, there's no denying that. Life is too short for vegetable oil."

"Life for everyone would be a lot longer if you switched to vegetable oil," Daniel said with a nod to Mr. Chips. "Me door is open whenever you come to your senses."

Siobhán felt as if she was losing control of the narrative. She turned to Liam. "Mrs. Chips was threatening you and your grandfather," she said. "That must have been distressing."

"She demanded money," Liam said. He was half turned toward the speedboat. "My grandfather started paying her. He thought that would be enough." He clenched his fist. "It should have been enough. This was her fault. She did this to herself!"

Normally Siobhán would have leapt to Vera's defense, but they needed Liam to boil like a tea kettle, and he was definitely on his way. She just needed to turn the heat up a tiny bit. "Mrs. Chips was depressed staying in her chipper all alone after the betrayals," Siobhán said, making sure to glance at Tara and Mr. Chips. "So she imposed herself on your grandfather *again* and procured a free room at the inn."

Liam edged closer to the speedboat.

"She took your grandfather's ladder while there and left her floppy yellow hat," Macdara said. "Did you conceive the idea for her murder when you went to her shed to get your ladder back?"

Liam stared, mouth slightly parted as if he was panting. He seemed to be debating between running and talking himself out of this somehow.

"It was all sitting in front of you, wasn't it? The ladder, the grease, the disguise," Siobhán said. "And once again, had you not been able to help yourself, I would have thought your grandfather was the killer. I was almost convinced." Liam nearly got away with it. And he would have manipulated Gráinne in any number of ways. The thought made her run cold.

"What do you mean 'Had you not been able to help yourself'?" Liam asked.

"My wonderful detective sargeant husband reminded me that dead men don't try to drown you and they can't throw rocks." She stared at him, the man who'd held her under the water, the man who made her think she was going to drown. He looked away first.

"You were also trying to spread a little suspicion Sheila's way," Macdara said. "Dropped Vera's ladder at the fishery—"

"Which then your grandfather picked up again," Siobhán said.

"He shouldn't have," Liam muttered. "You never even figured out it was Vera's ladder!" he added excitedly, sounding oddly proud.

"And you just had to throw a rock through Daniel's window to make it seem as if he knew more than he was saying," Macdara said.

Daniel rose from his seat. "Are you going to pay for that? That was an entire wall of windows." He caught the look Siobhán and Macdara were giving him. "Right, so," he said. "Not important at this moment." He sunk back into his chair.

"I would have gotten away with all of it if you two hadn't come to town. You were supposed to be on holiday!" Liam's face was scrunched in rage.

"Me wife," Macdara said sadly, "does not know how to holiday."

"I am the worst," Siobhán said. "I have a lot to learn."

"Wearing a trench coat with the floppy yellow hat wasn't that smart," Macdara said. "I suppose you didn't think it all the way through." They had found the trench coat in Liam's flat as well. His own bravado had convicted him. It never occurred to him that anyone would dare search his flat.

"You were able to mess with the CCTV tape so we couldn't see you slip inside Vera's flat that morning," Siobhán said.

"You retrieved the ladder from the shed—the one she'd taken from your grandfather's inn—then greased it with the beef fat, set it up with twine from this fishery dangling from underneath a heavy bag of flour, and hid in the secret room until the evil deed was done." Macdara shook his head. "It gives me no pleasure at all to arrest one of our own. But justice doesn't discriminate."

"You already had a plan to make sure Mike McGee would never inherit the inn," Siobhán said. "You were going to find someone else to leave it to. Someone you could charm."

"Is that why you were suddenly all over me, like?" Sheila asked.

Given Liam wasn't about to answer, Siobhán nodded. "When you rejected him, he didn't know what to do. That is, until we came to town." Gráinne blew her nose loudly.

"You figured Gráinne would fall for you and you'd get the inn back in your name, but in case that didn't work, you had a backup. Eoin was set up as the fall guy," Macdara said.

"It was the worst feeling of me life," Eoin said. "Thank you," he said to Siobhán and Macdara. "Thank you for clearing this up."

"You should thank Liam too. He made several mistakes," Macdara said.

"Did I, yeah?" Liam scoffed.

"You couldn't help but write *fried* on her forehead," Siobhán said.

Liam was taken aback. "What? You're going to test my fingerprints?"

"That wouldn't work, and I'm sure you wore gloves," Siobhán said. "But we might have thought it was an accident otherwise."

"That's because no one else was ever going to see it," Liam said. "I was supposed to be the lead investigator." He jabbed himself in the chest. "*Me.*"

"If it weren't for our holiday," Siobhán said, "you would have gotten away with murder."

"I didn't kill me grandfather!" Liam said. "The plan was going to work. Someone else must have poisoned him, and it sure wasn't me."

"It wasn't you," Siobhán said. She took out the page from his diary that they had copied.

Dear Liam. The ban garda with the red hair is asking way too many questions. She's close to figuring it out. I'm too old to go to jail. She wants a killer, so give her one. There are two castor plants in me garden. I've been dosing meself a little a day, not sure how long it will take. I've left a confession in me ledger as well. Let everyone think I killed Vera. Take back the inn. And for the love of all that matters, please stop gambling. Love, Pappy.

Liam bolted for the speedboat. Shocked heads looked to Siobhán and then to the guards, wondering why no one was following him. Moments later the engine roared to life. "Hey!" Daniel said. "Why aren't you stopping him?"

The speedboat shot out into the water, and for a few seconds it skimmed the surface with startling speed. But then it started to sputter. It sputtered until it died, and there sat Liam bobbing along without any gas. In the distance, just in case he somehow made it, the coast guard waited. Onshore, the guards moved in.

"Why did you let him do that?" Sheila said. "You knew he wasn't going to get anywhere."

"It's a lovely day for a holiday boat ride," Siobhán said. "I wanted him to enjoy his last few moments in the sun."

Chapter 31

They were all packed in, standing on the beach to watch the sun rise. Siobhán held Trigger in one hand and Macdara's hand in her other. Ciarán and Ann ran up and down the water's edge, racing. Eoin was eager to get back. He'd just received word that all his permits were in. Soon the O'Sullivan Six—or The Six, as people in Kilbane were already calling the restaurant—would be open for business. And Siobhán knew what James and Gráinne were going to say before they said it. Liam and John Healy had no other living relatives. Gráinne was the official owner of a seaside inn. And James was going to help her run it. And, of course, chase after a certain fisherwoman.

Gráinne, over the moon about this fantastic development, was already making plans for the future. "We'll have a spa too, and I can do fashion consults and makeovers!"

"I think I can do most of the work the inn needs," James said. "At least a good portion of it."

Gráinne wagged her finger at Siobhán. "And next time you come, there will be no murders, do you understand me?"

Siobhán laughed. "No murders," she repeated.

"Good," she said. "Because in my world, it's love before murder. *Always.*"

Macdara squeezed Siobhán's hand, and Trigger licked her face. The sun made Ann's blond hair gleam, and Ciarán's laughter carried across a warm breeze. Siobhán felt it, she felt the love. And for once, she knew she was doing it right. She suddenly felt like a woman on holiday.

**Please turn the page for an exciting sneak peek of
Carlene O'Connor's next Irish Village mystery
MURDER IN AN IRISH GARDEN
coming soon wherever print and e-books are sold!**

Chapter 1

"Would you please repeat the question?" Siobhán O'Sullivan drummed her fingers on their farmhouse kitchen table, something Macdara had already somewhat politely asked her not to do. Her study-weary husband sighed. Camped out next to her, a pile of books teetered like the Leaning Tower of Pisa. Preparing for the detective sergeant exams from home with that commotion going on outside was turning into an absolute nightmare. Chainsaws, drills, workmen barking orders—it was madness. But it was too late to find a quieter place now, she'd already promised Eoin that she would keep an eye out for a special delivery. His restaurant, *The Six,* was going to have its soft opening in two days. If that wasn't enough, he had rented out the field in front of it to a contestant for Kilbane's Top Garden Contest. Cassidy Ryan. Tomorrow was the first day of the contest and the town was abuzz with excitement.

"Officer Healy is on patrol," Macdara said. "It's evening and he's nearly finished for the day. He's strolling down the street."

"I thought he was *walking*."

Macdara gave her a look. She had a feeling they were building up to their first big fight as a married couple. He took a deep breath and she had no doubt he was counting to three in his head. "Walking, strolling, there's no difference."

"Of course there's a difference."

"Do tell."

"Why is he strolling if he's on duty? He should be less relaxed and more alert."

"Fine. Officer Jennings—"

"Healy."

"Right. Officer *Healy*. It would be easier to remember if I could get through the question at least *once* without interruption." He stared at Siobhán as if daring her to say something. She was doing a lot more than counting to ten in her head, but she kept her gob shut. Exams were hard, but there were days that marriage was even harder. "Officer Healy is walking down the street, as alert as he can possibly be at the end of a very long day, and here comes your fella Mike. Mike waves Officer Healy down—"

Macdara was paraphrasing and talking too fast. These questions were ridiculous. There was no choice but to interrupt again, she was the one who would be taking the test and she needed clarification. "Why does

Mike need to wave Officer Healy down if he's already approaching him?"

Macdara threw the manual down on the kitchen table. "We're not getting anywhere! I haven't even gotten to the accident." He stood and headed for the kettle.

Siobhán glanced at the practice manual, and imagined setting it on fire. "What accident?"

"Exactly!" Macdara said, as he rummaged around in the cupboard for box of tea. He continued to talk as he set about preparing two cups. "Mike tells Officer Healy that he saw a man named Joe plow into a cyclist and take off."

Apparently, her over-achiever husband had memorized the question. There were days she would have found this an attractive quality. Today was not one of them. She tapped her pencil on the table, it helped her think. "Does this Mike fella wear glasses?"

Macdara frowned as dropped tea bags into the mugs. "That's nowhere in the scenario!"

Siobhán crossed her arms and stared at her notes. "It should be. I would think that would be very important, don't you?"

"For the love of curried chips will ya please just shut your gob until I finish the question?"

Siobhán's jaw tightened. She was going to blow before the kettle. She didn't even bother to count this time. "Did you just tell your wife to shut her gob?" She gave him one those looks only a wife can give when he turned toward her. "And before you answer I'll be adding me own crime question to the list if your answer is yes."

"You will, yeah?"

Siobhán nodded. "'If a wife kills her husband but he totally had it coming because he egged her on by telling her to *shut her gob* when she's trying to study for one of the most important tests of her career—is she really responsible for his death?'"

"Yes," Macdara said. "She most certainly is." He paused and cocked his head. "How would you do it?"

"I'd slip something into your tea." Macdara stared at the mugs on the counter. Siobhán grimaced, pulled the manual toward her, and skimmed it. "'Joe saw Mike plow into a cyclist and drive away. Luckily the cyclist is not harmed. His name is Kevin. Mark chats with him and finds out he's forty years of age, with a wife and two sons.'" She pushed it away again, disgusted. "What on earth does that have to do with being hit by a car?"

"I didn't write the question and you didn't finish it." She gestured for him to do so. "He chats with your one, then fifteen minutes later Officer Healy is driving about, and he sees the car—"

"Wait. How could he see the car? You didn't even say the color, make or model."

"He obviously knew all of that."

Siobhán shook her head. If only she could meet with these men—and she knew it was men—who designed nonsensical practice questions, she'd murder them too. "It's not obvious at all."

The kettle whistled and Macdara wet the tea. He stirred in milk and sugar and brought them to the table. "Sans poison, dear wife." He set hers in front of her and gently touched her shoulder. "I know you're nervous. But this is never going to work if we can't even get through a single question."

He was right. She hated when he was right. "Fine."

Macdara eagerly sat down and sipped his tea before pulling the manual toward him. "He stops the car, they pull to the side of the road, and he orders him to get out. Now. Ready for the question part of the question?" She pursed her lips and nodded. "Is Officer Healy within his rights to conduct a breathing test?"

"Yes if—"

Macdara held up his index finger and wagged it. "It's multiple choice. I haven't read the choices." Siobhán crossed her arms, slouched in the chair, and patiently waited. "A: No. He has no right to tell him what to do and he shouldn't have stopped him in the first place. B: No, he has no proof the accident even happened—he only suspects it happened. C: Yes. But the test must take place within or close to an area where the requirements for Joe to cooperate can be imposed."

Siobhán pounded her fist on the table. "What in the world does that even mean?"

"Or D: Yes. Officer Healy can do whatever he wants because he's a police officer." Siobhán opened her mouth and there was her husband's index finger again. It wasn't the first time she thought about biting it. "Don't do it Siobhán," Macdara warned, "do not say D."

"I cannot answer the question if I do not understand what in the world they're trying to say in answer C."

"Well that's unfortunate because explanation C is the correct answer."

"What?" She was starting to wish there was whiskey in her tea.

Macdara began to mansplain. "Since Officer Healy has spoken to the cyclist hit by the car and confirmed the accident—"

"It didn't say he confirmed the accident. It said he confirmed your one was forty years of age and married with two sons."

"If the cyclist didn't confirm the story I'm sure it would have said that cyclist denied it. Why would they even write up this question if there was no accident?" By now they had both risen to their feet and were competing to project their voices over the commotion outside. Siobhán was wondering exactly where this argument was headed when someone banged on the front door. Had they disturbed the workers outside? *Saved by the bang.* Siobhán hurried to the window above the kitchen sink and peered outside. Planted at the front door was a deliveryman and next to him was an enormous wooden crate. It had to be for Cassidy Ryan and her garden design. Siobhán opened the window.

"That goes to the white tent," she said, startling the poor man. He whipped his head around and raised his cap. He was a *baby*. Nineteen at the most.

He glanced nervously in the direction of the large tent. It was big enough to house a circus. All the gardens had tents erected around them so that their gardens would be hidden until the official unveiling.

"Where exactly would you like it?" His voice started off deep and then squeaked.

"You're not going to like me answer," Siobhán said.

"Join the club," Macdara piped up.

The poor lad looked terrified. "I'll take you over to the tent," Siobhán said. "If the recipient isn't there I can sign for it." She glanced at Macdara. "I need some fresh air."

Macdara rose and grabbed the manual. "Not a bother, I can walk and talk."

Ugh. He was relentless. They headed outside and Siobhán once again glanced at the enormous person-sized crate. It was propped up on a rolling dolly. "Is it an elephant?"

The lad leaned forward and glanced at a sticker on the crate. "Statue."

The lad shrugged. "She's going all out." Cassidy Ryan had already caused quite a bit of trouble with the other gardeners, and not just because she was a blonde bombshell who flirted with every male in sight. She was the only *professional* landscape designer of the group and the other gardeners were incensed. Unfortunately, no one had thought to write a clause barring professionals into the bylines so they were stuck. It wasn't just the test questions that were aggravating. It was life. Rules and regulations. Everything revolved around rules and regulations. As Siobhán led the way she could hear the wheels of the dolly squeaking and bumping as they headed for the tent.

Macdara continued to yammer behind her. "If Officer Healy has reasonable grounds to believe Joe hit the cyclist, then he can ask for the breath test." He was committed to her passing these exams and using tough love to accomplish it. Was he worried it would be a poor reflection on him if she didn't pass the first time around? And why was this flustering her so much? She was normally an excellent student. Her head just wasn't in it. Did she even want to be a detective sergeant? Wasn't one in the family enough? "Can we put this on hold?" she called over her shoulder.

"The Road Traffic Act basically states that if an accident happens as a result of a motor vehicle on the road, and the officer believes that this person was in charge of the vehicle when the accident occurred, then the officer has legal authorization to administer a preliminary breath test." Macdara waited for her to respond.

"There was an accident?" the delivery lad asked when silence stretched. He sounded worried.

"See?" Siobhán said. "That's what I said."

"I didn't write these questions," Macdara said. "You asked for my help."

"*You* took the test, didn't you?" Siobhán asked. She was getting her back up, but she couldn't help it. Why couldn't they just take a break?

"I wouldn't be a detective sergeant if I hadn't taken the tests." He paused. "And you won't be either."

He did not just say that. In front of this delivery-baby no less. Siobhán eyed the crate again. It was big enough to stuff her husband into—maybe she could convince the lad to haul him away. "You could have at least given headquarters feedback on how idiotic these questions are."

"You're blaming me for *taking* the test? I don't have to help you study you know. I do have other things I could be doing."

"Like what?" Macdara was off for the week following their holiday at sea in Lahinch, and he was still trying to be a "Man of Leisure."

"Don't you worry about it."

"Consider yourself officially dismissed." They reached the tent. It was situated across from Eoin's farm-to-table restaurant, a short stroll away. Once the garden was unveiled, restaurant guests could walk through the installment either before or after their meal, and it would remain throughout the summer. It was ingenious of Eoin to think about doing this, even if it had gotten him in some hot water with the other contestants. Now that they were near the tent Siobhán was surprised that all was quiet. "Hello?" she called out. "Cassidy Ryan? There's a large delivery here. Some kind of statue?"

There was no reply. "She must be on break," Siobhán said. "Would you like me to sign for it?"

The lad glanced at his paperwork. "It clearly states that only Cassidy Ryan can sign for it."

"A rule follower," Macdara said. "Good man." He gave Siobhán a pointed look.

"Wait here then and I'll see if me brother knows where she is." Siobhán ignored Macdara and headed for the restaurant.

Macdara followed her. "Let's try another question. Susan is walking to work one morning—"

"Not strolling?" Siobhán shot back.

"Two men suddenly come up behind her—Harry and Joe."

"Is this the same Joe who struck the cyclist?"

"They say, 'We won't hurt you as long as you give us the bag!'" Macdara was getting into it, acting out the role. Just as he was speaking, the restaurant doors opened and a young woman emerged with a camera slung around her neck. She had not only caught the tail end of his statement, but Macdara was acting as if Siobhán had a handbag and he was going to snatch it.

The young woman's eyes were panicked. "Leave her alone!" she yelled, running toward Siobhán. She started to tug on Macdara as she screamed at Siobhán, "Where's your bag?"

"I'm not carrying one," Siobhán said. She glared at Macdara. "And neither was the woman in that scenario."

The woman let go of Macdara and stepped back, confusion planted on her pretty, young face.

"Of course, she was carrying a handbag," Macdara said. "How could they try and rob it off her if she wasn't?"

"Then why doesn't it clearly state that she's carrying a handbag? Good old Harry and Joe just said, 'Give us the bag!' For all I know it was a SuperValu bag."

The young woman's eyes ping-ponged between them, her shiny pink lips slightly parted. She was slim with straight brunette hair past her shoulders, and her dewy face was dotted with freckles. "Do either of you want me to call someone?"

Macdara turned to the young woman. "We're reading test questions," he said. "My stubborn wife is studying to become a detective sergeant." He shook his head. "Or should I say she's actively *avoiding* studying."

Siobhán put her hands on her hips, realizing that to this young woman she probably looked like a typical Irish wife nagging her husband. But some things couldn't be helped. "And my Detective-Sargeant-Husband is drilling me with practice questions that do not make an ounce of sense because they were written by men with limestone for brains!" Siobhán could feel her blood pressure tick up. She wanted to hit something. Preferably him.

"Stop overthinking every single little detail," Macdara said. "When you become a detective sergeant you can lobby to change the questions. But if you don't get out of your own stubborn way you're never going to pass the exam!"

"How many times are you going to call me stubborn?"

"As many as it takes to get through to you!"

The woman backed away slightly, her hand going to her camera. If she started to film them, Siobhán was going to yank it off her neck and stomp on it. She was dying for the woman to start filming them.

"Please excuse my rude husband," Siobhán said to the woman.

"Rude?" Macdara said, his face reddening. "Rude?!"

"We just returned from our honeymoon, isn't it obvious?" Siobhán said.

"The honeymoon's over," Macdara said, throwing his arms out.

Siobhán turned her back on him. "We're sorry we frightened you," she said to the woman.

"Not a bother." She looked around as if she wanted to flee.

"We're looking for Cassidy Ryan. But first things first. I'm Siobhán O'Sullivan-Flannery and the rude old goat behind me is my husband Macdara."

"Fantastic," Macdara said. "I'm a rude old goat. Noted."

"And I'm a stubborn wife. Noted."

"Say less and you'll hear more," Macdara said.

"You know what?" Siobhán whirled around. "I will say less. In fact, for the record, I am officially giving you the silent treatment." She mimicked locking her lips and throwing away the key.

"It's my lucky day," Macdara said. "I love the silent treatment!"

"Molly Murphy," the woman said, taking out a pad of paper and biro. "For the *Kilbane Times*. I'm the reporter and photographer for Kilbane's Top Garden competition."

"You are?" Siobhán blurted out. She looked like a baby too. Everyone looked like babies. Twenty-something and bright-eyed. Siobhán was getting old. And cranky. "Brilliant." They had just had their first big row in front of a reporter. *Typical.*

Molly jotted something down on her pad, her tongue sticking out of the corner of her mouth. Siobhán could hear Macdara breathing. No doubt he was fuming. But he was the one who just couldn't give things a rest. This wasn't her fault.

Eoin emerged from the restaurant. His ginger hair was slicked back, and he was wearing a white apron, white shirt, and black denims. He looked sharp. Long gone were the days where acne dotted his face and he wore American baseball caps backward. He was a man now, clear complexion, nice hair… *handsome.* And she was bursting with pride. All her siblings were grown up, although she still thought of Ciaran as a baby. "What's the story?" he asked. "Did I hear arguing?" He raised his eyebrow and took in the pair.

"There's a delivery lad by the tent who needs Cassidy Ryan's signature," Siobhán said, gesturing. "Would you look the size of that crate?"

They began to walk back toward the crate, and the young reporter tagged along. "I haven't seen her yet this morning," Eoin said. "She's not answering calls or texts either."

They reached the outside of the tent and the delivery lad looked at them expectantly. "Sorry, luv," Siobhán said. "Cassidy Ryan isn't here."

The lad stared at the crate and groaned. "If she doesn't sign for it I have to take this back." He lifted his cap and stared at it with dread. Sweat glistened on his forehead. "It's really, really heavy. Even with the dolly."

"I don't know what to tell you," Siobhán said. "But if you'd like to wait a bit, you could come into the restaurant." She turned to Eoin. "Right?"

"I can get you a tea or coffee," Eoin said. "And maybe whip up an Irish brekkie if you're hungry."

The delivery lad glanced at the crate again. "I really can't leave it." He gazed at the restaurant. "But a coffee would be nice."

"We'll all wait then," Siobhán said. "Although not *everyone* needs to be here," she said to the field.

"It's a grand fresh day," Macdara said. "I think I'll stay."

Siobhán should have reworded it. He was the stubborn one. *Stubborn* old goat.

"I'll put the coffee on." Eoin said. "Anyone else?" Siobhán raised her hand. Eoin nodded.

"Thank you Eoin for the very kind offer," Macdara said. "I will use my words and politely decline."

Oh, no he didn't.

Eoin laughed. "Whatever the pair of ye are smoking—don't pass it on." He ambled away.

"Looks like we've got time to kill," Molly said as if she was suddenly part of the family. She turned to Macdara twirling a strand of her hair. "What's the rest of the test question?"

Seriously? Was the entire Universe conspiring against Siobhán? The reporter was a little instigator. Siobhán wanted to throttle her.

Macdara didn't hesitate. "Harry grabs Susan, he puts a knife to her throat while Joe tries to snatch her handbag." He began to act out the scene. "She fights back. She starts to run away—they chase her—she trips and bangs her head on the pavement. She's dead."

Molly gasped.

"What?" the delivery lad said, joining the party. "Who's dead?"

"She should have just given them her bag," Molly said. "No matter what kind it was."

Did she *want* a punch in the face?

Macdara nodded his consent. "The question is—"

"Somebody tell him we all know what the question is." Siobhán held up her index finger. "The answer is *yes*. They can be considered liable for murder if their actions led to her action of running away, which it obviously did."

"I knew it!" Macdara turned to Molly. "Someone knows all the answers. She's just being stubborn because she doesn't like how they're worded. Now. Which one of us is the real goat?"

Fuming. She was absolutely fuming. She needed to go for a run. Otherwise she was going to get in her car and it was going to go for a run, and then she'd be the one liable for murder. Road Traffic Act, her arse.

"You two are an interesting couple," Molly said.

"You can be liable for murder, even if you don't actually murder someone?" the delivery lad chimed in, his voice squeaking.

"If your actions lead to the murder, absolutely," Siobhán said. "You can be prosecuted at least."

"Jeez." The lad grimaced. "Tough break."

Molly cocked her head and stared at the lad with a smirk. "Did we ruin murderous plans of yours?"

"What?" He looked and sounded stricken. The world was going to eat him up. "No. Of course not." He gulped.

Eoin returned with two mugs of coffee. Just after he handed one to the delivery lad, his phone dinged.

Siobhán took the other mug and wrapped her hands around it. She loved the smell even if she didn't need another cup. "Cassidy Ryan," Eoin said, holding up his phone. "*Finally.* She's given me permission to sign for the crate and she says a crew is on its way to install . . ." His eyes lingered on the crate. "Whatever it is." He showed the text to the lad and then grudgingly the lad handed him the paper to sign.

"Cassidy won't even tell you what's inside?" Siobhán asked.

"Other than it's a statue, no," Eoin said. "And before you suggest it we are not going to take a peek."

"It's against the rules," Molly said.

Siobhán so wanted to peek. She was starting to wonder if she was a bad person compared to this rule-following lot. Maybe that was another reason she wasn't fit to be a detective sergeant. And wasn't it just more paperwork? Did she want more paperwork?

"I cannot wait until tomorrow," Molly said. "We kick off in the town square." Her eyes shone with excitement. "This is my first feature assignment."

"Well done," Macdara said.

"Congrats," Siobhán added. She knew her tone didn't convey excitement, but that was the best she could muster.

Eoin whipped a ticket out of his pocket. "Speaking of which . . . Siobhán, I was given a VIP ticket for the opening, but with my restaurant set to open as well, I just can't spare the time."

"She has to study," Macdara said.

"I would love to go." Siobhán snatched up the ticket.

"One has to stop and smell the roses," Siobhán said.

"Thorns and all," Macdara muttered.

Siobhán threw open her arms. "Who doesn't love flowers?" She could act as well as the rest of them.

"Not just flowers," Molly interjected. "This year each garden has to incorporate a water feature—and there will be shrubbery, and statues and garden sculptures—I can't wait to see what everyone has created!"

Everyone slowly turned to stare at the crate.

"Whatever it is," Eoin said, "Cassidy Ryan swears it's a real showstopper."

Visit our website at
KensingtonBooks.com
to sign up for our newsletters, read more from your favorite authors, see books by series, view reading group guides, and more!

BOOK CLUB
BETWEEN THE CHAPTER

Become a Part of Our
Between the Chapters Book Club
Community and Join the Conversation

Betweenthechapters.net

Submit your book review for a chance to win exclusive Between the Chapters swag you can't get anywhere else!
https://www.kensingtonbooks.com/pages/review/